Medea

The Persephone Adventures Book 1

JOHN NOBLE

For Rachel who knows what it means to love others.

Contents

Chapter 1
Gemini

Jessie narrowed her eyes, her thumb anxiously tapping the cards, then finally asked the critical question. "Do you have any queens?"

Jackie grinned. "Go fish."

Jessie reached down, pulling a seven from the top of the dwindling deck. Oh great, a seven. That meant–

"So, do you have any sevens?" Jackie asked for the third time.

Jessie puffed out a sigh and reluctantly handed it over. This game always felt silly when it was just the two of them.

Across from her, a gloating Jackie didn't seem to mind as she triumphantly laid down yet another set of four cards. That gave her seven to Jessie's two, which meant–

"I think you won." Jessie nodded across to her sister's cards.

Jackie frowned. "You don't want to finish?"

"Not really." Sitting cross-legged, Jessie perched her chin on her palm, idly staring at the cards for a moment.

Jackie let out an exasperated puff. "But I thought you liked Go Fish."

"Well, usually we…" her voice caught like a knot in her throat, all the questions from earlier surging back.

Usually they played with Mom, so they had three players. Except now, Mom was…

Across from her, Jackie tensed at even the averted mention of Mom. Suddenly all of her excitement at winning stole away, replaced by a flash of irritation. Jessie stared at the cards, avoiding her sister's eyes. Her mind found its way back to last week, when they'd played Go Fish at home, except laughing and smiling and...

Across from her Jackie had set to determinedly shuffling the cards.

Meanwhile Jessie stood, wandering over to the small bed where she'd left her phone face down on the sheets. Slouching down on the mattress, she unlocked the device with a flick. Her thumb danced across the screen to check her messages.

Not that it mattered. There was no service here, but she kept refreshing and hoping they might get a single bar of signal long enough for a few texts to leak through. She found herself staring at their last message from Mom.

(Mom)
Pizza and salad for dinner?

(Jackie)
We're doing the sleepover at Kammie's tonight, remember?

(Mom)
Oh right

(Mom)
Text if you need me.

(Jessica)
Okay, love you mom :)
(Unsent: Tap to try again)

Jessie tapped the message for about the billionth time, watching as her phone tried... and failed to send it. A horrible feeling clawed at her insides. It was her fault the text hadn't gone through. Yesterday, she'd been so nervous that she'd forgotten to send the message until they were here, and now it was too late. Now Mom would never know that they still loved her and…

Seated on the edge of the bed, the awfulness of it all poured over Jessie like ice water. Had they made a mistake? All her misgivings from yesterday came rushing back in a cold torrent. "Jackie," her breath came sharp, her voice barely a whisper, "I don't know if I can do this."

For an instant the words hung in the air, until, "Jess, just relax."

She glanced up to see her sister glowering.

"But…?"

Jessie's voice died in the face of her sister's exasperated scowl. Jackie's lips drew tight. "It'll be fine. Okay?"

Would it though? Really?

Jessie felt a horrible anticipation puddling in the pit of her stomach. And not the nervously optimistic, first date jitters sort. This was more like when Mom brought home whatever boyfriend she'd dug out of the gutter that month. They'd all have to sit around the table and eat dinner together, everyone on pins and needles, waiting for a wrong remark to set off a fusion bomb of screaming. She'd sit in her room beforehand, trying to do homework, but really just dreading the prospect of dinner.

"It'll be fine," Jackie repeated, insistent.

Jessie stared at the floor, her hands suddenly cold and sweaty. "You don't know that."

Jessie looked up, only to see Jackie glaring back at her with that determined, almost insane certainty that her sister could muster when she was upset. "Jess, it *will* be okay. Not just okay, *better*."

Something about Jackie's cavalier attitude unleashed another tsunami of remorse.

"Jackie, how can you say that?" Jessie blinked away tears as an image of Mom back at the trailer darted through her mind. She could see it clear as day, Mom's worried panic building to a crescendo as she desperately tried to find them. For an instant Jessie couldn't breathe past the awful regret. What were they doing? "We can't just leave Mom like this."

Jackie's expression hardened to an icy veneer. "Why not?" She demanded in a vicious, biting voice. "Seriously, Jess, what did she ever do for us? You want to hang around this dump until she ruins our lives too?"

Jessica hesitated, trying to piece together a coherent response. But she found herself struggling to think past the confused worry stabbing at her chest. Her eyes darted around the room, the warm beige walls suddenly tightening like an anaconda around her ribs.

"No, but…"

"Well, then get a grip," Jackie snapped. "We're doing this, alright? Besides, you always wanted to leave too."

"Not like *this*," Jessie desperately tried to summon up the right words to explain. "Jackie, I wanted to go to Chicago, not…" she couldn't force the words out, "not…"

Just the thought sent a whole new set of worries cycloning through Jessie's head. What was Mom doing right now? Had she called Kammie's parents yet? Had she realized they weren't there? Did Mom think they'd run off?

Had she found the note?

Jessie choked back a sob, the tears flooding her eyes. Would… would they ever see Mom again?

Jessie slumped down, her elbows on her knees and her face buried in her hands as the sobs came. "I just… I can't do this." Jessie shuddered, "I'm sorry, Jackie. I can't."

For an instant Jessie sat there, drowning in a tsunami of shame. Shame that she was too scared to go through with this, that she was even thinking about leaving her twin sister alone. But also shame that they were just abandoning Mom. Did she really deserve that?

Jessie felt a shift on the mattress beside her. Familiar arms wrapped around her, and Jackie's voice whispered in her ear, a little less confident than before, but somehow more reassuring. "Jess, I know this isn't exactly what we planned, okay? I know it's scary, and it's not where I thought we'd go, but this is our shot. *Right now.* We can get out." For once there was a plea in her sister's voice. "Please."

Jessie heard the words, and in a way they made perfect sense. She and Jackie had talked about this a hundred times before. Where they would go, what they would do, how wonderful life would be if they could just get out. But always in a fantasy, *what if we won the lottery* sort of way.

Except now it wasn't a fantasy. Now the dream was real. Now they were leaving home, and going so far away that they couldn't come back. No matter what Jackie said, Jessie knew, deep down in her heart, that if they did this, they might never see Mom again, except on a screen. And now that she was staring her dream right in the face, it looked an awful lot like a nightmare.

Jessie felt like such a coward but…

"I can't." She pulled away from her sister's embrace, "I just…"

This time she heard hurt disbelief in Jackie's words. "So you're going to turn down the chance of a lifetime?" she demanded. "You'll throw it all away for–"

"IS IT?" Jessie threw back in her face. "Is *this* really the chance of a lifetime?" She gestured around the small white room with two simple cots, no windows to so much as check the time of day, and just a polished, slightly intimidating steel door for an exit. "How do you even know? Some lady tells you she's got a restaurant job on Mars and suddenly we're off across the solar system to–"

"At least I tried!" Jackie retorted hotly. "I did *something*."

Jessie's tone lowered to a furious whisper. "And it doesn't bother you that we're not even old enough to…"

"SHUT UP!" Jackie cut her off, abruptly standing as though that ended things. For once Jessie glimpsed fear in her sister's eyes. She hadn't asked what Jackie had done to get the two fake IDs they'd used to pass as eighteen. Maybe she didn't want to know. All that mattered was they had them, they'd lied, and apparently the lady here had bought it.

Jackie glowered down on her, breathing hard. For an instant the confident mask came off and Jessie glimpsed the desperation in her sister's eyes. She suddenly felt sick. What had they gotten into?

"Can we even leave?" Jessie demanded, a sudden caged panic chilling her veins.

"What do you mean?"

"I mean if we wanted to leave *right now*," Jessie pointed at the door. "Would they even let us? Or are we trapped here until…"

The door handle clinked and Jessie went dead silent as the door opened inwards. A middle-aged woman with flowing black hair poked her head inside. "Is everything alright?"

For an instant, neither answered. Ms Davani was… well… Jessie thought she seemed nice, or at least she smiled a lot. Maybe that wasn't the same thing.

Ms Davani pushed the door the rest of the way open and stepped inside, her gaze lingering on the two of them. When they'd arrived, Ms Davani had told them to change out of their old clothes and into matching ivory-white shirts and pants. Now Jessie deliberately glanced away and wiped her cheek with one sleeve to scrub off the dampness in her eyes. She sniffed and tried to look like she hadn't just completely lost it. Next to her, the mattress shifted as Jackie slid back down beside. Her angry scowl from before had abruptly vanished, buried beneath that familiar, neutral, *everything's fine* expression.

Jessie must not have done a good job hiding her tears. After a moment's pause, Ms Davani strolled over and delicately sat down on Jackie's bed, across from the sisters. Her angled features lent her an effortless severity, but she still wore a warm, friendly smile.

"What's wrong, girls?"

"It's nothing," Jackie muttered, shooting Jessie a veiled, *shut up* glower.

Okay, it wasn't *nothing,* Jessie fumed. They were moving to the other side of the solar system and abandoning Mom and their friends. She just wanted to make sure they weren't making a giant, colossal, irreversible mistake.

"Can we leave?" The words slipped out before Jessie could dwell on them too long and decide they were a mistake.

Even before Ms Davani could speak, Jackie jumped in, "She doesn't mean that, alright? Jess always gets jittery, and it always goes away. We just need a minute to–"

"NO!" Jessie nearly screamed. "I'M NOT OKAY!"

Jackie's words ground to a horrified halt and Jessie's gaze flashed from her sister's furious face to Ms Davani, somehow calm as a statue. For a second she fought to catch her breath. When she spoke the words were halting, but Jessie said them anyway. "Can… we… leave?"

"There's no *we*," Jackie snapped bitterly. "Just her."

The words cut Jessie like an icy blade, "Oh, so that's how–"

"You two, stop." Ms Davani barely even raised her voice, but Jessie froze anyway. It was freaky, how the woman could be so calm and firm without shouting. By now Mom would have blown up at her and Jackie. Jackie would then start screaming at Mom, and Jessie would be the one left to pick up the pieces. Yet with Davani, the familiar routine felt… very off.

Ms Davani leaned forward an inch, her voice still tranquil as a lake. "Jessica, in answer to your question. I don't want you doing anything you're not comfortable with. If you want to leave, that's completely fine."

A part of Jessie kind of expected her to say that. Sure she could leave, right until she tried walking out the door. "Then I want to go," she demanded.

Jackie desperately interrupted, "No, she doesn't mean…"

Ms Davani raised a hand and her sister's voice trailed off. For an instant, Jessie caught a flash of disappointment on Ms Davani's face, but then it passed and the woman nodded. "Alright," she said with a sigh, "I'll get your clothes, and you'll need to sign a few forms. Then you can leave. It'll take a few minutes. Sound good?"

Jessie gave a tiny nod and didn't dare look over at her sister. Across from them, Ms Davani rose and nodded towards the door, "Come on, Jessica."

Jessie heard the words, but it took a second for the realization to strike her like lightning. Every muscle froze.

She was leaving Jackie.

Jessie glanced over at her sister, and a lump like lead dropped in her chest.

Jackie stared at her, betrayal in her eyes, and behind that… she was scared. "Jess, please," Jackie pleaded. "Please, don't."

Jessie almost couldn't swallow and the tears brimmed in her eyes. What was she doing? She… she couldn't just leave Jackie here… alone.

"Jessica?" Ms Davani's voice sounded far away.

"Jessica?" Amid the pouring tears she felt a firm arm around her shoulder, Ms Davani's voice close by. "Let's go take a walk, alright? You can tell me what's wrong, and we'll figure it out together. Does that sound good?"

Jessie gave a weak nod and a moment later Ms Davani helped her to stand. The woman guided her towards the door. "Come on. It'll be alright."

The heavy door shut with a clink and Jessie dimly registered the brightly lit hallway beyond. They were in a small building. A reception area up front led back to this hallway with four doors branching off. One door opened into their own room, she was pretty sure another led Ms Davani's, and the third contained a bathroom. When they'd arrived yesterday, a lady doctor had taken them back, one at a time, through the fourth door, into an exam room. The woman had spent several hours poking and prodding them with all the standard physical exam stuff, along with a few more… *invasive* tests. But at least they were finished now.

Afterwards, Ms Davani had given them their current set of snowy white clothes and told them they needed to drink a lot of water and wait 24 hours without eating so they could get one more test finished.

That had been about twenty hours ago, and except for when they'd been sleeping, Ms Davani had come in every hour like clockwork bearing two bottles, either water or zero-sugar Powerade. She'd then stuck around with her concerned teacher sort of glare until they both chugged it down.

Jessie sighed, feeling some of the fear from before drain away, replaced by an empty numbness.

Outside the sun shone down, but Jessie knew it would still be cold. Her and Jackie's puffy jackets were hung on the rack by the door, hers a dark purple next to Jackie's bright, *right in your face* red. Both seemed oddly out of place beside Ms Davani's stylish, gray, button-up overcoat.

When Ms Davani opened the door, a crisp chill rushed in from outside, nipping her face. Fortunately, with the sun out, it wasn't really that much colder than the trailer when Mom didn't pay the power bill.

An oversized black pickup truck sat in the parking lot with a man inside. He was lounging in the driver's seat, which had been tilted halfway back, and glanced at them when they walked out. The man only watched for a second though, then he went straight back to staring at his phone. Jessie swallowed, "Who is…"

"He's mine," Ms Davani said, untroubled. "Mostly for peace of mind. I'm sure you and your sister aren't bothered by this sort of place, but I prefer to stay on the safe side. It's surprisingly cheap to get a private detective to keep an eye on things for a couple of days. I suppose if he spends the whole day reading that's a good thing,"

Oh. A part of Jessie wondered if there was a veiled burn in there about her town being slummy, but then again, they *were* trying to leave.

For a moment they walked in silence, Ms Davani leading her around the side of the brick facade building. They came to the back, where a grove of towering pine trees soared upwards, their needles still green even in the cold of winter. There was something strangely calming about the sight of trees. Maybe it just reminded Jessie of home, but…

"Talk to me, Jessica," Davani said softly. "What has you so nervous?"

Everything, was Jessie's first thought. But the more she considered the question, the more she struggled to nail down an answer. She was nervous, but that was normal given the circumstances. She was a little scared, but…

"I guess I'm just worried about Mom." Jessie picked at a long strand of her hair as she honed in on the one concrete thought she could articulate. She knew she had to be careful what she said. Ms Davani still believed they were eighteen and ready for an adventure, not sixteen and…

"I don't know what she'll do without us," Jessie mumbled.

The olive-skinned woman nodded. "That's normal."

Jessie swallowed. "Is it?"

"Of course," Ms Davani said. "Your sister was worried about the same thing."

Jessie blinked in surprise. "She was?"

The older woman nodded as though it were obvious. "I know it may look terrifying right now, but this trip doesn't have to be a bad thing."

Jessie stooped down, grabbing a fallen pine twig off the ground with a few brown needles still clinging to it. She began absently picking them off one by one.

Ms Davani continued, "I have the sense that your sister and mother don't get along very well, but one of Jackie's first questions was if there was a way to send money back home."

"Really?" Deep down, Jessie wasn't that surprised. Jackie and Mom screamed a lot, but she always saw the frustration afterwards. The part of Jackie that cared, and cried, and wished things could be different.

"I'll tell you the same thing I told her," the older woman said. "They need people out on Mars, and if you're willing to go, there's a lot of money for the taking. A life-changing amount of money, for you two and your mother."

Ms Davani let the words hang for moment before adding, "If you really don't want to go, that's fine. I understand this isn't for everyone. But I'd very much love to have both you and Jackie along, and I don't want you to miss this chance. Mars is like the old west right now, you can go there and be anything. That's rare, it's an opportunity that only comes along once every couple of generations, if that." She paused, "And I know Jackie will miss you."

For a moment Jessie stood there, shivering in the breeze while her chilly fingers plucked the pine needles, one after another. What was she supposed to do? She could leave, but either way she had to give up someone.

The hurt look on Jackie's face flashed through her mind, and she felt her worries begin to melt. Mom would be okay, but Jackie was going so impossibly far away, and…

Jessie shook her head, she couldn't leave Jackie. What would her life be anyway? She'd be stuck at home, tiptoeing around with Mom and pretending that everything was just fine. She'd sit there, desperately waiting for a softball scholarship so she could get into a real school. A scholarship that she knew in her heart would never come.

For a moment Jessie saw herself a month from now, lying on her bed and wishing she hadn't abandoned the one person in her life who really mattered. She saw herself wondering what would have happened if she hadn't been such a coward.

"Okay," Jessie whispered, her mind suddenly made up. "I'll go to Mars."

Ms Davani shot her a skeptical look. "Are you sure, because it's…

"No, I'll do it," Jessie insisted. She had to. She couldn't leave Jackie alone.

"Alright." Ms Davani seemed pleased. "Come on, let's get out of the cold."

Back inside she guided Jessie into the room, and reassured a visibly shaken Jackie that everything was fine now. Then she produced a board game that was, suitably, about building railroads in the old west. "It'll be fun" Davani insisted, before briefly stepping outside then reappearing with two *more* bottles of water for them to drink. "It'll help pass the time."

Jessie was hesitant at first, but after Jackie creamed her and Ms Davani in the first round, she started feeling more competitive. Ms Davani got a call and bowed out for the second game, but for a couple of hours the two went at it, trading games back and forth. For a little while Jessie wasn't even scared anymore.

Both girls finally looked up when the door handle clicked open. Ms Davani strolled in with her usual bright smile, and a pair of shot glasses nestled in one hand.

"Alright girls, last one. Doctor's orders."

The woman handed them both the diminutive cups. Jessie stared at it for a moment, watching the liquid inside fizz like soda and catching a faint waft of carbonation and… maybe lemons. It was only then that Jessie noticed she was oddly thirsty. It dimly registered that Ms Davani hadn't been back with the last few hour's water bottles.

"I'm sorry to say it won't taste very good," the woman warned.

Jackie just shrugged, tipped back the glass and swallowed, her expression puckering into a sour face as it went down.

All eyes turned to Jessie, who reluctantly downed hers, fighting not to gag. Uggg, it tasted awful, an overbearing citrus flavor mixed with a chemical bitterness. Nothing like soda.

Thankfully, Ms Davani produced another water bottle and deftly topped off both their cups to help wash away the foul aftertaste.

"Alright." The woman nodded with a little spring in her step. "You girls wait here. The doctor will be in soon."

She left, and for a few moments, the two were alone. Jackie perched on the edge of her bed, one knee bouncing in excitement, "This is great. I'm really glad you're coming Jess."

"Yeah." Jessie still wasn't a huge fan, but this was best for everyone. And maybe she would come to love it? That was how these things typically went, Jackie drug her into a bunch of crazy plans and… they usually turned out alright. Usually.

Sighing, Jessie blinked as a sudden wave of dizziness hit her. Oh… dang, she really did need to eat. Where was that doctor?

Across from her, Jackie covered a yawn. "Ooooh, I think I need to lay down."

Wait a second. An alarm bell rung in Jessie's head. That was a bit weird. Her gaze drifted down to the little shot glass in her hand, and a question blossomed in her mind. What exactly had been in that drink? She tried to focus, a little voice deep down warning her that something was wrong, something was wrong, something was…

Jessie yawned too, and the warning voice seemed to forget whatever was so urgent. She just needed a nap and…

No, no, something was wrong. Across the room Jackie was already blissfully laid out on her cot. NoNoNO! What was happening? Jessie tried to force her eyes open. She had to do something, she had to…

Jessie wobbled and suddenly couldn't stop herself from slumping backwards, landing on her pillow with a horrifying feeling like she was trapped in a nightmare. She dimly willed her arms to move, to get up and–

The door clicked open. Through cloudy eyes, she saw Ms Davani followed by the man from the truck earlier.

Jessie tried to move, tried to speak, but she couldn't. She was so tired.

Through her bleary eyes, Ms Davani's ever-present smile seemed to transform into a wolfish grin. And she dimly heard the man call, "Catherine, I'll get these two, you fold up the beds."

The man grew tall as a giant as he walked over. Then Jessie's vision turned to darkness.

Chapter 2
Cara

Kristina despised Exodus Week. It meant people actually wanted to buy things, and as a store owner, that was completely unacceptable.

"I don't see what's wrong with pink," the blonde woman insisted, holding up a miniskirt with a grin like the skirt was about to start talking and answer her.

Kristina had to bite her lip to hold the words in. *Maybe because it makes you look like you're off to middle school cheerleading tryouts*? She was still puzzling out a tactful way to suggest that when the woman's friend thankfully chimed in with an iota of sense.

"Anna, don't you think it makes you look a bit… young?"

The blonde frowned. "I thought that was the point, Jamie? You keep saying that's what Brendan wants?"

"Yeah, but like, twenty-two young… not sixteen." As if to emphasize, Jamie subtly nodded towards the far side of the store, where some *actual* sixteen-year-olds were browsing the jewelry aisle, one of them sporting a remarkably similar skirt with a rosy pink top.

Anna's expression fell with a quiet, "Oh…"

Kristina turned and strolled a few paces away, fighting back the niggling urge to stab herself with the nearest clothes hanger and end it all. This was absurd. And it wasn't even her real job.

She had actual, real world, life or death problems to attend to up here.

Well… maybe not *life or death* per se, but a girl could hope.

Plus, she still needed to figure out which of her people was stealing from her. That was probably more important than, helping a pair of fashion-clueless engineers buy a dress for Mars. Not even for Mars really, mainly for some silly, puppy-dog-eyed romance on the Persephone.

Who knew? Anna might never wear the dress. She didn't seem to get out that much, and Kristina sincerely doubted that anything she sold here could pass for appropriate in a reactor room.

"Ohhh, what about this?" She glanced over to see Anna grab another skirt off the rack. The woman must have been dead set on the cheerleader look, because this one was a school uniform style, red and black tartan that didn't match *anything* else she'd looked at.

Kristina sighed. Deep breaths, she murmured to herself.
Deep breaths.

She felt the instinctive urge to halt the awful fashion-crime that was in progress, but forced herself to pause. Maybe she'd let Jamie talk her friend out of that one. What was the phrase? If you can't say anything nice, don't say anything at all. Unfortunately, she was rapidly reaching the point where she'd just have to shut up for the rest of the day.

It was a shame too. Anna had a perfect figure and gorgeous, golden-blonde hair that almost glowed in the light. Except she'd apparently been raised by wolves and couldn't choose an outfit to save her life. If she could just settle on some colors that worked together and didn't bleed desperation, she could have this guy wrapped around her finger in an instant.

Frowning, Kristina thumbed through the nearest rack of skirts, her fingers rubbing the smooth fabric as she flicked past each in turn, *no, no, no… definitely no*. The worst part was, deep down, no matter how many times she claimed this wasn't her job and told herself she didn't care, a treacherous little part of her sensed exactly what Anna needed. Stepping over to the next rack, Kristina expertly flicked through the hangars looking for… *that one*. She pulled out a dark burgundy skirt that she actually stocked in adult sizes.

Spinning and taking two more steps to another rack, her fingers danced across a row of fine cotton tops. It should be right… *there*.

Her hand emerged clutching a slender, cream blouse. She held it up for an instant. The cut ought to be right for Anna. Burgundy would match the Mars theme, and the off-white blouse laced with rose designs would set just right with Anna's strawberry blonde hair.

Hurrying back to the two women, she forced a pleasant smile. "How about these?" she offered. "More subtle, and with sleeves instead of straps."

She might have been dangling a diamond the way both engineers' eyes lit up. In a flash, Anna was posing with the ensemble, while Jamie admired her with an encouraging nod. For an instant, Kristina felt a glimmer of satisfaction as the two women cooed over the outfit. Rack up another win for elegance.

Then she caught herself… and remembered where she was. Exiled to most backwater assignment in the solar system. Some of the lightness in her chest vanished, and her lips drew flat as she glanced around her store. Kristina wasn't claustrophobic, but it still seemed like the walls shrunk in slightly around her. And she wished that, for once, just once, something genuinely exciting might happen.

***

Thirty feet across the sales floor, Cara glared at the same shaky-cam video replaying on her phone for about the sixtieth time in as many minutes. At this point, just seeing the thumbnail made her want to puke, yet her eyes were glued to the screen regardless.

That bitch.

Literally, the second day since she'd left, and Amy was…

A supernova of rage churned in Cara's chest. If she ever saw Amy again, she was going to… to…

16

"What do you think of these?" Maddie's bubbly voice sliced into her brewing revenge plot.

"Huh?" Cara looked up to see her friend holding a pair of polished platinum hoop earrings with her usual buoyant grin.

"Do you think they're cute?"

Cara cocked a skeptical eyebrow. "You don't think they're a bit gaudy?"

"Well… maybe," Maddie's expression crumbled. She stared at the earrings another moment, disappointed, before turning back to the jewelry turntable and rapid-fire shuffling through the boxes. "What abouuuut– these?"

She enthusiastically held up a pair of dangling amethyst crescents. "Do they look good?"

Nope, still gaudy. Cara glimpsed the price tag on the jewelry box and winced. Apparently they were stupidly expensive too. Not that money had never stopped Maddie before. And admittedly, the *right in your face* style fit her friend's personality like a glove.

"I… they're fine," Cara said, distracted. She spent a moment flicking through her own turntable of bracelet and necklace boxes, deliberately ignoring her phone as it buzzed for the hundredth time.

"You really think so?"

"Sure, whatever." Cara focused on a ruby necklace so Maddie couldn't see her roll her eyes.

"Great, I think I'm going to get them."

Cara almost choked and had to cough to cover it. Just like that? Had Maddie even *looked* at the price?

"Mom said I could grab something before we left for Mars," Maddie continued. "These would be perfect. They're very – bold."

"Yeah," Cara gave a noncommittal nod. *Bold*, that was one way to put it. For a moment she pretended at being busy, at least until Maddie's persistently cheerful voice chimed right in her ear.

"You should get something too."

"I'm fine," Cara snapped, her eyes flicking back at her phone as it buzzed yet again. Another message flashed across the top of the screen and she felt a renewed stab of fury when she caught Amy's name. Frick, it was still six AM back home, didn't people have sleep, or cross country practice, or… anything else to do?

Maddie must have glimpsed the message also, because her voice abruptly softened. "Hey," she touched Cara's shoulder, "it'll be okay, Cara. Just give it a few days and–"

"Don't you have some earrings to buy?" Cara cut her off, turning away with a cold scowl. Not now. She didn't need another one of Maddie's counseling sessions. Or to talk about things, or… or…

Right now, unless it involved ruining Amy's life, Cara *really* didn't care.

And apparently that wasn't okay either.

Behind her, Maddie's voice turned frustrated. "Cara, I'm just saying, you can try to ignore it."

"Yeah, Amy is awful, but she's already a thousand miles away, and obsessing over–"

Her voice died as Cara spun and fixed her friend with a venomous, *shut up* glare.

Maddie went dead quiet as Cara successfully murdered the conversation. Stepping past her friend, Cara let out a breath she hadn't realized she was holding, and absently combed a hand through her hair, the anger ebbing from a raging forest fire to a more controlled simmer.

She glared down at the same ruby necklace from before, fuming. Sure, just ignore it, brush it off… don't worry. Easy for Maddie to say. She wasn't the one who'd been completely humiliated. She hadn't seen *her* life turned into an utter joke. She didn't have to watch everyone she cared about turn on her, watch her best friend just…

Almost of its own accord, Cara's hand clutched hard at the box with the ruby necklace. She momentarily stared into the gemstone pendant, allowing her eyes and her fury to lose themselves in the strange magnetism of the glittering geometric facets.

No one spoke.

Finally Maddie piped up, a willful optimism in her voice, like she was forcing the happiness back into the store, even if it didn't want to be there. "You should get something, Cara. It'll help."

Also easy for Maddie to say, Cara thought with a stab of resentment. That required money.

"Seriously," Maddie insisted, "retail therapy will make you feel better." Her voice turned devious as she added, "Plus, you can always rub it in Amy's face."

Cara hesitated at the last bit. Her focus mentally locked on the image of Amy squirming in envy.

"Just find something cute," Maddie encouraged. "It never hurts to look."

Slowly, Maddie's relentless positivity quenched the worst of Cara's fury. Enough, at least, for Cara to squash down her seething frustration. Her fingers slipped from their death grip on the ruby necklace box, and suddenly Cara felt strangely tired. Maybe Maddie was right, a part of her dimly conceded. It never hurt to look.

For a moment, Cara surrendered and took Maddie's advice. The ruby red necklace wasn't quite her color, so her eyes roved across the turntable racks of jewelry. A nice selection... for outer space at least. Spinning the turntable, she found a rainbow mix of colors – jade, opal, onyx, garnet – her eyes hesitated as they fell on a pearl bracelet.

That one.

Cara had told herself upon coming into the store that she wasn't getting anything. Just a glance at the prices in the window had been enough to let her know that whatever she might find would be a hard *No* from Mom. But before she could stop herself, she'd snatched up the bracelet. The string of pearls was cool to the touch, and gently rubbing two together, she felt a hint of grittiness. She held it up, noting a little blemish on one pearl that marked it out as real. The bright store lights caught the milky orb and for an instant she froze, the lustrous glow drawing her in.

Maddie's expectant voice interrupted, "Well, are you going to try it on?"

She shouldn't. Cara already knew she couldn't afford the bracelet. If Mom were here, she'd give a dissatisfied *hmmm*, walk away, and that would be it. Cara had been there before. If she tried to protest, Mom would fix her with an evil eyed glare until she reluctantly put it back. But Mom wasn't here... and the mental image of rubbing something new and flashy in Amy's smug face hit her like a shot of caffeine straight to the arm. She could already read the caption text in her head, *Living the High Life Up in Space*.

Cara draped the bracelet over her wrist, the magnetic clasp snapping around her wrist with a satisfying *clink*. Next to her, Maddie was all grins. "It's perfect. Definite buy."

Even given the dour day, Cara couldn't escape a smile as Maddie added a conspiratorial, "I bet the boys up here will love it too."

Cara spent a moment admiring it from a half dozen different angles. It *was* perfect. There was even an *Authentic - Sustainably Grown Thai Pearls* tag. She could guarantee Amy didn't have anything close to this. All her jewelry was the trashy, discount store kind.

Then Cara flipped over the tag to see the price stamped on the back...

Oh... she bit her lip at the number. That would explain why Amy didn't have it. Couldn't afford *that* when your dad was a First Sergeant. Unfortunately, the price was also steep enough to earn her a good old-fashioned grounding when Mom saw it pop up on the bank statement.

Cara stared one lingering moment, suddenly wishing she hadn't blown all her money on that goodbye bash last week, especially given the way everyone had sold her out the moment she'd left.

Next to her Maddie was still grinning. "Well?" she demanded. "Are you going to get it?"

Not if she had to pay for it, no.

There was another way, but...

Cara sighed, her resolve wavering. Her fingers twisted at a loose strand of amber brown hair. She shouldn't, she shouldn't, she...

If she got caught, Mom would murder her.

But then again… she glanced around the store, taking the lay of the land. One girl at the register, another in a purple cardigan helping two women towards the back, a single camera up top.

She wouldn't get caught.

And besides, it wasn't like Mom paid enough attention to even notice her suddenly sporting something new and cute and…

Her phone gave another irritating buzz. Glancing at her screen, Cara saw Francesca making snide little insinuations that Michael had never really loved her. Never mind that they'd been together for the last year, and they'd done Halloween as matching Oreo halves.

For a beautiful moment Cara found an escape, an image of the miserable scowl on Amy's face when she saw the bracelet.

Next to her, Maddie was grinning in anticipation, and Cara felt her last walls of resolve melt.

Yes, definitely yes. She'd get it and jam it right up Amy's backstabbing nose.

Aloud though, she said, "I can't." Cara shook her head and unclamped the magnets, gently laying the string of pearls back in its box.

"Yes, you *can*," Maddie whispered like a sly shoulder angel. But when Cara finally did set the box back on the table, Maddie's face creased in a frown. She mumbled a put out, "Oh, come on, Cara."

"Maybe later." Cara gave her usual excuse.

Maddie let out an exasperated huff and turned to examine the rack behind them. "Well, what about…"

Cara wasn't listening. Instead, her gaze rapidly swept the store. Purple Cardigan was still talking with the two women, register girl was just finishing checking someone out, a trio of glitzy college girls were excitedly poking through tops two racks over. No one was even looking at her.

She deliberately avoided staring at the tinted camera bulb studded into the ceiling towards the back, dead give-away. Instead, she picked up a box with the slim ruby necklace and drifted over a step like she was just browsing until she was blocking the camera's view.

The secret was to confuse the shoplifting AI. Most stores didn't actually track individual pieces, weights… all that. Way too expensive with all the sensors. Instead, they usually compared before and after images, to flag if something, say a bunch of white pearls, mysteriously vanished after she walked by. Thing was though, people were messy, they shuffled stuff around, re-stacked boxes, put things back upside down, and the AI was designed to ignore that. Which meant…

Cara's hand snaked out, and in a flash the pearl box was empty. The bracelet nestled perfectly in her wristlet purse, and she daintily set the ruby necklace box on top of it to confuse the camera. She'd done this before, but even so, it all happened so quickly that she surprised herself. It always felt like it should have been more complicated. Except it wasn't. It was a bit of a rush, actually. She felt her cheeks warming in excitement. She'd just done it…

Behind her Maddie spoke up, eagerly, "What about this, Cara?"

Cara started, but quickly recovered and turned to see her friend holding up a silver bracelet studded with polished jade circles.

"See, it'll match that skirt you have."

"I'm not sure jade is really my color." Cara shook her head, suddenly eager to get away from the place. "Seriously, Maddie, maybe later. I'll think about it."

Maddie pouted with an exaggerated, "Whatever." She got over her disappointment fast enough though, and a moment later was bouncing off towards the register to flash more of mom and dad's money. One of the perks of being a private contractor over being in the actual military, it definitely paid a lot better.

Cara's hand drifted to the distinctive lumps where the pearls were crammed in her wristlet purse. She glanced around the store, a sudden hunted worry churning in her gut. No one was marching angrily towards her, though.

Chill, she whispered to herself, *just don't act suspicious.* That was easier said than done. Her first time shoplifting had been a phone case. Mom wouldn't buy it so she'd… improvised. Her legs might as well have been jelly walking out, but she'd gotten away. And she'd improved since then. This time she relaxed her shoulders and let out a long breath, forcing her stomach muscles to unclench as she edged for the exit.

She'd always felt a little twinge of nervousness walking out of a store without buying anything. For some reason, her mind always wondered if the clerks would assume she was stealing. But this time, she could fricking swear everyone was watching her. Being on a space station, even a big one, didn't exactly reassure her either. If she screwed up, there was nowhere to run. But despite the feeling like someone was playing a symphony on her nerves, no one stopped her. *Just walk normally.*

She felt a building wave of exhilaration as the exit loomed up ahead. Then she stepped out past the threshold into the bustle of the Medea Station promenade.

Boom, she'd done it. To either side, the giant ring station curved upwards in the distance like a vast bowl. Up along the curve, she caught sight of a hamburger place she remembered passing earlier, *Ring World Buns* or… whatever. It would probably be–

"Hold it right there, hun."

A firm hand grabbed at her shoulder and a jolt like lightning hit her heart. "What the…"

She spun around, breaking the grip, only to find herself facing down the purple cardigan woman from inside. Oh, crap.

The woman's lips split in a fierce, bobcat grin. "I think you're forgetting something."

Cara swallowed hard, but didn't flinch. She *wasn't* getting caught. After the beer run fiasco back at Christmas, Mom would legitimately end her. Fortunately, back before Amy had been a traitorous bitch, the two of them had been trapped in this exact same spot before, staring down angry store employees with illicit things crammed in their pockets. The secret to escape was easy. Confidence.

"What's your deal, lady?" Cara snapped angrily. She took a step back, affronted. Usually employees backed off if you got angry. When she'd worked a stint at the mall last summer, they'd actually been flat out told *not* to get involved and just call security, which rarely did anything either.

Surprisingly, the woman didn't back down. Her brown eyes narrowed and her hand latched back on Cara's shoulder. "I believe you have something of mine."

"Well, you're wrong." Cara tried to pull her shoulder free, but the grip just tightened. "Let me go!"

"Or what?" The lady mocked in a patronizing tone, like she was daring Cara to try. "You'll go cry to mommy and daddy? Throw a tantrum?"

The same part of Cara that had spent the last hour stewing over Amy bristled at the woman's casual arrogance, like this was all some sort of joke. Unfortunately, she'd hit her breaking point a while back. "Don't touch me."

"Oh, is the little thief angry?" The woman's grin widened and her eyes narrowed like a tiger. "How about you return everything you stole, and I'll *consider* being merciful."

Cara felt a surge of anger at the woman's patronizing tone and let it power her. She twisted, throwing her entire body weight against the woman, and the hand slipped free. Cara danced back–

Then slammed to a halt.

The cardigan woman's other hand snaked out and snatched her wrist with a ferocious strength. The last thing Cara saw was the woman stepping close, then her world twisted into a blur. When everything crashed back into view, she was face to face with the station bulkhead, her cheek smashed against the cold steel paneling. Her whole face stung, and her arm had been wrenched back, screaming like it might pop out of its socket. The woman crushed her against the wall with her entire body weight, and Cara gasped at the pain.

"Now then," the woman's smug voice declared somewhere near her ear, "Let's try this again, hun. You have a stolen bracelet of mine, and I'd rather like it back. Does that sound about right?"

Reality crashed over Cara like a cold tsunami. NoNoNo…

"WHAT THE HELL LADY!" Maddie shrieked from nearby. "YOU LET HER GO!"

Cara heard a dull *thwump* and a sharp, "OWWWW."

The woman swore. "Kid, stay out of this." From the corner of her eye, Cara dimly saw Maddie lashing at the woman with her handbag. Then the woman caught the purse and jerked Maddie close. The pressure on Cara's arm tightened, and she screamed at the pain, her world turning to a haze as the two grappled with each other. "STOP IT!" Maddie shrieked. "YOU'RE HURTING HER!"

An instant later the pain dimmed. Through the agonized tears brimming in her eyes, Cara saw Maddie stumbled a few steps backwards, tripping and ending up flat on her butt. Their eyes locked, Cara's friend staring at her, stunned, furious.

"Your friend's a thief," the woman snapped, pressing Cara against the wall. "Isn't that right? *Thief.*"

"Screw you!" Maddie screamed, scrambling to grab her wristlet purse where it had skidded across the floor. "Cara, tell her that's stupid!"

Cara barely heard. In the back of her mind a desperate voice was screaming in full on panic. She couldn't get arrested. "Let me go!" She tried to squirm free and threw her entire body back against the woman, and for an instant the woman finally seemed to budge–

But only for an instant.

The woman shoved her back and Cara's head banged against the bulkhead with an impact that left her forehead and her nose both stinging. Cara gasped for breath as the horrible woman twisted her arm just to the point of stabbing pain and held it with a mocking, "Tsk, tsk, I didn't say you could go… *thief.*"

Cara's world blurred in agony. Tears poured down her cheeks, unbidden, and even trying to move just amplified the flaring pain in her shoulder. She could only dimly hear Maddie, still screaming, and when the woman's steely grip on her arm finally relaxed, she didn't feel any relief at all. The tears didn't stop.

As the vicious pain eased, the void left behind flooded with a cold, dread at what Cara knew came next. This woman was absolutely insane and…

Behind Cara, the woman murmured, "Oh don't cry yet. Let's see your purse, then we can call your parents. Save the tears for someone who cares."

Chapter 3
Gilded Cages

Seated on a plush couch in the break room behind the dress store, Cara rubbed her eyes, and tried to pretend she was anywhere else. She tried to pretend Mom *wasn't* sitting right next to her. She also tried to ignore the furious shouts that leaking past the closed door to Kristina's office. "What in all the stars is wrong with you, Kristina!"

"I told you, Perry, she tried to shoplift."

"So you *attacked* her?"

"*Apprehended.*" Kristina's voice came back irate, peeved, and oddly haughty, given who she was talking too. "Technically, I did warn her to stop. But when the little brat tried to run, I had no choice."

The only response was a moment of dumbfounded silence from the office.

Staring at the floor, Cara tried to ignore the worried butterflies bouncing around her stomach. Instead, she busily scrubbed her cheeks with a hand towel, cleaning off the blush she'd applied this morning, and which her tears had streaked beyond recognition. She tried to make a show of been busy, all while avoiding eye contact with Mom like she was Medusa herself.

After several wipes though, Cara hesitated at seeing part of the hand towel come back still snowy white, instead of a light crimson. For an instant, a part of her almost wished Kristina had slammed her against the wall just a bit harder. That might have given her a legitimate bloody nose, instead of one that just stung to touch. At least that might have earned her more sympathy from Mom. Maybe then they'd be in the infirmary, not… here.

As it was, she could feel the silent, icy rage radiating off Mom, enough to send a chill scuttling down her spine. With little else to dwell on, the dread of what came next sank into her bones. She was *soooo* screwed.

She'd hoped Dad would come instead. He'd be furious for a bit. But then he'd ground her, she would cry a bit, and it would be over… more or less. Mom though–

Camped on the floor at Mom's feet, the twins were somehow blissfully ignorant of the livid scowl on her face. Instead, they were busy with some stupid game that involved punching each other. Eli whacked Leo on the shoulder. "Owww." Leo winced, pulling back his arm to–

Mom hissed, "*You two, STOP.*" Her cold expression twisted in a furious snarl.

The twins froze and Cara pulled her arms a bit closer at the icy bite in Mom's voice. She wished the plush couch could just swallow her up and end things already.

Inside the office, Perry's voice rose again. "Kristina, *no one does that!*"

"She was getting away!"

"To where? We're on a space station!"

"So what then? I'm supposed to roll over and do nothing?"

"Yes!" Colonel Perry swore, his words dripping frustration. "Look, Kristina, I don't have time to deal with your psychosis, alright. I have actual problems. But you need to ease off by about *five thousand percent*. Got it? Next time someone tries to shoplift, you call the duty officer, show him the video and we'll take care of it."

An expectant pause.

"Is that understood?"

Kristina's voice was sullen and completely unconvinced. "Yes, sir."

The door swung open, and Perry strode out with a dark scowl. "And next time cut the attitude.

Kristina's voice transformed to a prim, sarcastic, "Of course, *sir*."

Eyes still fixed on the floor, Cara stared at Perry's polished boots as they took a couple steps, then paused in front of Mom. Down at Mom's feet, even Leo paused his idle, *I'm bored*, whacking at the couch cushions, and looked up.

"I guess I'll leave this to you, Major." Perry let out an exasperated sigh. "You have a handle on it?"

"Same as always, Colonel," Mom remarked, with a strained breeziness to her voice. "I appreciate you uhh… deescalating things."

"Of course," Perry hesitated a second. "Is Ian not…"

"Conference call. The usual handover problems at the old post."

"Ahh," Perry gave a half-hearted chuckle, "fair enough." The boots took a half step to leave, but paused. "It's good to see you again, Karen. A nice brood you two have there."

Mom's answer was cold enough to make Cara wilt, "We'll see."

Perry left, and Mom stood, snapping at Cara, "Get up."

She reached down, grabbed Leo and Eli's hands and briskly hauled the two little boys up to standing with a sharp jerk.

Mom might have left the service when the twins were born, but the Space Force hadn't really left her. She'd certainly lost none of her terrifying Major's tone. From the way she ran the house, Cara sometimes wondered if Mom had really just gotten a new command. One that happened to include two six-year-olds, along with her as the senior noncom.

Either way, she stood, sniffling and wiping at her eyes but willing herself not to cry. No point making things worse. She glance at Mom, who nodded towards the door, and Cara's heart sank as she realized she wouldn't even get the petty solace of slinking in dead last.

A part of her almost didn't move. Kristina had basically assaulted her after all. If Mom was so eager for this meeting, then she could go in first… except, Cara also knew she wasn't going to win that fight. She'd probably just burn whatever embers of sympathy Mom still had for her…

She hazarded a glance at Mom's frigid expression… that was, assuming Mom had any sympathy left at all. As she hesitated, Mom's foot began tapping at a rapid clip on the floor, like a bomb timer counting down to detonation. Cara knew from experience she had about five more taps until things got *really* bad. Taking a deep breath, she forced her feet towards the door, stepped inside and a moment later she was working overtime not to make eye contact while Mom introduced herself.

"Karen Rosenfeld."

Given how heated everything had just sounded, the woman seemed remarkably warm and friendly as she introduced herself to Mom. "Kristina Andrews."

The Kristina gestured for them to sit across from her at a utilitarian, metal-framed desk. Unlike Kristina's temper, the desk was neatly arranged. A folded down work tablet and thermos sat at one end. Meanwhile the sleek silver base of a holo-wardrobe projector sat off to the side, idly cycling through a menagerie of different gowns. Kristina dropped down into a rolling chair across from them with a polite, "It's good to meet you, Ms Rosenfeld."

Cara sincerely doubted that, but she followed Mom's lead and took a seat.

There were only two chairs, so Leo and Eli both wasted an awkward moment squabbling for a spot on Mom's lap until she swatted them down, "Sit down, and stay quiet." She shot both little boys *The Glare*, the extra scary one she reserved for special moments, and instantly the twins went silent as field mice.

"I assume you and Cara have already been introduced," Mom continued brusquely. "I'm deeply sorry for any trouble my daughter might have caused. I thought we raised her better than that, but…"

Mom's voice trailed off with a burning glare in Cara's direction. Apparently she'd gotten the jist of the situation over the phone, so they hadn't spoken much since she'd stormed in ten minutes ago. Regardless, Cara knew what to say. "I'm very sorry," she mumbled, trying not to sound too perfunctory and swallowing back the miserable resentment burning in her chest. "I shouldn't have tried to steal… It won't happen again."

Technically that was true, she was sorry… sorry she'd gotten caught.

"Well, I'm sorry too," Kristina nodded, her politeness seeming more than a little forced given the context of how things had gone down earlier. "It's become apparent I overreacted and uh…" Staring at the table, Cara watched Kristina's fingers drum an irate, not particularly apologetic symphony. "I might have used substantially more force than was strict necessary."

Oh right, Cara mused indignantly, that's what almost dislocating someone's arm was called.

Mom continued, "Well, that's good to hear. Hopefully we can put all this unpleasantness behind us."

As the women talked, Cara found her eyes idly regarding Kristina's things. She stared at the thermos and the tablet, both of them a pastel purple to match her cardigan. Odd, the thought danced through her head, purple didn't quite feel like Kristina's color. Too subtle.

Her focus snapped back to Mom as she caught, "…and of course I'll make sure Cara here is adequately punished. Her behavior was completely unacceptable. You should know she'll be spending most of her remaining time on Medea in our cabin. I'll make certain she isn't allowed to bother you again."

What? Cara blinked at Mom's words. She swallowed back a feeling like the life was being sucked from her chest. A sudden weight pressed her back against the chair. Spend the rest of her time in the cabin? Seriously?

Sure, she'd tried to walk out of a store with a bracelet. Yeah, it was bad, but it wasn't *imprisonment* bad.

"Sounds excellent." Across from them Kristina gave a small nod. "Hopefully that will hammer the lesson in."

"Yes," Mom remarked dourly, and even without looking up, Cara could feel her glare. "We can only hope."

"If you don't mind my asking, how long are you here for?"

"Saturday evening," Mom said.

"Oh…" Kristina's tapping fingers paused, and daring to look up, Cara caught a flash of surprise on the woman's face.

Yeah, *oh*, especially given it was Monday. The sourest pill was that she'd briefly been excited at the prospect of a layover. That had been the sole bright spot in discovering that Dad was being sent to Mars and she'd have to abandon her entire life. At least she'd have five full days with Maddie to explore one of the world's biggest space stations. They could browse all the shops, sample the local cuisine, and take in the twirling views of Earth. She'd been planning on spotting out the Great Wall and the Giza Pyramids. She'd also heard that thunderstorms were particularly spectacular from above. It had almost sounded fun.

Mom simply nodded at Kristina's surprise, masterfully covering over all the irritation Cara had seen her display in private. "Military timing and all. You learn to live with it."

"Of course," Kristina said, betraying nothing and going quiet. Cara looked up only to meet Kristina's calculating eyes, which bored straight into her. She averted her gaze to the tabletop, but Kristina didn't budge, the silent intensity between them building like a noiseless scream. Cara fought back the urge to slink down in her seat as the moment drug out into a painfully awkward forever until…

"What if I had an alternative arrangement?" Kristina finally broke her soul probing glare and looked back at Mom.

"As in?"

"I've been a tad short on help the last couple of days, especially with the Mars crowds and all. What if I took Cara off your hands and put her to work? It's nothing exciting, lots of scut work honestly, but…" Kristina paused, "I'd pay her, of course. I've done enough free work to not be a fan of it."

Wait, what? Cara froze, horrified. She glanced over and caught the way Mom's expression had instantly brightened at the mention of *scut work*.

"And you're okay with having her around, even after…"

"Oh, I think she's learning her lesson. This might help it sink in. Besides, it's mostly backroom stuff."

No, No, NO! Cara wanted to scream. Working for Kristina was the absolute last place she wanted to be. That might be worse than the cabin. And why would Kristina even want her?

In desperation she tried to speak up, "I don't know about–"

"It'd only be for the week," Kristina added helpfully.

"But I don't have anything to wear."

"I've got a charming jumpsuit that should fit," Kristina said, with a panther gleam in her eyes.

"But–"

"Quiet," Mom snapped, eying her with a plotting expression that Cara had long since learned meant trouble.

For an agonizing second, Mom said nothing, until, "You really don't mind, Miss Andrews?"

Cara bit back a curse.

"Of course not. Like I said, I've got plenty for her to do. And keeping an eye on her shouldn't be a problem."

Mom nodded, her lips twisting in a cold smile. "That might be just the thing she needs. You can keep her during the day. She can earn her own money for a change, and I can have her watch the twins in the evening. That actually sounds like a perfect punishment. What do you think, Cara? Does that sound appropriate?"

Appropriate, no. It sounded like her own personal hell. She caught Mom's glower though, and knew better than to argue. Otherwise Mom would just tack on something even worse to the pile.

She swallowed back a frustrated lump in her throat. She'd guessed that *something* awful was rushing down the pipe. Apparently she'd been correct. Cara sighed. "Yes, ma'am," she mumbled sourly. "Sounds about right."

Chapter 4
Stellar Coffee

Cara's stomach twisted with dread, and the waiting was only making it worse. With her punishment out of the way, Mom and Kristina chatted a few more minutes. Cara noted that the two now seemed to get along famously, nothing like bonding over ruining her life. Eventually though, Mom rose, collecting the twins and leaving without even a word of goodbye, just a frigid, *you deserve this* glare. Then it was just her and Kristina.

"Come on then." Kristina stood and made for the door, curtly gesturing her to follow. "We don't have all day for you to lounge around."

The whole situation felt surreal, like living in a dream where she'd just been disowned, but Cara numbly stood and followed. Outside, Kristina took a sharp left and paused in front of a utilitarian shelving unit adjacent to the restroom. She knelt down to the bottom shelf, thumbing through the layers of neatly folded clothes before pulling out something grey and tossing it to Cara. "Put that on, it should be about your size." She flicked Cara towards the bathroom, "Now."

"But…" Cara froze, her eyes widening as she held up the bundle and a baggy, puke grey jumpsuit unfurled before her. All it needed was a few white stripes to fit right in at a prison.

No. Absolutely – fricking – no.

She glared at Kristina, with a sarcastic, "I think I prefer my normal clothes."

"Well, too bad," Kristina remarked with a merciless smirk. "If you work here, you wear a uniform."

Cara's mouth dropped open in indignation. *"Seriously?* I didn't notice anyone else wearing this *uniform."*

"Well, nobody else here is a juvenile delinquent either." Kristina shrugged and nodded to the bathroom door with a patronizing, "If you prefer, I can probably find something worse."

Oh, screw her. Cara's cheeks flushed in a wave of flamethrower hot fury, and a single venomous mutter slipped out, "Bitch."

From Kristina's terrifying, almost triumphant smirk, the word might as well have been a compliment. "Why don't you try on your new outfit?"

Kristina roughly nudged her towards the restroom. A moment later, Cara found herself standing in the cramped lavatory that smelled faintly of lavender. She numbly stared at her new *uniform,* trying to ignore Kristina's foot tapping like an impatient metronome outside. Frick. This couldn't be happening, this couldn't be happening, this couldn't–

"Are you done in there yet, hun?" Kristina's sarcastic voice cut in. "If you're obsessing about your hair... I wouldn't bother."

Cara's gut twisted in another boiling urge to do... something. But if she ran, Kristina would call Mom and...

A frustrated sigh slipped out as she glumly realized there was really only one thing she could do... she closed her eyes, winced, and slipped on the prison suit.

Stepping back outside, Cara was painfully aware that she looked like an escaped inmate. But Kristina regarded her outfit with an excited grin that sent a chill down the girl's spine, *"Perfect."*

Kristina abruptly wheeled and started towards the front. "Come on. We don't have all day."

On the short walk, she continued, "Just so we're both on the same page, I only have two serious rules here. First, work hard.

That should be a given. Second, you will not, under any circumstances, enter my office alone. You can knock, pound on the door, Melody has my number to call if you need it. But you *stay out* unless I tell you. If you can manage that, we'll get along... better." Kristina paused, turning to fix Cara with a laser glare, "Do you understand?"

Cara nodded, not trusting what would come out if she opened her mouth. That earned her a second glare from the shop woman. "Third rule, you'll use words when spoken to," Kristina added condescendingly. "Get some value out of that high school education."

It was like Kristina was *trying* to be infuriating. For an instant, Cara didn't care what happened. She came within a hair's breadth of slugging the vile, patronizing woman right in the face. Right until she remembered how their last confrontation had gone. Reluctantly, she tried to squeeze her rage back into its bottle for later.

"Yes, Ma'am," she nearly spat the words out. "Understood."

After entering through the dress store, Cara was more than a little surprised when Kristina pushed through the next few doors and they emerged out into... a coffee shop next door? Did Kristina own both?

They were standing behind the serving bar, and at twelve noon, the place was packed like a mall on Christmas Eve. The moment they stepped though, a harried looking Hispanic woman wearing a blue and gold apron darted over. She was toting a white coffee mug in each hand, one black and steaming and the other with a mountain of whipped cream on top. "Ms Andrews, the creamer didn't make it up on today's shipment."

Kristina's face creased, "You're sure?"

Coffee-girl nodded, "Military bumped the general supplies pallets today *and* tomorrow. Some priority gear. That was all Aaron would tell me."

Kristina sighed, "How much do we still have stocked?"

"At this rate, we'll make it through tomorrow morning."

Kristina's face creased in a frown. "Alright, start only handing it out on request. I'll light a fire under Aaron and remind him what a mutiny they'd have if they ran out of coffee supplies up here. Anything else?"

Coffee-girl snapped her finger twice, as though trying to remember, then pointed, "Dish soap."

"Right," Kristina nodded. "I bummed two cases off Miranda at Trio. We just need to pick it up."

Coffee-girl nodded, took two steps over to the counter and called, "Leon? Skinny black? Catherine? White chocolate mocha?"

She barely paused to hand off the drinks, then spun back to Kristina. "Alright, but Stephan won't be here for another hour and a half, and I don't know when either of us will have time to make the run to Trio."

"I've got you covered there." Kristina nodded towards Cara. "Melody, I want you to meet Cara. She'll be here the rest of the week. She's working as a punishment, so feel free to use and abuse her as you see fit. Probably starting with a supply run."

Melody's eyes widened with a, *what did you do to piss her off* look. Apparently she'd missed the show next door.

Fortunately, Melody was too busy to pry. Instead, she gave a curt nod and focused her very business-like gaze on Cara as Kristina wheeled to leave. "You know where Trio Pasta is?"

Cara opened her mouth to—

"Never mind, you wouldn't, would you." Melody barely paused, and set to pacing in the tiny space between the serving bar and the coffee machines as she spoke. "Okay, get the Medea Map app, take a trolley down to Trio, and tell Miranda that Kristina sent you for the soap. Then get back here ASAP."

For a second, Cara could swear her brain straight up decoupled from the rest of reality. She was supposed to do what…?

An hour ago she'd been on vacation. And now she was stuck here in a chaotic mess of a coffee shop, and people expected her to go places and get things and–

"Well?" Cara was dimly aware of Melody staring at her like she was an idiot. "Get moving. You need to get to Trio before the lunch rush starts or we're going to run out of mugs."

"I…"

"Alex? Coffee Frappuccino?" A loud barista's voice punctuated their conversation.

A second young blonde in the same distinctive blue and gold apron brushed by. "Melody, I could use a hand. Number two needs the filter changed."

"On it." Melody spun off in her frenetic style. Then, as though she'd forgotten something important, spun right back, pointing at Cara. "Trolleys are outside the stockroom. Take them out the back door. Code is 1133." Melody executed a final dizzying heel turn and strode over to the giant, polished-chrome coffee machine.

Cara stared, her mind as blank as her expression while the bewildering haze of people on both sides of the counter bustled by. She tried to keep all that in, but she already had a mild sense of panic that she'd forgotten something important.

She blinked, somehow more worried and stressed than before. What had she landed herself in now?

***

"Hello? Anybody?" Cara pounded on the back door of, what her phone assured her, was Trio Pizza for the third time. Were they just ignoring her?

She stepped back a moment, arms crossed, glaring at the door and willing it open.

Nothing.

"Seriously, open up!" She banged her fist on the door, setting it to shuddering with a loud BOOM.

Still no one.

Cara let out an exasperated huff. She glanced back down the endless, unmarked service hallway to where it followed the arc of the ring station, curving upwards and vanishing in the distance. Already the worried thoughts were setting in. How long until Melody expected her back? What if she complained to Kristina? She really didn't want to get chewed out… again.

Cara puffed out her cheeks and slowly let them deflate. She *could* go around front, but then everyone would see her in this awful prison suit. She scowled. Maybe that was Kristina's plan all along, to humiliate her as much as possible.

Frustrated, she punted at the door with a BANG that left her toes smarting.

"OWWW!" She hopped on one foot, swearing. Screw this whole stupid station, and Kristina and Mom, and Amy, and… and…

"GRRHHH!" She let out a frustrated shriek, her hands clenching in pent-up fury, ready to choke someone.

In the stillness the shout seemed deafening, but died away to an almost eerie silence. The service hallway remained as deserted as before, the only sound the ever-present whirr of the vent fans.

Even in the stillness, it took Cara a minute to calm down from her furious supernova to more of a red dwarf simmer. Finally though, she took a deep, deliberate breath. Okay, so it was either return in ignominious failure, get screamed at and potentially have Mom called *again*. Or, leave the cart and find somebody. Couldn't be that hard, right?

Right?

It was a several hundred foot backtrack to the nearest crossover back onto the Medea promenade. Then came a far more embarrassing hike back through the crowd. Cara wandered past an endless stream of restaurants and shops that sprawled out like a vast airport terminal. All the while she tried not to wilt in humiliation under the bemused stares of servicemen and the scattering of civilians streamed by.

Fortunately, with an enormous flashing pizza slice out front, Trio was hard to miss. At a glance, the place appeared to be a standard pizza-by-the-slice bar, with the lunch rush line already piling up. Unfortunately, she didn't see anyone to talk to beyond the cashier. She also wasn't in the mood to wait all the way through the line just to ask a question.

Cutting right to the front, she lasered in on a thin, gangly sort of boy wearing a ridiculous pizza themed apron and manning the register. Always trust a nerd to know where to go.

"Excuse me." She stalked up with a storm cloud frown and more or less elbowed in front of his next customer. "I've been knocking on the black door for the last *five minutes*."

The boy blinked in confusion. "Okay?"

"I guess no one thought to answer?"

The boy stared at her with a cockeyed frown. "Well… you're supposed to order up front. Also, you really can't cut the line like this."

Cara's cheeks flushed. "Look," she hissed, "I'm not here for a slice of pepperoni. I'm supposed to pick up some soap, so how about you point me to someone who actually *knows* what's going on. Sound good, Pizza Boy?"

Back at school that snark and the *don't screw with me* glare would have cowed him and gotten her anything she wanted. But surprisingly, the boy's eyes narrowed. A half empty bottle of Purell sat by the register, and he slowly nudged it towards her. "Does this work? Or are you too dirty for that to be enough?"

Cara's face went so hot that she was surprised her hair didn't burst into flames. "Tell me, *Pizza Boy* do you actually *enjoy* being stupid, or is it just that you can't help it?"

His voice kept an emotionless, *would you like a drink with that* tone, "Only around *some–*"

"Everything alright, Sebastian?" Fortunately, *for him,* an older woman, also in a burgundy, pizza themed apron, picked that moment to stroll up.

"Umm… yeah," he nodded towards Cara, "She says she's looking for dish soap?"

Cara smoothly name dropped. "For Kristina."

The woman regarded her in momentary surprise, "Oh, so you're the girl she caught shoplifting?"

Cara's heart dropped straight to the floor, then kept right on falling. The boy, Sebastian, stared at her, open-mouthed, the other woman watching in obvious amusement. "Yes," Cara mumbled, her cheeks flaming a furious scarlet as she tried to ignore the line of people behind her.

"Alright then," the woman nodded at Sebastian, "I'll take the register." She gestured for the next person in line, "I'll ring you up here, sir."

She flicked for Cara to step behind the counter. "Sebastian, go help her load up. It'll be two cases of dish soap," the woman fixed Cara with a warning glare, "no more."

No worries there. Cara had to struggle to keep from sneering. Just what every girl wanted – a bunch of industrial grade cleaning supplies.

She followed Sebastian back through the swinging door into a bustling narrow kitchen. Both of them squeezed to the side when a messy-aproned chef hurried past with a platter of fresh breadsticks.

"The soap is back here." Sebastian pushed through a second door into a cramped storeroom and pointed towards a cluster of gallon jugs plastic-wrapped into multipacks and stacked in a free corner.

Cara blinked. Everyone had been talking about cases of soap, but for some reason she'd been thinking in terms of two-pack bottles of Palmolive at the store. Not like… Costco six-gallon megapacks.

"You'll need a trolley to move them." Sebastian stated the obvious.

"It's out back," Cara said, then added a frosty, "if someone would ever answer the door."

A moment later she'd wheeled her cart inside, and gave one pack an experimental lift. It was heavy. *Really* heavy. Her arms strained just to get it off the ground. Cara half-lifted half-dragged the bundled soap two unsteady steps before her fingers slipped and she stepped back with her hands on her knees, panting.

"So, let me get this straight," Sebastian wore a mocking grin as he leaned against a shelf stacked to bursting with flour packages. "You tried to steal from the coffee shop lady, and now you work for her? How'd that happen?"

"It's only temporary," Cara muttered, taking a deep breath before giving the case another sharp tug, that slid it next to the trolley.

"Yeah, I bet so, especially when your boss hates you."

Cara glared at him, breathing hard while he lounged around. "You going to contribute Pizza Boy, or are your stick arms too wimpy for that?"

For an instant his face creased in a scowl, then in a flash, he marched over, grabbed the six pack and lifted it onto the trolley without so much as a grunt.

"That answer your question?"

Yeah, it did actually. Cara grinned to herself, one down. Before he could wander off, she'd grabbed the other case and put some desperation strength into dragging it over to the cart, "You mind?"

Sebastian bit his lip, frowning like he suspected she was using him, but he grudgingly obliged. In a moment, both packs were nicely centered on the trolley. Perfect.

Cara flashed him a taunting, *thanks for the help, loser,* smile as she hauled the suddenly heftier cart towards the door. Maybe he'd appreciate it. He probably didn't get many smiles from girls. She tugged the cart out and into the long service hallway that curved up in the distance. "See you around, Pizza Boy."

He strolled over to the door, with a nod, "You too, Klepto."

Cara's mouth dropped open, right as Sebastian promptly slammed the door in her face. For a second she glared at the grey steel, fuming. Oh yeah, she'd see him around, and Pizza Boy was going to get burned.

She had the whole slogging trip back to check her phone, which mostly just proved her world was still in the process of rapidly imploding. If it hadn't stung so much, she'd have marveled at how quickly all her friends had bailed on her. As it was, she threw her frustrated energy into dragging the cart back to Kristina's, where she barely managed to unload the collective twelve gallons of dish soap in the storeroom.

She was just finishing up when Melody wandered through, glancing at the translucent plastic jugs, brimming with green soap. "We need one of those up in the kitchen."

Frick, seriously?

Melody must have seen the look on Cara's face, because she added, "Just a gallon is plenty. You've got some scrubbing to do."

Scrubbing was an understatement. Walking into the wash room with Melody chatting away, Cara froze when she saw the sheer mass of dishes racked up and awaiting her.

"Consider this your life now," Melody chimed cheerfully. She walked to an oversized stainless steel sink, grabbed a pair of long rubber gloves and tossed them to Cara. "Wear these. You'll wash and dry all the mugs, plates, silverware, etc. We try to avoid disposables up here. Usually, Ruth or I will get the dishes during off hours, but you'll notice we're a bit behind this week. So this is all yours now."

Cara finally caught the gloves her eyes going wide, "But how do I…"

"You ever used a sprayer before?" Melody asked, grabbing a metal wand and squeezing the handle to send a brief jet of water slicing into the sink.

"Uhhh…"

"It's pretty simple. Basically, spray everything down and try to scrub off all the stuck-on food. Once you've prewashed an entire rack, throw it in the machine." She gestured towards a silvery steel boxlike contraption mounted on the countertop next to the sink. "Just slide the rack underneath, pull down to seal and let it do its cleaning."

That was all a lot easier said than done. Melody had about two minutes to show her how the setup worked before Ruth poked her head in with a curt, "We need you up front."

Then Cara found herself alone, staring at a room full of dirty dishes. More numb than anything else, she finally grabbed a white mug. Several dark smudges marred the rim and a thin puddle of black ooze swirled in the bottom, exuding a strong scent of black-coffee. Someone had like… put their lips on this, she realized with a budding horror, like… all over it. She glanced around the kitchen, the enormity of her task sinking in. Even wearing gloves this felt like putting your hands in a hundred different people's mouths. She'd been a little grossed out the first time she'd kissed her boyfriend, but this was a whole other level of nastiness.

She tried to use the sprayer, but the water splattered back in her face, leaving her with a miserable mist drenching her cheeks. And after trying to wipe it off a couple times, the arms of her jumpsuit were soaked through also. When Melody poked her head in ten minutes later, Cara wanted to scream in frustration.

"Is that still your first rack? You know dragging your feet doesn't make the dishes go away, right?"

"I'm trying, OKAY?" Cara insisted, spraying down a plate and getting another spatter of water on her face, before finally shuffling it aside.

Melody strolled over and picked it out. "This isn't clean," she declared, thrusting the plate right back at Cara and pointing at a speck of… some sort of caked-on goo near the rim. "That'll just bake on if you throw it in the washer."

Cara reached for the sprayer.

"Don't just water blast it," Melody said, sharply, "use your hands. That's why we hire *people* to do this job. That, and hold it low. Tilt away from you when you're spraying. It'll keep you from taking a bath all shift."

Cara took the plate, staring at the nastiness. Finally, she screwed up her face, and winced her eyes closed as she tepidly scrubbed it off with a sponge. This was so disgusting.

Next to her, Melody gave a disappointed snort.

"WHAT?" Cara whirled on her.

"Really? Have you never touched a dirty plate before?" Melody shook her head.

A furious Cara rinsed the plate, spot gone, and slammed it back in the dish rack so hard she was surprised it didn't shatter. "THERE, HAPPY NOW?"

Melody sighed, obviously not. Cara wanted to scream. So what, she was trapped here now, pawing through the whole station's germs with no one to help or… Cara blinked back frustrated tears, her voice desperate. "Please, isn't there *anything* else I can do?"

"Look, Cara," Melody calmly fixed her with a serious stare, "I know you don't want to be here. But you *are*. And unless you can memorize the drink menu in the next five minutes, this is the only job you're even *remotely* qualified to touch. So you're doing this. You can either do a good job and be part of the team, or you can sulk and make everyone else miserable too. Your choice."

Melody didn't wait for an answer, instead she wheeled and headed back up front. Once again Cara was alone, staring blankly at an endless pile of dishes.

Where to even start?

Maybe she should just leave, a little voice in her mind nagged. It wasn't like anyone was stopping her. She could always walk out… but then she'd have to face Mom. Her heart sank a little. She couldn't hide out in Maddie's cabin forever.

It felt like she was betraying a little part of herself, but slowly, Cara reached for another plate… and started rinsing.

Chapter 5
The Hub

The next day and a half blurred into an exhausting haze of mugs, plates and caked-on food. In the evenings, Cara found herself trapped with the twins while Mom and Dad enjoyed two consecutive date nights.

The second evening she'd staggered back from work, bone tired, and basically passed out on the couch after her parents left. Thankfully, the unsupervised twins hadn't worked out how to light the cabin on fire. But that nap had still earned Cara an old-fashioned screaming from Mom. For once she'd been too tired to care. Her arms hurt, her feet stung when she walked and she'd been forced to just sit there and absorb the brunt of Mom's ire.

When Mom finally tired of chewing her out, Dad had gestured her off to bed with a disappointed frown. Cara had slumped into her cot, with the cabin lights still on and the twins making their usual racket. She'd tried to tune out the madness. Yet it seemed she'd only just closed her eyes when she jolted awake to the blaring screech of her alarm.

Rolling over, she checked her phone– six in the morning. Okay, she could lay there for a few extra minutes and…

Dad mumbled from across the darkened cabin, "Get to work, Cara."

Next to him, Mom yawned and added, "There are clothes on top of your suitcase."

Oh, how fricking considerate.

Somehow she rolled out of bed, threw on something, and staggered her bleary-eyed way down to Kristina's. After changing into the prison suit, Cara found Melody, just in time for the woman to thumb her towards the kitchen with a scowl. "Cutting it close, are we?"

Then it was back to dish hell as the breakfast tsunami struck.

In the endless haze of wash, rack, repeat, Cara lost track of time, and jumped when Melody tapped her on the shoulder. "Clean up," the woman nodded toward the back. "You've got another delivery to do."

Ten minutes later, Cara stood at the entrance to the Medea Station service elevator, peering inside as the doors glided open. Sadly, there were no seats. She stared a half second in glum disappointment before finally wheeling her trolley inside. The spartan elevator was simple enough, basically a metal box with a door. The walls to the left and right were marked with gigantic arrows, one painted to point Up and the other pointing Down.

Before allowing her to set foot outside the coffee shop, Melody had doused her with an interminable lecture on how to use a fricking elevator. Cara suffered through the talk on which arrow to stand next to, how to position the cart, what to expect... blah, blah. And of course, Melody ended with, *don't forget the creamer,* because apparently, creamer was the only thing that *really* mattered on this station.

Tugging the trolley towards the *Up Arrow* wall, Cara maneuvered it lengthwise against the polished metal plating. She hesitated, running down a mental checklist as the door automatically closed behind her. The cart was braced, nothing would slide into her, and... she was definitely standing on the correct side. She reached for the button to start the elevator up towards the Medea Station hub, when the door gave an abrupt *ding* and slid open.

Pulling a trolley in backwards came a gangly looking boy with tousled black hair, and the burgundy back half of – what she could guess – was a pizza apron.

"This elevator's taken, Pizza Boy."

Sebastian spun around, his eyes going wide when he saw her glaring back. "Oh, perfect," he mumbled.

"Just what I was thinking," Cara agreed coolly, rather hoping he'd take the hint and find somewhere else to exist.

Unfortunately, Sebastian pulled his trolley inside with an exaggerated sigh. "Well, this is going to make for a fun ride."

"You could always find another elevator?"

"Actually, this is the only one we can use," he snapped. "And it's a five minute wait for it to get back down." Cara felt a scowl slipping onto her face as he pushed his cart over next to hers. "Trust me, I'd rather not be stuck in here with you either," Sebastian said. "I guess I'll just have to stare at the wall for a distraction."

He meant it as a burn, but Cara nearly laughed. Oh please, a boy who could keep his eyes to himself. That was a good one.

She punched the button marked *Hub - Cargo Bay,* then slumped down on the floor next to her cart while she waited. The last three days of running errands and standing to wash dishes had left her feet throbbing. For a moment she closed her eyes, relishing a moment of pure bliss as the pressure vanished from her heels.

Beneath her, the elevator gently began to rise, and gravity abruptly shifted onto an angle. If the transition hadn't been so smooth, it would have been terrifying. It almost felt like one elevator cable had snapped and they were dangling lopsided. As it was though, Cara just leaned back against the Up-Arrow wall like a recliner.

For a moment she lounged back into serenity– the gentle hum of the elevator, and the wonderful sensation as the aching in her feet faded. Then came a persistent metallic tapping, and her eyes popped open.

Pizza Boy was staring at her, idly tapping a finger on the elevator wall.

"Well, that was short lived," she remarked dryly.

"Huh?"

"Whatever happened to all that, *even the wall looks better than you do* talk?" she demanded smugly.

Sebastian's expression twisted in disgust. "Of course, because even in space the entire universe revolves around *you*."

"Well, then stop staring," Cara dared him.

"Stop acting weird."

"I'm trying to *relax*. Okay?" She primly folded her arms. "This is the first moment of quiet I've had since I woke up. Except now I'm trapped in here with you and your ADD." Her gaze pincered on his tapping finger, "Could you *not* do that for like... two minutes?"

After standing there, one hand idly tapping at the wall the entire time, Sebastian abruptly halted, frowning like he hadn't realized what he'd been doing.

Finally.

Cara watched him out of the corner of her eye. It was almost comical. She could see he was trying *really* hard not to make noise. He squirmed, like the fidget was crawling around in his stomach, trying to escape. Eventually, he settled on folding his arms and silently tapping on one elbow.

"So, what did *you* do?" Cara asked, her head bumping back against the wall.

"What did I do to...?" Sebastian left the question hanging.

"To get trapped up here, slaving away at that pizza place? I assume manual labor is Medea Station's favorite punishment, so what did you do?"

"Uhhh, I applied." Sebastian cocked an eye in her direction. "Not everyone up here is a jailbird you know."

Cara frowned, "But you're... what? Sixteen?"

"Seventeen," Sebastian corrected. He paused but must have read from the confusion etched on her face that wasn't a satisfactory answer. "My dad pulled a some strings so I could come work here for a couple months. They needed help with the Mars crowds, so he talked to Miranda. She said sure, and... here I am." He muttered the last bit with a definite dose of sarcasm, like the station wasn't quite what he'd been hoping for.

"And your dad is...?" Cara probed.

"An officer–" he added as an afterthought, "with the Space Force."

"Huh. Mine too." Cara nodded, letting a bit of curiosity out. "Anybody I'd know?"

She caught a flicker of hesitation on his face before, "Probably not."

He sighed, then added. "What about you? How did you start out robbing Kristina, then end up as her… servant?"

Cara allowed her head to bump back against the elevator wall as she spoke. "Bad luck, I suppose. It was Kristina's idea, and Mom was more pissed than usual yesterday."

"Huh," Sebastian nodded. "So is this your first time stealing or…"

"Well, I usually don't get caught," Cara remarked dryly. "And typically Mom never notices. That makes things easier."

Her voice trailed off, and she looked back to see Sebastian staring at her, mouth agape. It was enough to make her want to shrug. "What?"

"You actually are a klepto," he said in amazement.

"Am not."

"Might want to check a dictionary on that one."

Cara rolled her eyes, so he wanted to be clever. "Well, since you obviously don't know, *technically* kleptomania is a pathological condition," she declared primly. "They can't help themselves from stealing. *I,* on the other hand, just like nice things."

"Wow, I can definitely see the difference." Sebastian shook his head.

While they talked, the gravity in the elevator car leveled back out as it coasted to a stop, but even sitting, Cara could feel the change from down below. She wasn't quite floating, but she was close. Most of Medea Station was laid out along a gigantic ring several hundred feet below, which constantly spun to create artificial gravity.

If the rest of the station was one mammoth wheel, the shuttle bay sat right at the hub. This close to the center, gravity was barely a fifth its usual strength.

Standing, Cara fairly bounced upright, the flimsy gravity taking her by surprise. She'd been dreading getting up, but now her feet barely even felt the weight. "Wow."

"Yeah," Sebastian reached for his cart as the door dinged open. "If you ever wanted to do some hardcore parkour, this is the place." He nodded to the short, stocky sentry standing guard outside the elevator. "What's up, Victor?"

Wheeling his cart out, Sebastian flashed his wrist past the check-in panel and was rewarded with a pulse of green. Cara followed, the sentry eying her as he asked, "And you are?"

"Cara Rosenfeld," she said, cautiously eyeing the muscular man with a surprisingly deep voice. Suddenly she was a bit less resentful of Kristina forcing her to repeat what she was supposed to say. "I'm with Kristina Andrews." She fumbled to pull out the badge tucked inside her jumpsuit. "I'm just here for a few days so they gave me this instead of changing my implant."

She slid the badge near the prox sensor and was rewarded with a green flash of her own.

Even so, the man regarded her for a couple seconds, before nodding. "If you're with Kristina, then she still has some sacks from yesterday waiting for pick up. You too, Sebastian."

Sebastian frowned. "I thought they bumped the supply pallets yesterday?"

"They bumped the pallets for space," Victor said, "but they were still underweight, so they wedged in some bulk stuff. From the smell, I'd say it's coffee and flour. It's over in LTS. Can you uhh…" He nodded towards Cara.

Sebastian gave an exaggerated sigh, "Yeah, I'll show her."

He turned to leave with Cara following, her steps hesitant in the flimsy gravity. It pained her to have to ask, but finally, "So, where are we going?"

"It's this way," he said cryptically, adding, "Watch your step. Gravity up here takes some getting used to."

The cargo bay was packed, creating an industrial landscape all its own. A large beam crane sat idle on rails far overhead, while a couple of forklifts were parked off to one side. Everywhere enormous piles of beige-grey plastic crates towered like sloped mountains. Medleys of blue, green and white barrels dotted the floor like groves of squat trees, while metal framed totes were mounded up in little hills. The place was a labyrinth. And Cara couldn't escape the sensation that she had just stepped into the seedier side of Medea.

"Is all this for the Persephone?" she asked, a hint of amazement creeping into her tone.

"Not all of it," Sebastian navigated ahead, "but a lot." He paused by one crate, nodding to a band of purple tape wrapped around it. "You can tell from the tape. Purple is for the Persephone, red is Medea, I think blue is for the fleet, and green is civies."

Cara glanced around, noting that most everything was, in fact, banded Persephone purple, with maybe a scattering of blue.

"Main drop-off is down there." Sebastian pointed down an aisle between two canyon walls of crates. At the end, Cara saw a wide clearing with a series of grid lines neatly taped off on the floor. "Each store gets its own square where they pile up all the supplies that come in. It's pretty easy. Just grab your stuff and go."

"If you miss a pick up though," Sebastian continued, leading off down another weaving path, "then they dump everything over in long term storage. Which is this way."

Wandering through the confusing maze, she only caught glimpses of people, a couple men gesturing at a stack of crates, a woman with a tablet examining totes. Meanwhile, the hanger echoed with the occasional far off, *Beep Beep Beep* of a forklift backup alarm.

"So, is it normal to have the supply pallets bumped?" Cara asked.

"For the last week or so, yeah," Sebastian nodded. "It's like everyone left all the important stuff until the last second. Last Thursday it was a bunch of perishables, Saturday it was a literal *ton* of electronics. As for yesterday and Monday, all I heard was something classified, so… who knows."

Sebastian turned down another path that finally opened up and let Cara look beyond the endless walls of crates. Cara froze at the sight, blinking to ensure her eyes weren't tricking her. Down in the outer ring, Medea Station's curvature was gentle enough to be comprehensible. She might have been standing in a broad valley where the walls bowled up around her. Here though, the arc was tight and the ceiling high enough that she could see the floor curve steeply upward in the distance. Cara stared at a tower of crates barely two-hundred feet away, but leaned over at an insane, sixty-degree angle. It nearly gave her a headache.

"Pretty cool, isn't it?"

Cara blinked, forcing away the momentary dizziness. She noticed the boy looking back and watching her with an amused, *gets'em every time* grin.

"Sure." Cara swallowed back a flash of nausea and tried to focus on the path ahead.

Another turn took them back into the maze, and she caught echoing voices up ahead, growing more distinct "…what idiot put them *here*?"

"Well, you never said they'd look like this."

"What did you *think* they'd look like?"

"Not… whatever. Either way, we have to move them before—"

The two rounded a corner to discover two men in Space Force blue-and-black cameo. Cara almost instinctively picked out the insignia, a Major's golden oak leaf and the inverted chevrons of a Master Sergeant. Both men looked up at the sound of the trolleys and Cara swallowed at their glares. Had they taken a wrong turn?

"What are you two doing here?" The major strode up with a scowl.

Cara had been on the bad end of her mom's glowers enough to wince and stare at the floor, but surprisingly, Sebastian didn't budge. "Just picking up stuff for downstairs." He pointed past the major and made to wheel his cart on by, "Over there."

The man physically stepped into his path though, catching the cart and roughly shoving both it and Sebastian a half step back. "Too bad, this area's off limits.

"Since when?" Sebastian shoved right back but the man barely budged

"Since, *now*," the major growled, nodding them back the way they'd come with a dangerous tone. "Why don't you two make like a pair of trees… and get out of here."

Cara blinked. What? That didn't sound right.

"Now hold on," Sebastian argued, "you can't just shut off this whole area. All we need are–"

"Hey," Cara grabbed his wrist. "Let's just go, okay?" Sebastian might not recognize the pattern, but she had this exact same argument with her mom, like… at least once a day. Fighting it out never ended well, and there was a much easier solution. So long as he didn't make too much of a stink, that was.

"No," Sebastian fumed, clearly angry, "if we don't go this way we can't–"

"*Come on*," Cara pulled his arm. "Let's just go. We'll sort it out later."

Reluctantly, he let her tug him back a step. She could see from his posture he was still ready to fight it out, but… seriously, there were easier ways.

The major gestured them off with a disparaging flick of his hand. Cara shot him a stink eye, but she turned her cart and the two wheeled off anyway.

"You know, for a thief, you sure fold pretty easy," Sebastian hissed, once they were out of earshot. "You realize that's the only way to–"

"Will you *shut up* and let me handle this?" Cara snapped.

Sebastian did, but cocked an eye at her, like she'd better explain.

She let out a huff. This wasn't *that* complicated. "Look, Pizza Boy, you getting in a shouting match with the major won't change his mind, alright? Trust me, I've tried – a lot. If we cave though, he'll think he's won."

"And…?"

"And obviously he hasn't," Cara declared. "But let's get the rest of our stuff, give those two a few minutes to clear off, *then* we head back. Sound like a plan?"

"Well…" Sebastian paused frowning like he wanted to object. He didn't though, and Cara got the sense he was mainly just salty at being called Pizza Boy. Eventually his indignation won out, "Alright. Daily pick up is back this way."

"Perfect." Cara flashed him a smile.

***

Fifteen minutes later, Cara peeked her head around the same corner, her gaze casting across the piles of boxes scattered about before gesturing ahead. "We're clear."

"Great," Sebastian trundled his cart on through, "let's get the bags and get out of here."

Cara had been waiting for his congratulations, which of course hadn't materialized. Not that she'd really expected it, but still a, *Thanks for your genius plan, Cara,* would have been nice. Whatever. At least Kristina and Melody wouldn't chew her out.

Pushing her own cart ahead, Cara trailed the scruffy-haired boy through the futuristic cargo-scape of Medea. For being off limits, the area sure seemed pretty open to anyone who walked by. Overhead, the bright LED lights glared down, while a few shouts echoed around the cargo bay. A dozen different varieties of plastic crates lay piled up like giant Legos and…

What the–

As they wheeled down the narrow avenue, Cara's eyes jumped to where the two men had been standing earlier. Up close, she saw a row of one, two, three… eight crates. Each was chest high, twelve feet long and wrapped in the purple Persephone banding. Normally, they would barely have registered.

Except that every crate was coated in a glistening layer of frost.

"What in the…?"

From the note in Sebastian's voice, this was new to him too.

Grinding to a halt, Cara stared in stunned shock. She felt like they'd been hiking in the forest and stumbled onto a real-life dinosaur. Who packed a bunch of deep-frozen crates to Mars? And why? And what had the Major so concerned that he wanted to move them?

The crates were right along the pathway, and after a moment's stunned hesitation, Cara finally stepped closer. Close enough to feel the arctic chill radiating off them. For a moment, she hovered a palm near one of the frostbitten boxes, feeling the warmth instantly stolen from her skin, before pulling it back with a glance at Sebastian. "What do you think they are?"

Sebastian regarded the box for a moment before stating levelly, "Probably a bioweapon."

Cara blinked. "*What*?"

"Well, what else do you transport in frozen crates heading to Mars? They're probably setting up a biolab there for a bunch of really dangerous research. That way it can't get out."

"Except on all of us colonists."

"Well… yeah," his words failed him, but Cara got the point. Compared to millions dead, a few thousand colonists barely qualified as collateral damage.

She sighed, "It might just be medicine?"

"Medicine that you need a security clearance to open?" Sebastian pointed to the word *CONFIDENTIAL* stenciled in bold blue on the side of the crate. "Just saying."

Cara rolled her eyes. Yeah, he was *just saying* it was a bioweapon. But that didn't make an ounce of sense. Nobody needed eight giant crates of bio-samples, not unless this was Jurassic Park and they were trying to clone a dinosaur army.

Cara nibbled at her lip, "It might just be tissue samples?"

"Yeah, tissue with the plague."

"No, genius. Tissue to clone animals and stuff. It's like a seed bank, except for animals."

Sebastian weighed the possibilities a moment before, "I vote for the plague option."

"Of course you do." Cara leaned in, feeling the chilled air flowing off the crates and puddling around her shoes. As it did, an idea took shape in her mind. She glanced around; no cameras that she could see.

"Well, only one way to find out."

Back at the daily drop off, she'd already picked up several boxes of stuff for Kristina. While rummaging through them to make sure she had the ever so crucial creamer, she'd also discovered boxes of coffee filters. Flipping open a one thousand pack, she grabbed a half dozen of the conical filters off the top and held them in her hand like an impromptu glove as she reached for the lid.

"Are you crazy?" Sebastian hissed and swatted her hand away, his eyes wide as he realized what she was about to do.

"What?" Cara narrowed her eyes, irate. "You know another way to prove yourself wrong?"

He stared at her, wide-eyed. "You *are* crazy."

"You're not curious?"

"The box is *Classified*. They send people to jail for looking at that crap."

"One, it's only Confidential. Two, they're not supposed to leave this stuff sitting out in the open anyway, so it's technically someone else's fault. And three, I'm just looking. They'll get over it. With her dad being a Colonel, Cara was pretty darn sure they couldn't do much anyway."

Sebastian glared at her with a scowl like she'd just suggested jumping out of an airlock. "Cara, you need to seriously recalibrate your danger meter."

She let out an exasperated huff. Could he shut up? They were under eighteen, the military wasn't going to lock them up for peeking in a suspicious box left out in the cargo bay. For all they knew, it could be a bomb. *If you see something, say something*. Right? That was the motto on base.

Heck, they might turn out to be heroes. Maybe this was her ay out of Kristina's work-camp coffee shop. Besides, she could always say they hadn't noticed the stenciling. Well... assuming Sebastian could manage a semi-convincing lie... so, maybe not.

Whatever, the box was probably locked anyway. At this point, it would be worth trying to open it just to see him squirm.

"Fine, we can fix my *danger meter* later," she snarked. "For now though–"

Before he could stop her, Cara grabbed the lid and pulled. To her surprise, it popped right open with only a crackle of ice sprinkling to the floor. She pushed the cover up, allowing the light to flood in, and her mouth dropped open at what lay inside. She was staring at a sleek cryopod, its glass canopy flecked with frost. And beneath the gentle dusting of snowflake white, Cara saw…

A girl?

Chapter 6
Cold as Ice

"Hoooooly shit!" Sebastian muttered over her shoulder.

Cara hurriedly pushed the lid the rest of the way over, until it flopped open with a bang. "Who is she?" Cara mumbled in shock, her hand hovering a finger's breadth above the glass.

The cryopod looked brand new. It was the sort of *Find Your Future Today, Fountain of Youth* trash they sold to rich old people who wanted to wait out cancer in a deep freeze. But the girl was… maybe sixteen. And she definitely didn't look like she was dying.

Leaning in, Cara's eyes traced over the pod. The canopy was heavy glass an inch thick. Inside the girl was laid out, hands at her sides, clothed in pure white with frosty pale skin and an expression of utter calm.

For an instant, the girl's strange serenity drew in Cara's entire focus. Only the far off beeping of a forklift jolted her back to reality. A persistent burning sensation registered in her hand hovering near the glass and Cara pulled it back, massaging her ice-cold fingers. Frick.

Next to her she noticed Sebastian still staring, enraptured, his hand drifting towards the glass, a little boy wanting to tap and smile and wave to see if the strange girl waved back.

"Don't." She caught his wrist, snapping him back to reality, "It's too cold to touch."

He blinked, "Right."

He moved towards the end of the pod, but his eyes kept flashing back to the girl. "She's like… our age."

"Yeah, I noticed." Cara folded her arms, one finger anxiously tapping at her elbow, and finally muttered, "Frick."

"Agreed," Sebastian murmured.

The cryopod was arranged in two parts. The glass canopy occupied most of the space, but a box shaped control podium was built into the pod at the end near the girl's head. The podium looked like it housed all the actual equipment to keep the pod chilled and stable. Somehow, the controls were the only part of the pod that *weren't* actually frozen, and Sebastian stepped down towards the end, tapping at a few buttons.

"What are you doing?" Cara hissed and followed him, worry bleeding into her voice.

Sebastian kept typing, "I'm just seeing if this thing has any info about her."

An instant later the console gave a friendly ding. Sebastian's face lit up with the echoed light from the screen, while a physical button on the console began to gently strobe with a soft red glow. Sebastian mumbled the whole time. "Alright, password is… *password*?"

Beep, beep.

"Okay, then… *password123*?"

Beep, beep.

"Capital P *Password*?"

Beep, beep.

While Pizza Boy showed off his, decidedly bottom tier, hacker skills, Cara stepped back, her eyes drawn to the word stenciled on the side of the box. *CONFIDENTIAL*, that made no sense. There was nothing classified about a girl in cryosleep. "What do you think the military wants with her?"

Sebastian glanced up at her, "I mean, it's pretty obvious."

"Is it?"

"Yeah, she's a super soldier, or well – some sort of experiment. Possibly telekinetic."

Cara crossed her arms, "I'm being serious."

"Yeah, me too." He looked up, seeing her still unconvinced. "Have you never seen a *single* sci-fi show?"

"The frick does that have to do with this?"

"Well, if you had, you'd know exactly what's going on."

"Oh please, do tell."

"Look," Sebastian let out an exasperated sigh, "don't take this the wrong way, but this sort of thing is freakishly common."

"Just off the top of my head: Star Trek - Generation Two, Khan is a genetically engineered super soldier who's been trapped in cryostasis. Ringworld intro vid, Pillar of Spring is being chased by aliens, discovers the Ringworld and defrosts Master Sergeant who is, you guessed it, a literal super soldier."

"Then there's Quantum Effect 2. The main character got frozen and preserved for two years after a shipwreck, and they're bringing him back to life as a biotically enhanced super soldier. There's The Void, Season 2 where they've turned immunodeficient children into alien proto-molecule enhanced super soldiers in pods that the bad guy intends to launch at Mars.

You also have Warp Gate. They discover an alien girl frozen in Antarctica who has pseudo-telekinetic powers. And of course, Warp Gate Pegasus. One of the main characters goes back in time and waits in a stasis pod to save the other main characters in the future. That said, time travel into the past isn't seriously realistic, so... yeah, that just leaves super soldier or telekinesis."

Cara blinked. "Well, it's a good thing your reality has *some* limits," she finally managed, bouncing between amazement and sarcasm.

What the frick? She shook her head, still sifting through all that nonsense. Did space do something to your brain to make people up here extra crazy? Or was this just Pizza Boy being normal?

Sebastian tried another password, *"Beep, beep."*

Okay, this was getting waaaay out of hand. "Sebastian, stop."

"Hey," he shrugged, "you're the one that opened Pandora's box here."

"Yeah, and it was supposed to be locked, and not have like…" her hands gestured frantically, "a person inside. So let's just shut it."

"I'm just trying to figure out who she is."

"Why?" Cara demanded, the frustration bleeding into her voice.

For once, Sebastian didn't give a pithy answer. "Cara we can't just leave–"

"Sebastian," Cara snapped, "if she is a super soldier, then even I know not to let her out."

"I'm just–" His hands moved for the keypad.

"STOP!" Cara grabbed at his wrist and jerked it away.

"LET GO!" Sebastian was stronger than her. The two wrestled for a moment, fighting over the console. Arms smashed at the console and something flashed on screen, rapid fire snapping through about three different prompts. Then he broke her grip. Cara stumbled back, her eyes widening in panic. Across from her, Sebastian was staring too.

The button. The big, red flashing button that no one even understood. They'd just hit it, probably a half dozen times. Frick.

From the console a friendly feminine voice chimed, *"Emergency Thaw Sequence Initiated. Time to Completion, Eight Minutes. Please Standby."*

Something beneath the console hummed to life, and a horrified Cara buried her mouth in her hands, a dozen obscenities going off rapid fire in her head. Frick, Frick, FRICK.

Five feet away, a white-faced Sebastian stared at the pod as a gentle hiss of white fog flooded the canopy. After a moment, he mumbled a curse.

"Well, that was just genius," Cara hissed, furious.

"Oh, this is *my* fault?" Sebastian retorted. "If you hadn't–"

"*Yes*, it is," Cara cut him off. "You just *had* to start pressing buttons and–"

"Yeah, not *that* button. Maybe if you'd kept your hands to yourself and didn't have to control every–"

"Don't pretend this isn't your fault! I warned you to stop and *nooo–*"

"Well, if you hadn't opened it!"

"It was supposed to be locked!" She nearly screamed back. "And why would you try to–"

"SHUT UP, CARA!"

The sudden fury in Sebastian's voice came as a shock, and she took an involuntary step backward. For a moment the two stared, both breathing hard. Slowly Cara's fury seemed to bleed away, leaving just a cold, miserable panic deep in the pit of her stomach.

What were they supposed to do now?

Sebastian swore, then shook his head, starting a steady pacing. Finally, his tone turned slightly more practical. "Well, okay, we can't just leave her here."

"Oh, yes we can," Cara said. She quickly stepped around to the back and grabbed the crate's lid to seal the cryopod back inside. This was one problem she *did not* need in her life right now.

"Cara, we unfroze her," Sebastian moved to stop her shutting the pod back up, "we can't just–"

Cara pointed at him. "*We* did nothing. *You* unfroze miss super soldier here."

Sebastian glared back, pointedly refusing to take the bait. "She is *our* problem, Cara."

There was a real, almost scary intensity in his eyes, enough to make Cara hesitate for once. Finally she glanced away, fuming, "Look, let's just get our stuff and bail. We know Major Grumpy and his sergeant friend are going to come back soon. She can be *their* problem. Let the Space Force handle her."

Sebastian starred at her with an aghast frown, like she'd just suggested shooting a dog or something, "Really, Cara? That's your plan? Walk off, let the Space Force catch her, and shove her right back into cryo-sleep. Then they just ship her off to some black ops laboratory on Mars and she gets to live out her life as an *experiment*?"

"You don't know that." Cara snapped, "There are all sorts of reasons they might—"

"Like what?" he demanded, clearly upset. "Seriously, name one? Because we are way beyond tissue samples here." He hesitated, and Cara pursed her lips, but couldn't think of anything.

Sebastian shook his head, his voice turning more concerned, "Cara, whatever they're planning for her on Mars, I guarantee you it's not good. If it was, the Space Force wouldn't have gone through all the trouble of having her classified, and they probably could have just done it back on Earth."

"So, what then?" Cara hissed. "You want to go fight the entire Space Force over something we don't even understand? How do you think that's going to end?"

"I don't know, but we can at least try. What would you want if that was you in there and her out here? Would you want her to just walk away?"

The condemnation in those words stung, and for once, Cara wasn't sure what to say, "Well…" she mumbled, feeling every ounce of control slipping away around her. She wasn't sure where to go with that sentence though, and for a second her gaze lingered on the frost flecked canopy.

The Space Force wouldn't be experimenting on kids? Would they? Just asking the question though, she was struck by the depressingly obvious answer.

Frick, that was exactly the sort of twisted idea the military would dream up. And they'd probably go to extraordinary lengths to hide it as well, like secretly sending their test subject to a research lab on another planet.

As much as she didn't want it to, Sebastian's explanation made a scary sort of sense. And deep down, a little voice inside murmured what she already knew; something was very wrong, and she couldn't just abandon…

"Frick." Cara kicked the wheel of her trolley in frustration. Why did this have to be happening now?

For an instant, she struggled just to get the words out, a part of her still kicking and screaming that this was a giant mistake. Nothing good ever came of getting involved. But finally, "Fine," Cara nearly spat the words, "we'll do… something. But let's at least get our stuff first. We've still got a few minutes."

***

When they returned to the strange crates, seven were still marked out by the white film of frost. But on the one they'd opened, the frost on the outside of the crate had disintegrated into a puddle on the floor. The pod's glass was speckled with a dewy layer of water droplets that left the canopy wet to the touch. The machinery inside hummed at a low whine, and the pervasive noise crept into Cara's chest. All the frantic worry knotted up, gnawing at her until she thought she might puke.

Down in the pod, the haze of white still obscured the strange girl, but touching the glass canopy, Cara could feel the newfound warmth emanating from the cocoon within. "How much longer?" She glanced at Sebastian.

The boy stared at the console, "It doesn't say, but it's showing what I assume are brain waves, so – probably soon."

Cara ran a hand through her hair, seriously wishing she'd just, given up, gone back to the coffee shop and told Kristina to go scream at the military about her missing stuff.

Oh well, she mused grimly, at least now she'd have a wild story to tell the twins when she got permanently grounded.

At her feet the humming grew suddenly louder. The mechanical whir took on a layered tone as some other pump spun to life. A blast of clear gas vented into the canopy, pushing away the billowing clouds of white and… there the strange girl was. Her skin was a natural peach tone now, instead of the ghostly pale of earlier, and her face was dotted with beads of water. Monitoring electrodes studded her body, with two right on her temples and several more snaking into her shirt.

The pod let out a gentle beep. As if on cue, the figure inside abruptly breathed. Her chest rising and sinking… once… again… and again. Her eyes were still closed but soon the girl's chest had settled into a gentle rhythm.

Then there came a sharp hiss from the canopy and Cara nearly jumped backwards as a blast of air puffed out, the seal broken. The humming abruptly died like a computer when you turned it off by holding down the power button, and suddenly everything grew terribly quiet.

Glancing at Sebastian on the other side, Cara took a cautious step closer. She peered down, to see the girl's eyes flutter open, then drift shut again. Her lips mumbled something indistinct through the glass and for a moment all Cara's earlier reservations evaporated like water in the Sahara.

She reached for a handhold to open the canopy. "Come on, let's get her out."

Sebastian followed suit, but warned, "Careful though. Cryo-sleep may have left her pretty messed up."

Right, Cara dimly nodded, as they both grabbed at clamps on opposite sides of the canopy. "On three," she said. "One, two, *three…*"

They lifted and, quite to her shock, the thick glass canopy smoothly glided upward, pushed aloft on preloaded springs.

Cara leaned down next to the girl. "Are you okay? Can you hear me?"

It took a breathless second, but finally the girl's arms stirred, and she mumbled something that sounded vaguely like "*Airmi?*"

Cara bit her lip and looked up at Sebastian, who just shrugged, equally lost. "Can you hear us?" he asked again.

This time the answer came back faint but distinct, "Yeah."

The girl's eyes weakly struggled open, staring at nothing in particular before drifting back shut.

"They probably sedated her before the cryosleep," Sebastian said.

"Sedated?" The girl murmured, the confusion in her tone mingling with what Cara could only peg as a rural sort of accent.

"You've been in cryosleep," Cara whispered.

"What?" Her voice turned more agitated, and her eyes struggled open, blinking and slowly focusing on Cara's face. "Where am I?"

"It's okay." Cara took the strange girl's hand. "You're on Medea Station. Do you remember what happened?"

The girl's grip was weak, but even so, Cara could feel her hand tighten at the question. The girl's face creased in panic, her eyes shifting like she was desperately trying to recall something, until…

The girl blinked, tears brimming in her eyes. "No," she whispered, horrified, "I don't remember anything."

Chapter 7
Daughter of the Lethe

"Hey, it's alright," Cara whispered, giving the shivering girl's hand a reassuring squeeze. Inside though, her panic meter jacked straight up to eleven. Had the girl been dying, and that was why she couldn't remember? Had they just killed her by waking her up? Or was this all expected and…

She tried to keep a brave face, but her gaze danced across the pod to Sebastian, expecting him to have some answers. The boy just stared back, dumb as a rock, "What?"

"Is this normal?" Cara hissed, trying to keep her voice down not that it mattered much with the strange girl right there.

"I don't know," he replied at a typical, clueless-boy volume. "Why would you assume I'm an expert on cryopods?"

Cara winced at his answer, loud enough to wake the dead, which… frick, they sort of had. She nodded towards the girl with a pointed, *can you keep it down* glare. "Well, you sure had a lot of opinions while she was still in there," Cara fumed. "For an idiot, you've been doing a passable job imitating a nerd."

Sebastian sighed, lowering his voice to a whisper. "It's probably cryosleep. I'm sure being frozen takes a toll on your body. And I'd wager the brain takes a while to… I don't know, reboot? Fire up all the right neurons? If you think about it much, it's a miracle her body even remembers how to breathe. And who knows, maybe it's some residual sedative they gave her."

Cara sighed. Great, so nobody had a clue, and this whole situation was devolving into a mess of a CDC episode. The girl was teary-eyed and…

"Hey," Cara gently leaned close, smiling and trying to do what little she could. "What's your name?"

"Huh?" The girl sniffled and looked at Cara.

"I'm Cara, and that's uhh," she almost introduced him as *Pizza Boy*, but caught herself. "That's Sebastian. What's your name?"

The girl gulped, but finally managed, "My name is…" her expression screwed up like she was trying to remember until, "Jessie," she said. Her fist tightened like it was the only thing she had to hold on to, "My name is Jessie."

"Awesome," Cara nodded. "Do you want to get out of the cryopod, Jessie?"

The girl glanced around, like she was just realizing where she was. "Yeah," she said, with a hint of determination in her voice. "Yeah, I do."

Before Cara could offer to help, Jessie pushed herself up to sitting, then gasped, "Oooowwww."

"You okay?"

"Yeah," she mumbled, wincing, "just… everything feels like… like–"

"Like you just unfroze and all your joints are rubbing really badly?" Sebastian guessed, hurrying around and offering her a hand.

"Something like that." Jessie bit at her lip and accepted his hand. She puffed out a few long breaths before attempting to get out. It took a couple of tries, but eventually she made it up to standing, and judging from her more measured breaths, the pain seemed to have dimmed.

Glancing around at the sprawling cargo bay that curved up in the distance, her mouth dropped an inch. "Where did you say we are?"

"Medea Station," Sebastian offered. "We're up by the shuttle bay, which is why gravity is a bit funky."

Jessie blinked, "Like… the space station?"

Cara nodded and Jessie's hand covered her mouth, her eyes going wide in shock, "But... how?"

Well, at least she still knew general stuff, Cara mused.

"What's the last thing you remember?" Sebastian probed, steadying her.

"Umm..."

The question set off an alarm in Cara's head, and she abruptly glanced around. That sergeant from earlier had said he'd do something about the crates, hadn't he? She doubted he'd meant defrosting everyone, so probably move or hide the pods. In which case, when would he get back?

"Hey, guys," Cara interrupted, "Maybe we should work out all the details somewhere that's... not here."

***

Ten minutes later, Cara stepped out of the girls' restroom to find Sebastian anxiously pacing next to their two carts. "Is she alright?"

"She's fine." Cara shot him an amused glance. "Besides, she's a super soldier, isn't she?"

Sebastian didn't seem to appreciate the humor. "What if someone else goes in there?"

"Well, I don't know how it is in *boys'* restrooms, but girls don't typically peer under the stalls at each other. As long as she keeps quiet, I doubt anyone will notice."

Sadly, that was the only part of their haphazard plan that was going well. Over the last ten minutes, what to do with Jessie had morphed into a massive headache. The simple reality was that they needed to get her downstairs, out of the cargo bay, and away from the military. Unfortunately, Jessie looked like she'd just stumbled out of an old school psych ward. The bizarre combination of no shoes and snowy white clothes absolutely screamed that something was wrong. Cara also doubted Victor was dumb enough not to notice *three* teens leaving as opposed to the two who had arrived.

The temporary solution had been to leave Jessie in the women's restroom – alone. It was... well, it was kind of stupid.

70

But, locked in a stall, Cara figured no one would bother Jessie, at least until she could return with some clothes that wouldn't stick out quite as badly. She still wasn't sure about the whole *getting past the guards* part, but it was a baby step.

Sebastian still didn't look entirely comfortable leaving Jessie behind. But before he could object, Cara grabbed her cart and pushed towards the elevator. "Come on. Kristina and Melody are already going to be wondering where I am."

Heading to the elevator, a part of Cara was quivering even worse than when she'd tried walking out of Kristina's shop. What if Victor knew? What if he asked what had taken so long? What if…

She tried to force the thoughts down beneath a simple mantra, *Act Calm.* She was *supposed* to be here, so act normal.

Clattering along next to her, Cara caught Sebastian looking shaky too. "Just chill," she cautioned.

"Easier said than done."

Cara allowed herself a grin. "You'll get better with practice. I know I have." Her smile widened as she saw his face twist at the insinuation.

"Let's be clear, this does *not* make me a thief."

"I don't knooow," Cara teased innocently, "We just stole a classified super soldier and stashed her in the bathroom."

"It's not stealing if it's a *person*."

"Abducted then," Cara mused, cheerily. "I suppose that's worse."

Sebastian glared daggers at her. "This isn't helping."

Oh, it was *definitely* helping. He might be ticked, but the abnormal tightness in his shoulders had vanished, and now he was pissed instead of scared. Big improvement.

The two turned the corner, and she saw Victor up ahead. Cara couldn't resist the chance for one last dig. "Just try not to stress, Pizza Boy."

His expression creased in a scowl and Cara accelerated a couple paces ahead, giggling to herself. Turned out she wasn't that nervous anymore either.

"You two find everything?" Victor had already hit the call button upon seeing them, and the door glided open as they walked up.

"Not exactly," Cara said breezily, "but we'll figure it out." She kept on and added, "I might be back."

She stepped past him into the elevator. It was only once she was inside, pressing her trolley against the down arrow wall, that she felt a twinge of anxiety prick at her chest. But then Sebastian was inside, the door slid shut and… boom, they'd done it.

The elevator car slowly began to move, gravity twisting onto an angle yet again. Sebastian slumped against the down arrow wall, letting out a relieved breath. "So, you're coming straight back, right?"

"Nah," Cara remarked deadpan, idly stared at her nails, "I think I'll just wash dishes for the rest of the day."

That earned her a sharp look, but honestly, they'd been over this already… twice. She'd go back, drop off Kristina's stuff, grab some real clothes, then come get Jessie and somehow improv a way out of this catastrophe. Her shift didn't end for another three hours, but whatever. Hopefully, none of her various bosses would notice that she was planning to be scarce for most of it.

Unlikely, but… she could always dream.

"Seriously, though," Cara added feeling his anxiety becoming contagious, "She'll be alright. If anything, I think Jessie needs the time alone."

She caught his skeptical side glance, "Oh, don't be like that. Imagine if *you* woke up in a strange pod, surrounded by strange people, that wasn't even on planet Earth. Then to top it off, you could barely even remember your own name." Cara gave a sympathetic shrug. "It's a lot to take in, you know."

For once her words seemed to connect and Sebastian slowly nodded, letting it drop with a quiet, "Yeah, I suppose."

He didn't add anything as the elevator whirred on its descent to the main ring. Now that they were actually away from Jessie and *relatively* safe though, Cara felt like a worried knot of questions. After a long moment of silence, one of them wormed loose.

"Do you think we ought to tell someone about...?" Cara noticed the camera up in one corner of the elevator with a start and left off the *her*. Hopefully no one was listening to their conversation too closely.

Sebastian finally looked up from staring at the floor, with a simple, "No."

Something about the raw bluntness of his statement rubbed Cara wrong, like a burr in her shoe. ""Sebastian, what are we supposed to do then? I'm leaving in... what, four days? And I know you can't be here that much longer either. What happens after we're gone?" She turned so the camera couldn't see her lips and dropped her voice to a whisper, "It's not like she can permanently live in the bathroom."

"I'm not saying keep her here forever." He met Cara's gaze, his own voice dropping to a hush. "But if we tell the Space Force... well, whatever she is, she's already classified. They'll probably just throw her back in the box and figure out a way to wipe our minds too."

"Not necessarily," Cara insisted. "Maybe... whatever the Space Force is doing with her isn't what we're thinking. I mean, wouldn't you expect a" she mouthed the words *super soldier*, "...shouldn't that be classed as Top Secret, not Confidential?"

There were three levels of military classification, *Top Secret* being the highest. That was followed by *Secret,* with *Confidential* at the bottom. So yeah, a little odd that a super-secret, legally dubious, genetic manipulation project wasn't *more* classified.

"Maybe," Sebastian agreed with a quiet shrug, "but that's assuming the military makes any sense normally, which..." He let the word hang, but Cara got his point. Never trust the Space Force to contain intelligent life.

"Look," Sebastian whispered, "the way I see it, if we go make a stink about all this, *maybe* someone believes us, and *maybe* something happens... for a couple hours."

"Then, someone way above us makes a few calls, and she suddenly disappears because they had to," he air quoted with his hands, "*send her back to Earth,* or something. In reality, it's straight back in the box, and if we ever talk about it again, bad things happen."

"Sebastian, you don't know that."

"I do, *actually.*"

"How? You can magically see what Colonel Perry's going to do?"

"Pretty close, yeah," Sebastian retorted bluntly.

Cara rolled her eyes. "How? How could you possibly–"

"He's my dad."

Cara blinked, "Wait, Colonel Perry is your dad?"

Sebastian nodded with a sigh.

"For real?"

There was a flash of irritation on his face. "Yes, for real."

A part of her did a mental backflip. "Are you fricking kidding me?"

This had all sorts of wild implications. To start, Perry clearly knew her own parents, which meant she and Sebastian had possibly met before. She must have been young at the time, but still. Regardless, it was fantastic news as far as not getting perma-grounded went. "This is great," Cara hissed, "you can talk to your *Dad* and save both our butts."

"Hate to say it, but given how busy Dad is, *you'd* probably have better luck getting a word in."

"Yeah, but you're his son."

"I don't know why you think that'll change things," Sebastian remarked glumly. "Would he agree with what's going on? No probably not. But if she really is some," he stole a page out of her book and mouthed, *super soldier*, "he's just going to tow the Space Force line. Clearly someone higher up the chain of command than him was involved to get her this far in the first place. I'm sure they'll have a bunch of really official sounding reasons why this is perfectly fine and extremely critical to national security. And that'll be it."

Cara caught a glimmer of frustrated disappointment in his eyes and decided, for once, not to pry. Sebastian might not be very sanguine on their prospects, fair enough.

However, it was also becoming painfully obvious that she had a lot more experience cashing in on daddy's rank than he did. As far as she was concerned, even if Perry wasn't at the pinnacle of the military food chain, being the station commander's son was still a pretty fantastic trump card.

That, and she had the niggling sense they'd *definitely* need to play it later. Just a question of timing.

Chapter 8
Jessie

Camped in the bathroom, Jessie's lips pressed into a tight, nervous line. There was something uniquely undignified about huddling on a toilet seat and just… waiting. Sadly, it seemed like *undignified* pretty accurately summarized the last half hour of her life.

Jessie's eyes wandered across the blue partition walls of the stall for about the dozenth time. When Cara had first pulled her in here, she'd honestly been grateful just to sit down. But with every passing moment she was beginning to worry.

The first ten minutes after she'd woken up, she'd felt so nauseous she'd nearly puked, and rushing through the cargo bay hadn't helped. Now though, the nausea had mostly vanished, leaving just a tangle of questions behind. And sitting here, wondering what was taking Cara so long wasn't helping. Instead, the worry was gradually mounting and her knee bounced rapid fire, one foot tapping an anxious tune on the floor, to keep from exploding with nervous energy.

Oh, and she was starving too. She'd been dying of thirst, so she'd gotten a big drink from the bathroom sink, which had apparently turned her stomach back on.

Bad idea.

It seemed that, not only had *she* forgotten her last meal, but *her stomach* had as well. Another insistent gurgle emanated from her midsection and she tried to ignore it, which was hard when you had *literally* nothing to do. She would have killed for a phone and a box of crackers right now.

The moral of the story, she decided glumly, was that cryosleep sucked. One hundred percent. She could definitely see why it hadn't caught on as the go-to transportation choice. Waking up was flat out miserable, and losing all your memories was… the awful thought gripped like ice around her heart and she nearly choked up at the riptide of emotion.

Why couldn't she remember anything?

Some stuff was still there. She could still speak English. She knew that fifteen plus twenty-seven equaled forty-two. She could even remember that the Declaration of Independence was signed in 1776 for some stupid reason. But when she thought of home…

A tear spilled down Jessie's cheek and she sniffled, scrubbing it away. When she thought of home she couldn't remember anything. Just… trees. Big puffy green… elm trees?

Don't ask how, but she was pretty sure they were elm. An image flashed in her mind, her staring at the leaf, a little green oval with serrated edges. She could dimly hear a girl's voice blurred in the background.

She tried to focus, but that just chased the memory away, and again, she was back at zero.

For a moment, she couldn't hold back the awful panic that crushed down on her. She felt like she'd lost… *herself.* Yeah, she had a name, barely, but if she couldn't remember anything else, then who was she? Really?

Not the same Jessie who'd climbed in the cryopod, that was for sure.

She wasted another several minutes trying to remember anything until…

Voices.

The bathroom door gave a whine as it swung open and two womens' voices strolled inside. "So he got suspended?" one asked, incredulous. "For that?"

"Yeah, I tried to explain that the boys were picking on Cleo. He was just trying to stand up for his own sister, but *nooooo*. It was like talking to a rock, a really stupid rock."

The soft whir of a faucet came from one sink, then another, the sound broken by the splash of washing hands.

"Then the principal wanted to have a conference tomorrow, and couldn't seem to grasp that I'm in *outer space*, so I can't make it."

"Sad to think *he's* in charge of teaching."

"I know, makes you wonder how the world still goes round."

The faucet flipped off, and Jessie heard an exaggerated sigh. "When's the next cargo shuttle rolling in?" the second woman asked.

"Sometime after lunch, but Milo's gonna get it loaded. It's some… I don't know, not our problem."

"That's good. I'm already sick of handling everything for–

The sudden, jet engine scream of one of the hand dryers flared to life, drowning out everything else.

But Jessie was barely listening anyway.

She remembered school.

Flashes at least.

Her standing outside a giant red brick building. Sitting at her desk, watching a laser pointer dance across a slideshow while she idly doodled on her tablet. The flick of a softball leaving her fingers as she flung it from the outfield toward second base. Sitting in the lunch room, eating a sandwich while a curly-haired black girl across the table complained about a geometry test. Meanwhile the sunny blonde sitting next to her leaned close with a conspiratorial whisper that…

Oh.

The bathroom door banged shut, and the puzzle pieces abruptly snapped together in Jessie's head.

She had a sister.

Jackie.

She didn't know where the name had come from, but she would have bet everything that it was right. For a second, she almost couldn't breathe. She had a twin sister and… another memory flashed in her head. Her and Jackie sitting on the floor with a board game between them. They were playing Ticket to Ride, and Jessie was wishing she'd done her hair up in a braid like her sister. It looked really cute, even wearing all white…

Jessie's heart froze in her chest, her hands covering her mouth. Jackie was wearing white.

Her gaze flashed down to her own white pants and long-sleeved shirt, the importance of it hitting her like a lightning bolt. If her sister was wearing white, then…

Then they must have gone into cryosleep together.

Which meant Jackie was up on this insane space station too. She must have been frozen in one of those other crates.

In a flash Jessie had pushed open the stall door, and a second later she stepped out into the valley shaped cargo bay beyond. The two women were just vanishing behind a pile of boxes off to her left, and she crouched a moment, staying out of sight. It gave her an instant to consider what a horrible idea this was, and also to decide that she didn't care. Cara had mentioned something about a man coming back to move the crates soon. Which meant that if she waited, she'd lose her chance to find the only other family she had… or at least that she remembered.

She could apologize later. *After* she'd saved her sister.

Thankfully, the route they'd taken to the bathroom was simple enough to backtrack. Straight, left, second right, then straight again. Amid the towering forest of crates, she could only catch brief glances to either side where the floor curved upwards. That was good, it meant no one could spot her sneaking around either, and if not for the constant reminder of the weak gravity, she might almost have been back on Earth.

Except for the noise.

In the donut shaped cargo bay, sounds seemed to come from every direction, and the place echoed like a mountain pass. It was quieter than earlier, but sharp *beeps* still pulsed in her ears. She was a few steps past the right turn when the cargo bay suddenly jolted with a loud, *BOOM-Boom….boom-boom.*

She froze, eyes flashing both ways, her heart in her throat. It sounded like someone had just dropped a box about four times in a row, and she was genuinely surprised the whole station hadn't shaken. Behind the clatter, a man shouted,

"SANJAY…Sanjay," his voice seeming to come from both directions at once.

Jessie took a deep breath, holding on to the reassurance that it was just this place, and not herself that was crazy. And even if she was crazy, saving her sister couldn't wait.

It wasn't until she got close to the cryopod that she separated out another noise from the wild echoes. The rev of an electric motor, then the piercing blast of a backup alarm for a few loud *beeps*. Creeping the last ten steps, Jessie peeked around the tower of crates.

Instantly her optimism sank like a brick. A forklift was already pulling up in front of the row of frost encrusted pods. The man driving it must have just arrived, because he screeched his forklift to a stop when he noticed her pod was no longer frozen.

Even from thirty feet away, she could hear the stream of curses as he hurried over. He pressed a hand against the side, gauging the temperature and swore again. Then Jessie watched as he jerked open the pod lid, looked inside, and went dead still.

Hadn't expected her to be gone, she realized. Dead, perhaps, she thought morbidly, but not gone and vanished. She wasn't entirely sure what to make of that, but it felt important. Maybe he knew–

"Rico, bring it down!– it down!"

Another bizarre double shout echoed from somewhere in the cacophonous cargo bay. The already jumpy man abruptly glanced her direction and Jessie jerked back behind cover, her heart pounding…

Had he seen her?

For an instant she pressed herself against the crate, barely daring to breathe and not sure what to do then…

Tap… tap…

Quiet footsteps, coming closer.

Shit.

She glanced right. It was a long way back down the avenue of crates to safety. And if she ran, she'd give herself away for sure. But she couldn't stay either. Icy panic gripped at her and she slowly backed several steps down the avenue, trying not to make a sound before…

The man swished into view five places away, and Jessie gulped, her whole body tightening. He wore a name patch that read *Carrington* and a disarming smile, which might have been more convincing if she hadn't seen him swearing up a storm thirty seconds earlier.

"Well there? Who are you?" His friendly tone was belied by the way his intense tiger gaze narrowed on her. "Did you get lost?"

"I'm sorry," she murmured, taking another cautious step back, even as the enormous bald man in military dress matched it with a step forward. "I should go."

"It's okay," he said, taking yet another pace closer. One hand edged infinitesimally towards her. "I'm not going to hurt you."

Yeeeeeeah, clearly.

Jessie's hands tensed into fists, her heart hammering in her chest as her left foot edged back another pace.

"Hey, just come with me," the military man coaxed, still smiling and taking a long step that brought him close enough to tower over her. "I'm sure you're confused, but I can help you understand everything. All you need to do is–"

Jessie spun to run.

Thick fingers grabbed her arm, "Get back here."

The man wrenched her to a screeching stop and flung her against the nearest crate.

Jessie's back struck painfully against the box. His meaty hand pinned her arm back as his face blotted out the lights in the ceiling above. "How'd you get out?" he demanded, all the friendliness vanishing from his tone.

Jessie shrank down, terrified, "Please, I don't…"

"HOW did you get out?"

"This is a mistake. I'm not supposed…"

The man's eyes bored into her like an icy laser. "You're *supposed* to be in your box, you little brat." He nodded towards the cryopod.

No. Jessie desperately shook her head. She wasn't going back in there. She couldn't lose herself in the ice again. She twisted, trying to free her arm, "Please just let me–"

CRACK

A hand whip cracked at her face and Jessie crumbled to the floor, tears brimming in her eyes and gasping at the fire that lit her cheek.

"Come on," the man snapped, hauling her upright with a jerk that nearly wrenched her shoulder from its socket. His grip crushed her arm as he dragged her along. Jessie gasped in pain and frantically tried to dig in her bare heels but couldn't find any purchase on the smooth station floor. In response the man simply scoffed and gave her arm another painful yank that sent her stumbling forward.

"Now, get back in your pod and–"

"NO!" Jessie swung at him.

He hadn't expected that.

He was taller than her by a head, but she could still reach. More by instinct than plan, she threw every ounce of strength behind a coiled fist aimed at his face.

It connected.

And her knuckles exploded in pain.

The man's head snapped to the side as she slugged him right beneath the eye. His steely grip slipped loose amid a string of curses. "You brat, you'll pay for that!"

Jessie danced back, the blood thundering in her ears and a wild haymaker whipped by inches in front of her. She spun to run but a weight like a freight train crashed into her from behind.

She tumbled face first to the floor, dazed. Thick meat-hook fingers clawed at her and icy dread slushed in her veins. In a panic, Jessie desperately hammered back with her elbow.

Once.

Again.

And again.

The fingers slipped.

Her elbow screamed, but she barely noticed amidst the adrenaline tsunami. Writhing loose, Jessie rolled away and scrambled to her feet, panting. She just had to get away and…

Two steps away, the man rose like a wounded colossus. His face screwed up in pain, one eye winced almost closed, but with absolute murder in his voice. "You bitch."

She stumbled back as he drunkenly lunged for her. One wild fist caught the shoulder he'd nearly dislocated a moment before, and her arm screamed in pain. In the low gravity, Jessie barely kept her feet.

The furious man swelled up in her vision and she stumbled backwards. Her tailbone bumped at against something rigidly hard. Nowhere to run… no, No, NO–

The man pinned her arms against the crate with an invincible strength, his body almost smothering her. In a haze, she lashed out with the one thing she could still move. Her leg.

Her knee snapped up, driven by pure desperation, and smashed home – right between his legs.

The monster of a man gasped, his eyes abruptly defocused and the crushing pressure vanished as he slumped to the floor.

Jessie didn't stop to stare.

She ran.

Tearing through the rows of crates, Jessie took the first right and found herself in an unfamiliar lane, panting for breath. She swerved down another left turn, and briefly caught a glimpse of the floor bowling up in the distance. Then she darted back into the cargo-maze with high walls of crates piled on either side. Straight ahead, a huge steel-gray cargo bay wall reared up behind another mountain of boxes. If she could get there, she could find the bathroom again and wait for Cara to get back.

Jessie skidded around the next right turn–

"What the…"

She crashed headfirst into a short woman carrying a tablet, their feet tangling. With so much momentum in the weak gravity, she went flying, hit the ground, rolled and scrambled back to her feet almost faster than her mind could follow. She glanced back to see a woman sprawled on the floor, hissing in pain.

"Watch it, would..."

The woman looked up, her voice dying, replaced by a wide-eyed stare as she caught Jessie's strange white clothes. "Hey, who are you?"

Jessie didn't really know. Not that it mattered. She didn't hang around to answer, and took off, fear pounding in her veins. She hurtled through the labyrinth of unfamiliar crates as the shout echoed behind her, "STOP! GET BACK HERE!"

Chapter 9
Logistical Complications

"What took you so long?" Melody snapped, poking her head into the storeroom where Cara was straining with the, suddenly *waaaay heavier than up in the cargo bay*, coffee sacks.

"They had some extra stuff from yesterday up there," Cara mumbled.

"Did you get the creamer?"

Cara nodded towards the cart. *Of course* she'd gotten the fricking creamer.

She took a deep breath, heaving to drag yet another bulky sack off the trolley, and trying to ignore Melody's probing, judgmental gaze.

"Well, I suppose you're not too far behind on dishes," Melody finally noted.

Apparently that was as close as Melody could come to, *you're not a total screw up today,* Cara mused, suppressing a frown.

She gave the heavy bag another resigned tug and was surprised to find Melody reaching down to lend a hand. They worked together a moment, lifting several oversized sacks and piling them in the corner. That left just a few of the lighter boxes to unload. Finishing with the sacks, Melody noted a bulky carton labeled creamer which she promptly scooped up. "Get everything else put away, then get back to the dishes. Got it?"

"Sure thing," Cara mumbled, a small part of her wanting to triumphantly announce that she had exactly zero intention of going back to the dishes. She had more important things to worry about.

Not the time though.

In a flash Melody had hustled back to the front and Cara found herself alone. It was mostly quick work to stock everything else, although she did waste a solid two minutes searching for where to store two gallons worth of mocha chocolate syrup.

Finally though, it was done. Before anyone could wander along and cast her back in the dish pits, Cara rolled the trolley over to the door that led into the break room behind the dress shop. Cracking it open, she hesitated, peering inside.

Nobody.

Perfect.

Moving slowly so as not to make a racket she pulled the trolley on through. The waiting room outside Kristina's office was dominated by sagging, overstuffed couch. Three uncomfortable looking wickerwork chairs lined the far wall and an end table sat near the door to Kristina's office. In her two days here, she had yet to see anyone actually use the space as a break room. Probably for good reason. Just the prospect of relaxing and idly chatting somewhere where Kristina could appear at a moment's notice was deeply unnerving.

On the far side sat another door, from which the crisp, slightly astringent scent of new clothes spilled out. Pushing it open, Cara's mouth dropped as she found herself gazing into... wardrobe heaven.

Dresses, blouses, jeans, leggings, skirts ... the sight was dizzying, and a little heady. If clothes had a magnetism all their own, then this was Medea Station's North Pole.

It was also chaotic. Kind of a jumbled mess, honestly.

Given how strict and precise Kristina usually seemed, Cara blinked at the confusing menagerie of colors and styles. Technically she *could* puzzle out a few traces of organization amid the fashion riot arrayed before her... *barely*... strong emphasis on the barely.

Racks upon racks of dresses in transparent plastic sheaths were crammed in on the left. Rows of tops, blouses, jumpers, rompers, crop tops, camis, and a dozen more styles hung in packed ranks on the right. Along the back wall, long shelves partitioned into cubbies towered almost to the ceiling, piled with neatly folded jeans and leggings. Meanwhile, in the back corner a moderately stable mountain of shoeboxes rounded off the chaos ascetic.

Kristina had warned her not to bother trying to put up the clothes and to just leave the trolley in the break room. Now Cara could finally appreciate why. Unfortunately, she needed an excuse to be back here, so if anyone asked, she'd just have to play dumb. Shouldn't be that hard to sell, given how little Kristina and Melody already thought of her.

Shooting a final furtive look around the room, Cara took a deep breath, as though nerving herself for the plunge. She took a pleated red skirt from one of the boxes to at least maintain the veneer of working, then dived into Kristina's manic dream closet.

The chaos of Kristina's organizational system definitely slowed her down. Cara thumbed through two dozen different hangars before finding a white spaghetti strap top that could work for Jessie. Then, down at the far end of the rack, she happened onto a forest green cardigan and checked the tag – adult small.

Excellent.

She pushed that rack aside to find the skirts tucked behind and started flipping through those. She could almost feel the moments oozing away as she hunted, and the hairs on the nape of her neck kept prickling in constant expectation of Kristina's sharp, angry shout from the door. But she was making progress.

After a moment, she found a floral print skirt that *might* fit Jessie. It was frustrating because the sizes had absolutely *no* organizational system at all. Smalls, mediums and larges weren't even racked together, so she never knew what she'd find if she kept flipping. Frankly, it was a wonder anything escaped closet land and made it up front.

She caught a noise like a door from outside and glanced back with a sudden jolt.

No one.

Frick, she couldn't just spend the rest of the day browsing like this. Sooner or later, Melody was going to peek back into the washroom and start wondering where she'd gone.

Making a snap decision, Cara grabbed the skirt. She'd tried to guess Jessie's sizes, and just to be safe, she stepped over to the leggings and grabbed a couple of backup pairs. Something in there would work. Throwing that all on the cart, she moved on to the shoes.

Socks were easy, but for shoes she'd actually had to swap hers with Jessie and guess at the girl's size. She'd narrowed it down to either a seven or seven and a half. In either case, the first box of sevens she opened was a pair of simple flats and right beneath them sat an identical pair a half size up.

She scooped up both boxes to be safe, piled them on the cart and did a quick double check. Tops, skirt, leggings, shoes, socks. That should cover the essentials.

Cara stared at her cart a moment, mentally guesstimating just how many dollars' worth of clothes she was… *appropriating* this time. A lot.

She glanced at the door and a part of her hesitated. Kristina was going to murder her when she found out. And it was *when* not *if.* She was currently breaking the most obvious rule in the book, don't steal things when people already suspect you.

The alternative possibility danced through her head. Technically, she could still walk away, put everything back, pretend like this had never happened and…

And what?

Leave Jessie sitting alone in the bathroom until someone stumbled onto her and threw her back in cryo.

A familiar memory of Mom's voice intruded in her head, *Remember the golden rule, Cara.* Even in her mind, the words sounded like Mom, strained, slightly irate, and condescending. She'd always told herself the golden rule was stupid. Yet here she was, about to be eternally grounded. All because of something Mom said.

Cara shook her head with a sigh and pushed the thought away. Yeah, okay… fine. She would also want somebody to help her if she woke up from a deep freeze on the wrong planet.

Stupid Golden Rule.

Taking a deep breath, Cara pushed her trolley for the door.

The break room was still empty. Stepping back into the coffee storeroom, she let out a relieved breath when she saw that Melody *wasn't* waiting to shout at her for once.

Before that could change, she headed for the back door, slipped out into the hallway and headed off towards the service elevator. Maybe she *could* get back before anyone noticed.

Maybe.

At least getting to the elevator was easy. Tapping the call button, she glanced at the time on her phone– half an hour since they'd left Jessie. That wasn't too bad. She tried not to notice the other message notifications begging for her attention. More social drama from the last couple days still piling up. Although, with all the madness of the last hour, she'd almost forgotten about it for a while. Surprisingly pleasant, actually.

The service elevator must have been sitting up near the cargo bay, because she waited several minutes before the door dinged open. In the meantime, she morosely flicked through her message backlog. Most of what she read just left her boiling. Despite that, she felt a sincere rush of gratitude when she got to Maddie's messages. Her friend had completely hushed up the whole Kristina debacle. Not only that, but based on what Cara was seeing, she'd also been doing an admirable job throwing up distractions with a barrage of Earth selfies spammed out to everyone and anyone.

After everything that had happened, Cara found something comfortingly normal about her usual social media maintenance. She picked out a smiling selfie from the day before yesterday with a *Lov'in the high life* caption and set Codex to do the automated send-out. Real life might be rapidly evolving into a fiery shuttle disaster, but nobody else had to know that.

The elevator dinged and Cara glanced up as the doors glided open. Pushing her cart inside, she tapped the button for *Hub - Cargo Bay* and…

"Hello, Cara."

A chill like ice dropped into her chest at the familiar woman's voice. She spun in horror as the absolute last person she wanted to meet strolled into the elevator with a smug grin.

Kristina.

"Frick." The mumbled word seemed to slip out on its own and hung there, very *very* awkwardly. But if anything, Kristina's bobcat grin only widened.

"Cargo bay." She nodded to the button panel as the doors coasted shut. "Interesting choice."

Cara's feet rooted to the floor and her eyes slid to her cart. All the evidence was piled right there for the world to see: two looted shoeboxes, socks, leggings and multiple different tops. And Kristina didn't so much as deign to glance at it. Instead she slid over to the UP arrow wall.

"You might want to stand here, hun." Kristina cheerfully gestured to a spot beside her.

The elevator shifted, and Cara stumbled over to the UP arrow wall, finding herself terrifyingly close to Kristina. How did she know? Like seriously… how? Was she magic? Or…

Cara covertly gave her arm a sharp pinch. Please be a dream, please be a dream, please be a dream…

She squeezed until the pain made her wince. Frick, she didn't wake up, even though being trapped in an elevator with Kristina was legitimately the stuff of nightmare fuel.

For a moment Kristina seemed content to let her suffer in the terrifying silence until, "I've been meaning to ask, how's the job going?"

Awful, especially if she included being trapped in an elevator with her boss and a load of contraband. That wasn't an appropriate answer, so Cara settled for a mumbled, "It's fine."

"*Really?*" Kristina remarked with a panther gleam in her eyes that made Cara gulp. "Huh, must be doing something wrong. You know, Cara, it's alright to say you hate your job. Most people do actually. I think it's a very American sort of sentiment."

Cara didn't answer.

Back when she'd still had a boyfriend, he'd shown her this video of a woman in India feeding a live chicken to a tiger. She'd thrown the squawking bundle of feathers over the fence, and one tiger had actually leapt up and clawed it out of the air. It had then grabbed the chicken in its mouth, ran off, and proceeded to toy with it for like… half an hour. All this while the chicken was still alive and occasionally making some spirited escape attempts. The tiger seemed to enjoy clawing it back in.

At the time, she'd mostly just thought it was odd that someone would do that for fun. Right now though, with Kristina less than a foot away and clearly relishing the moment… Cara was really starting to sympathize with that chicken.

***

By the time the elevator slowed to a halt, Cara had something that might resemble a plan. Well, that was if you squinted and turned it just right. To start, she was screwed. No two ways around that. She'd known that going in, but this reckoning was substantially more immediate than she'd intended.

That said, whatever witchy powers Kristina did have, Cara was about seventy-five percent sure her boss had no clue how crazy things *actually* were. That meant Kristina didn't fully know what was going on, and she was playing the chill game to see where this all went. Mom specialized in the same sort of insidious entrapment, and Cara had even pulled it a few times on the twins. Not that duping a pair of six-year-olds was some brilliant feat, but conceptually, same idea.

The elevator door inched open to find Victor still standing sentry duty. He cocked his head at seeing her. "You're back in a hurry."

"Uhh… yeah," Cara stammered, flustered. She'd had a fairly complicated sob story planned out for Victor, in which Kristina had shouted at her and demanded she return to grab a missing case of creamer. Obviously though, that idea wouldn't work now that Kristina was physically here.

91

Thankfully Kristina chimed in, "You how it is, new girl forgets things and so we–"

"Victor!" A woman's shout sliced between them, and Cara caught a dark-haired woman in Space Force fatigues dart out from between the crates, hurrying towards them. "Hey, did you let some crazy looking girl loose up here?"

Cara gulped down a sudden lump that felt hard as a rock. Oh no.

For some reason Victor looked directly at Cara, as though checking she was still there, before, "I don't think so, why?"

"Well, some teenager in white just ploughed into me out in the crates." The woman with a tech sergeant's stripes stumbled up, massaging the back of her head.

Victor chuckled, "Yeah, right. Good one, Amy."

Cara swallowed. Oh *frick, Frick FRICK*!

"I'm not joking," the woman snapped, irate. "Crazy girl crashed into me then just ran off."

Victor glanced around, as though maybe *he'd* see her. "Well, where'd she go?"

"If I knew that, I'd have found her by now," the woman retorted. "Whoever she is, I'm pretty sure she's *not* supposed to be up here."

Victor swore and puffed out a sigh. "Alright, I'll let someone know…"

Cara glanced at Kristina, who looked to be momentarily distracted at the news. "I need to use the bathroom."

Kristina blinked in surprise, but then, "Don't run off," she warned.

Cara almost had to pinch herself a second time as she took off with her cart, trying not to walk *tooooo* fast. Had that just worked? She glanced back to see Kristina still listening as Victor and the woman began radioing for backup. Well, at least she'd ditched her boss, but frick, what were they supposed to do with the whole Space Force bearing down on them?

It was a short walk to the restrooms, and poking her head inside, Cara swallowed hard when she saw every single stall door hung wide open. "Jessie?" she hissed, dragging the cart inside. "You here?"

Nothing.

No. She stopped in the middle of the restroom, her chest constricting in panic. Where had she gone? Could Jessie not sit still for…

The door banged open and Cara spun as Jessie bolted inside, panting hard, her blonde locks a disheveled mess.

"Where did you go?" Cara demanded.

Jessie knelt over, hands on her knees for a long moment, as she caught her breath. "I'm sorry."

"Jessie, they're looking for you. They're about to search the whole cargo bay."

"I know," she mumbled and Cara hesitated when she noticed the tears in the girl's eyes. "I'm sorry, but I had to. I was trying to find my sister."

Sister? Cara blinked but didn't ask. No time. "Look, I brought some clothes." She nodded to the trolley. "Find something that fits and then we'll get out of here before they do a…"

The bathroom door opened with a faint squeal. "Okay, Cara, this is getting–"

Kristina's voice trailed off and Cara froze in horror. Her boss stared at Jessie, mouth agape then mumbled a soft, "*Dermo*."

Cara's breath drew sharp as a knife. "Kristina, please, I can explain."

Kristina's eyes narrowed on her like a laser, and for a horrible instant, Cara was certain she was about to wheel and call for help. Except she… didn't. Instead, Kristina went dead quiet, her lips drawn tight and her tiger gaze honed on Cara like she was prying straight into her soul, until…

"Alright, Cara, I'll take the short version."

Cara blinked in stunned surprise. "Wait really?"

Kristina's gaze flicked across to Jessie. "The clothes are for you, right?"

Jessie gave a tentative nod.

"Good, get dressed." She pointed at Cara, "You. Start talking. Now."

Chapter 10
The Great Escape

Cara's explanation hit most of the morning's highlights.

"Her crate was marked classified, so we assumed going to the Space Force was a mistake," Cara said. "Sebastian thought that she might be…" she hesitated at the words *super* soldier and cast an anxious glance at Jessie's stall. Sebastian might have thought Jessie was a government experiment, but she'd already been through a lot today. Cara doubted that piling Sebastian's crazy theory on top of all that would help.

Thankfully, Kristina noticed and seemed to understand. She gave a curt, *we'll talk later* wave.

Cara sighed, relieved. "We decided to try and help her escape. But she couldn't blend in downstairs wearing all white."

"So you decided to do some unapproved borrowing?" Kristina arched her eyebrows.

Cara wet her lips, wishing they could have just glossed over that particular. She wasted a moment failing to think of a charitable way to put things before, "Yes," she said bluntly. "And I understand how that looks, but I didn't know what else to do. It was for a good cause."

Cara winced slightly in preparation for Kristina's imminent wrath. She didn't try to pretend at being sorry. She wasn't, and she genuinely doubted Kristina would care or believe her anyway. Shockingly though, her boss just nodded. "I assume you had a plan to get her out of here?"

Cara shrugged, "Sort of. I'd tell Victor you'd yelled at me and sent me back to find some creamer. Then, I'd ask him to come help so Jessie could get to the elevator."

That was a horrible plan, mainly because sentries weren't supposed to leave their posts while on duty. Ever. If it worked, she'd potentially earn Victor a court martial. More likely, he'd say *No*, and she'd get absolutely nowhere. From the expression on her boss's face, Kristina knew that also.

"I guess that's a C- for effort," Kristina mused sarcastically. "I think we'll–"

Kristina abruptly broke off as the bathroom stall squeaked open and Jessie stepped out.

Cara blinked in surprise. The transformation from last century psych ward inmate to normal girl seemed like a scene out of Cinderella. Cara noted with a hint of pride that she'd picked a decently classy ensemble. Except for some rumpled hair, Jessie suddenly looked like someone she wouldn't be embarrassed to sit with at lunch.

Jessie's face flushed at both of them abruptly staring at her. "Is this okay?" she asked modestly.

"Yeah," Cara nodded. "You look great."

Kristina reached into her purse, producing a brush which she tossed over to the surprised Jessie. "Except for your hair. Mind explaining why you look like you lost a fight with a couple of sparrows? Also, why is the Space Force suddenly tripping over itself to find you?"

Jessie swallowed hard, clearly nervous. "Well, like Cara said, I can't really remember…" Jessie choked up a moment and sniffled before she continued, "After everybody left, I kept trying to recall… anything, really. Then I just…" She paused, gathering her thoughts before, "I'm pretty sure that I have a twin sister, and I think she may have come up here in a pod also. I'm not sure why she–

"Short version please," Kristina interrupted in a brusque tone. "I'd prefer to finish *before* they find us."

"Ummm…" Jessie stammered, clearly taken aback. "I went back to the pods to find my sister, but some guy was already there, moving the pods. He saw me, he seemed to know who I was and tried to put me back in cryosleep, so I had to fight him off."

Cara blinked at the last bit. Wait, Jessie had done *what*? She was just out of cryosleep and she'd still….

Cara noticed Kristina's mouth dropped slightly in incredulity. "You *fought* him off?"

The girl simply nodded.

"What did he look like?"

"Tall, bald, he had a military uniform with a name patch, it was uhhh… C– something."

"Probably the same sergeant we saw with that captain earlier," Cara chimed in.

Kristina's eyes narrowed. "Carrington?"

"Yeah, that's him," Jessie gave an eager nod. "How do you–"

"Later, Ice Princess," Kristina snapped, pacing the room twice. Jessie shot Cara a nervous side glance and the best Cara had to offer was a sympathetic *It's probably okay* shrug.

Kristina abruptly twirled to point at Jessie. "I assume you have an implant?"

"Uhhh…"

Without any elaboration, Kristina stalked over. She pulled out her phone, and grabbed a surprised Jessie's wrist, swiping her phone across it to elicit a soft beep. "That's a yes."

Kristina looked at her screen and hesitated with a momentary, "What the…?"

She gestured for Jessie's wrist again, swiped her phone, eliciting a second *beep,* then looked even more confused.

"What is it?" Jessie asked, worried.

"Nothing," Kristina mumbled, shaking her head and poking at her screen for a moment. She abruptly pointing back to Jessie. "Wrist, please."

A hesitant Jessie stuck out her hand and Kristina swiped across the girl's wrist. This time her phone gave a more triumphant *ding*.

"Alright, Princess," Kristina continued with barely a pause, "do you at least remember how to run an elevator?"

Jessie nodded.

"Perfect. You'll need to leave the bathroom, turn left, and don't walk, *run,* until you see an elevator. That's the passenger elevator. There's a keypad with a scanner beneath it. Your implant has the code. Once the elevator shows up, I want you to get in, stand by the down arrow, and hit the button for Level 2. There'll be a little star beside it. That takes you down to the promenade. Once there, exit the elevator and go left until you see a side hall. Find a bench and sit there. *We,*" Kristina gestured to herself and Cara, "will find *you.* Understood?"

Jessie gave a nervous nod, "And if…"

"Nothing will go wrong," Kristina said curtly. "If it does, you're screwed, so discussing it won't make a difference." She nodded towards the door, "Now go, we're running out of time."

Jessie hesitated.

"NOW," Kristina snapped and a chastened Jessie mumbled a demure, *Thanks* as she vanished outside.

That just left Cara still trying to keep up and feeling more than a little irate at Kristina's abrupt assumption of control. The feeling compounded as Kristina smoothly folded Jessie's discarded white fatigues into a, now empty, shoebox, dropped it on the cart, then gestured Cara to the door with a flick. "Cara, time to go. They need to see us both leave the way we came in. Don't forget my cart."

"Wait, just like that?"

"Well, unless you *actually* need to use the bathroom."

The sarcasm just left Cara fuming. "But what if there's a guard?"

"Then they'll probably catch her," Kristina remarked bluntly. Her boss strolled over to the door and gestured her outside.

Something about her unconcerned, matter-of-fact tone left Cara hesitant. "Hold on," she demanded, indignant. "Did you just send Jessie to get caught?"

"Hopefully not," Kristina said pointedly. "The passenger elevator requires a passcode or a military ID to use, so they don't usually post a sentry."

Kristina's tone lowered slightly, picking up a cold menace as she added, "Now move, before I make you move."

That was also pretty matter-of-fact. And while it didn't make Cara feel an ounce better, she reluctantly grabbed her cart and followed along. "You know, you can be a real bitch," she mumbled.

"Likewise, hun," Kristina agreed icily as they walked. "And just so *you* know, perhaps try showing a tiny bit more gratitude to the woman who is working *extremely* hard to save your worthless butt."

That was a debatable depiction of events, but she didn't have time to argue. As they neared the service elevator, Cara saw the door slide open and a half-dozen men and women in dark patterned Space Force fatigues spilled out. By the time they rolled up, a burly young lieutenant with short cropped, brown hair was already interrogating Victor and the woman from earlier. "You said it was just one girl?"

"Yes, sir. She was dressed in all white. I didn't see where she ran off to."

"Alright, I'll get a few more squads up here to start..."

The lieutenant's voice trailed off, his eyes honing on Cara like razors, before jumping to Kristina with a pointed, "Who's your friend, Kristina?"

"She's not the girl you're looking for, if that's what you mean, Lawston." The woman shot him a sly grin, and Cara caught a flash of irritation on the man's face at how much she knew. Kristina added a cheeky, "May we go about our business?"

From the change in his expression, Cara wasn't sure if that last line thawed the lieutenant or frosted him.

"Did you see anything?"

"The inside of a women's restroom, so nothing you'd care about," Kristina remarked in a honeyed voice. She strolled over and hit the button to open the elevator door. "Should I assume you'll take your coffee up here this afternoon?" She added a flirty, "I can deliver it myself if you'd like. Two-thirty sharp? I can be quite punctual."

Lawston's face reddened, his stance relaxed, and he waved her and Cara inside. "I'm sure this won't take that long. And you know not to mention this girl–"

"Of course." Kristina gave a wink and a giddy wave as the door closed. "Mum's the word." Her voice turned to an airy alto as she added, "Later, Lawston."

Once the door closed, Cara shot her boss a surprised, "Him? Really?"

Her boss just shrugged, a grin tugging at her cheeks.

***

Kristina didn't say a word in the elevator, probably because of the camera staring straight at them. The quiet did give Cara a moment to realize something she'd missed though. Kristina had said the other elevator required a passcode to operate. So how exactly did her boss have military access codes ready to whip out of her back pocket?

The question circled like a hawk in her mind. For all that Kristina had scolded her for stealing, had *Kristina* also stolen the code somehow? And why would she just… have that sitting on her phone?

Speaking of which, why had Kristina helped them at all? An hour ago, Cara would have bet every cent she had on Kristina coldly turning her and Jessie in. But instead… it felt like the moment Kristina had seen Jessie, she'd decided to help them, even before Cara had explained anything. Which made no sense.

Frankly, it was stupid. If the Space Force figured out what they were doing, all of them would be in *extremely* hot water. And despite being psychotic, manipulative, and overbearing, she was quite confident that Kristina wasn't stupid.

So why was her mercenary boss suddenly feeling altruistic? Almost the instant Cara considered the question, a possibility hit her. What if it wasn't altruism? What if Kristina wanted something from Jessie too?

99

Ding.

Cara looked up as the elevator gave a friendly chime. Gravity had shifted back to Earth normal, and in front of her the doors slid open. The two stepped out, merging into the bustling crowd on the promenade. Compared to yesterday the station seemed noticeably busier as a steady stream of colonists piled into Medea.

Unlike the drab back hallways that Cara had been scurrying around for the last couple days, the Medea Station Promenade was a wash of mingled voices, flashing signs and the aromatic scents of food pouring out from a dozen different restaurants. Laid out like a giant mall, the spacious concourse arced upwards in the distance, following the curvature of the enormous wheel that formed the bulk of Medea Station. A couple hundred feet off, Cara could see the people strutting around like little ants, but strangely angled. It reminded her of one of those mind-bending movie scenes where the ground warped upwards until all the skyscrapers were sitting at impossible angles. Except real. Even having been here for several days, Cara still felt a slight *whoa* in her chest.

Kristina, meanwhile, had apparently been on Medea long enough to become completely inured to the scenery. She set off to the right at a brisk walk, talking as she went, "Earlier, what was it you weren't telling me about Ice Princess?"

"Huh?" Cara blinked and had to hustle just to keep up.

"In the bathroom, you didn't want Jessie to overhear something. What was it?"

"Ummm, it was nothing," Cara tried to cover. If Kristina really was hiding something, then maybe telling her about Sebastian's crazy or… perhaps not so crazy, super soldier theory wasn't the best idea.

For a second Kristina kept walking and Cara thought she might just let things drop until, "Hun, this all goes a lot easier if you *don't* lie to me. Especially when I'm trying to help you."

Are you though? Cara wondered silently.

Before she could wonder too much, Kristina turned to face her, coming to a full stop serious-faced, "Cara, whatever it is, it might be important."

Yeah, that was the problem. Cara sighed. Unfortunately, she still needed Kristina, maybe more than ever now that Jessie was down here with nowhere to stay, no money, zilch.

Standing in the middle of the concourse while other passers-by flowed like a river around them, Cara lowered her voice. "It's Sebastian," she explained quietly. "He thinks Jessie may be some sort of government experiment, possibly a super soldier or telekinetic."

If that wackiness did surprise Kristina, it didn't show in her posture. Wildly enough, she actually seemed to consider the possibility for a moment. "Hmmm, and that's based on?"

"Him playing too many video games," Cara remarked, a hint of disdain creeping in. "But the experiment thing makes some sense. She *was* in a classified pod after all. I just didn't want to pile that onto everything else that Jessie has going on right now."

"Fair enough," Kristina nodded. "I suppose you did the right thing then." For once she almost seemed to mean it. "I'll make a note to look into it." Kristina turned, breaking back into her quick strides and gesturing for Cara to follow.

"You know someone who might know what's going on?" Cara asked, hurrying to catch up.

"Well, since he's involved, I assume Milo Carrington has at least some clue," Kristina remarked as she kept walking.

Cara's jaw dropped a hair. "You're going to talk to *him*?"

"More like interrogate," Kristina remarked dryly, "but yes, I suppose that's the general concept."

Cara nearly missed a step. The frick was Kristina planning? No offense, but assuming Carrington really was the sergeant from earlier, having encountered him and his monster arms just from a distance, she was fairly sure Kristina wouldn't be doing the interrogating.

She followed a moment, not sure how to say it, but… "Kristina, you've seen the sergeant, right? Like, in real life?"

"Cara," her voice turned patronizing, "I run the best coffee shop on Medea. I see *everyone* at some point. So *yes*, I can handle Carrington."

Okaaaaaay, whatever. Cara made a mental note to stay on the down low until she saw Kristina alive again.

"Speaking of things that need handling," Kristina added, "are you comfortable dealing with Ice Princess?"

"What do you mean?"

"*I mean* the last time she was left alone, she nearly got herself caught," Kristina said. "I'd like to avoid a repeat performance. And since you still owe me for trying to rob my store – *again* – I'll be calling in that favor. I want you to stick to her like glue, get her food, figure out what she knows, track down her Codex account, anything. Her implant was completely wiped. All I could get off of it was a name, Jessica Fischer. Maybe start there."

"Wait, for real?" Cara frowned. Usually implants had loads of info on them. Just off the top of her head, hers had a home address, contact info, her Military ID so she could get around base, plus her student ID, and a bunch of other stuff she'd forgotten about over the years.

"Well, that's just the open broadcast directory. If you want to try cracking the admin password and see what else is there, be my guest. But it sure looks like someone tried to turn that girl into a ghost."

"So," Kristina continued, "now that you know, do you think you can manage Ice Princess?"

"I.... probably."

"Let's pretend you said *yes*. In which case, you're off dishes for the rest of the day." Kristina glanced at her phone then added, "I know you're off at two. Do you mind staying till five?"

Ditch the dishes and hang out with Amnesia Girl for the next few hours? Cara felt like there ought to be a catch, especially with Kristina involved. If there was though, she definitely couldn't see it. "Yeah, sure."

"Perfect."

Instantly Kristina whipped out her phone and a moment later had Mom on the line. "Ms Rosenfeld, hi... Yes, yes, Cara is doing fine, better than fine actually. I wanted to see if you'd let me keep her a bit longer today."

They chatted for a moment, until Kristina abruptly spun with a *behave yourself* glower and handed the phone to Cara. "She wants to talk to you."

"Mom?"

"Cara," Mom's voice had that cheery ring she always got when the twins finally consented to take a nap, "is everything alright?"

"Uhhh… yeah, of course."

"And you're *okay* with staying late." The intonation said it all. Cara nearly laughed as she realized. Trust Mom to be suspicious of her suddenly finding a work ethic.

"Mom, it's fine," Cara insisted. "I just figured, if I'm going to make money I might as well make as much as I can." A lightbulb abruptly flashed on in her head and a mercenary grin tugged at her lips as she added, "Kristina said she'd pay me overtime. That's not a problem, is it?"

She waited through the stunned pause on the other end of the line, trying to ignore a simmering irritation at the subtext. Wow, that really went to show what Mom normally thought of her.

Finally, "No, that… that's great, Cara," Mom said encouragingly. "Tell Kristina I'm fine with you working as much as you want."

The irony wasn't lost on Cara. The one thing Mom actually approved of, work, and of course she *wasn't* doing that. Frick, she *hated* doing that.

Cara held in her sigh. "Alright, appreciate it."

"Of course," she could almost hear the smile through the phone. "I'm proud of you, sweetie. Talk to you later."

Awww, thanks, Cara thought, the sarcasm ringing in her head. She tried to ignore the sting in those words, and settled for a simple, "Alright, bye."

Mom hung up and Cara handed the phone back to Kristina. "Mom says I'm good."

"Excellent." Kristina nodded, and pointed to where the station floor bowled up in the distance. Cara saw a blonde girl in a familiar skirt, standing around and visibly gawking at the scale of the mammoth space station. "Looks like Ice Princess

made it down after all," Kristina remarked. "In which case, your
new job starts now."

Chapter 11
Ghosts in the Shell

Cara had only been to New York once, but Trio Pizza definitely seemed to be aiming for that pizza by the slice, hole-in-the-wall feel. Wedged in behind a narrow storefront, it extended far back with a single row of booths lining the left wall while the kitchen had been crammed along the right. Fortunately, it was only 11:15, which meant she and Jessie had just beaten the lunch rush to order.

They found a spot about halfway to the back. Behind them the kitchen door ping-ponged open and closed as a steady stream of servers trooped in and out. Judging from her bright grin, Jessie was appreciating the experience, even if the restaurant didn't provide the best ambiance. Cara meanwhile, was still savoring finally getting to shed her hideous dishwashing jumpsuit back at Kristina's office. But even despite her relief at not having to walk around looking like an escaped inmate, Cara couldn't avoid a nervous worry that pricked at the back of her mind. Not scared so much as… anxious? When they'd first found Jessie, helping her out of the cryopod had felt like something out of a dream. It couldn't actually be happening. But now that the military was hunting them, it all seemed a lot more… real.

Regardless, Cara made sure to sit facing towards the front, where she could watch the crowd streaming by outside. If someone did come for them, they'd take the back way out through the kitchen. In which case, perhaps it was a good thing she'd been here earlier in the week.

They'd barely taken their seats and set their stand with the number 15 on the table, when Sebastian appeared. He was doing that restaurant thing where he expertly balanced the platter with just one hand. "Ladies," he nodded, and set out a basket of breadsticks.

His eyes went to Cara, "Everything go okay?"

"We made it. Didn't we?" Cara deliberately dodged the question. She wasn't sure how Sebastian would react to the Kristina news. Frick, she wasn't sure how *she* should react to the Kristina news.

"Cool," he nodded at Cara and flashed Jessie a grin. "Pizza will be out in a minute."

He hurried off to distribute more breadsticks, and Cara grabbed one, taking a tentative bite.

Across the table, Jessie was a lot less reserved. She more or less crammed half a breadstick into her mouth. "Oh my gosh," she mumbled as she chewed, "these are *amazing*!"

Not quite the word Cara would have chosen. If anything, they were a bit salty. But watching Jessie wolf down the first bite, then ravenously tear into what was left, Cara decided not to judge. If she'd stepped out of a cryopod, she might be starving too.

"Don't eat too much before the pizza gets here."

"I know, but it just tastes sooooo good," Jessie said, letting out a contented sigh. "I feel like I haven't eaten in days."

Cara nibbled on her own breadstick. "Well, technically you probably haven't."

"That's a good point," Jessie agreed, right as another server hurried by, balancing two platters crammed with pizza slices. He stopped at the next booth down, Jessie's eyes following him hungrily. She licked her lips and reached for the last breadstick. There had been three in the basket, which was an awkward number to share between two people. Jessie grabbed it, then paused halfway to her mouth, "Did you want…"

Cara waved it away, "All yours."

"Thanks," Jessie tore off a quarter and scarfed it down. In between bites though, she seemed to grow more thoughtful. "I wonder what all I missed while I was asleep?" She paused, swallowing, "It's still 2065? Right? I feel like it should be 2065."

"Yeah, February 28th." Cara cocked her head. At least Jessie hadn't been asleep too long. "Are you remembering more?"

"Not… sort of." Jessie frowned and finally stopped eating a moment. She let out a long sigh. "I think my memories from before are still there, but it's like I can't grab onto anything… does that make sense?"

Cara shook her head.

"It's like…" Jessie puffed up her cheeks and let out a long breath, "like trying to find something at the store, but you can't remember where it is, so you have to walk down every aisle until you find it. Then, sometimes you just notice stuff you'd completely forgotten about. When I first woke up and you mentioned we were on Medea Station…" She struggled a moment to put it into words, "I knew what Medea was, but if no one had told me, I wouldn't have remembered that I knew that. I'd still probably be wondering where we are and why all the floors are curved. If that makes any sense."

Cara shrugged and gave Jessie a sympathetic answer, "I guess." She tried to remember Kristina's advice, just hang with Jessie and learn what she could. Except, what if Jessie didn't know anything either?

Well, that wasn't entirely true, was it, her inner critic pointed out. Jessie remembered what the year was. Maybe she just needed some help to remember more.

"Jessie," Cara leaned in a bit, "what's the last thing you remember?"

Jessie nibbled at her lip. "The last thing is sitting across from my sister, Jackie. We're playing a board game, and she's in the same white shirt and pants that I was earlier. I feel like we're in a small, white-ish room and…" Jessie paused, her expression turning confused. "The thing is, I think she was really happy."

"Happy like…?"

"Like excited." Jessie's face transformed for an instant to intense concentration, then faded to disappointment. "I can't recall anything else though. But it must have been right before we went into cryosleep."

"And you're sure your sister was *excited*?"

Jessie nodded.

Well, that made zero sense. It also didn't help nail down when exactly she'd gone into cryosleep. "Do you remember anything from before that, maybe a big event like–"

"Hello again, ladies," Sebastian's upbeat voice interrupted. The boy strolled up with a platter balanced precariously on one hand. "Your pizza has arrived."

He made a wholly unnecessary show of depositing plates in front of them. Cara's held just a single slice of supreme, while Jessie had gone for three slices of Canadian bacon and pepperoni. She had a glow in her eyes like Christmas had come early.

"*Bon appetit*," Sebastian finished with a flourish and an overdone bow. He set aside the platter, then slid in beside Jessie who bit into her first slice with a rushed, "Ohmygoshthankyousomuch!"

"No problem." He tapped his fingers energetically. "So, what's the situation?"

Cara cocked an eyebrow across the table. "Don't you have work to do?" She nodded back toward the kitchen.

"Don't you?"

Jessie jumped in between bites, "Kristina let her off for the day."

Sebastian's expression mouth dropped a half inch. "Why would Kristina–"

"She knows," Cara said bluntly.

His mouth dropped open. "You told her?"

"No, idiot. She found out. She…" Cara didn't even know how to explain it. She couldn't exactly say that Kristina had magic powers.

"I don't know how, but she caught me. Anyway, I guess she's on our side now… sort of. She helped Jessie escape, and she's funding lunch."

Sebastian didn't look remotely mollified. "You know, Cara, you are the *worst* thief I've ever seen. Seriously, how could you–"

"Oh, that's rich, Pizza Boy. I don't see you trying to–"

"Guys, STOP," Jessie interrupted both of them with a frustrated hiss. "Look, she's not that bad, alright. And she's helping, and she bought lunch, so just… stop. Okay?"

Cara let out a long sigh. Right, *not that bad*. Just wait until Jessie *actually* got to know Kristina.

Across from her, Sebastian seemed to cool down some as well. After a moment's pause, he finally asked, "Well, what's the plan then?"

"I'm trying to figure out exactly when Jessie went into cryosleep."

Jessie mumbled through another mouthful, *"ats wat we wer ooing?"*

"Huh?" Cara and Sebastian both stared at her.

It took her a moment to swallow, then, "Sorry," she offered, red-faced. "I said, that's what we were doing? Also, this is the best pizza *ever*."

Sebastian grinned, "I'll let them know you like it."

Given how hungry Jessie was, Cara had the sneaking suspicion *any* pizza would have been the best pizza ever. But whatever.

"It was sometime this year. I was trying to think of a big event that she might remember? What abooooout… the inauguration?"

Jessie frowned, "Who watches that? I mean, I remember the election but–"

"Super Bowl?" Sebastian offered.

Cara sighed, why would Jessie be keeping up with–

"Yeah, I remember that." Jessie's eyes lit up in sudden excitement, "It was uhhh… Cincinnati and the blue team. Right?"

Sebastian frowned, his mouth hanging half open, "Well… I guess that's technically accurate. But you do remember it?"

"Sure," Jessie nodded, "We were…"

Jessie's voice abruptly trailed off, her eyes going wide and one hand covering her mouth as she sucked in a sharp breath.

"What?" Cara asked.

Her voice was breathless, "I… I remember."

***

The announcer shouted through the TV, "TOUCHDOWN COWBOYS!"

"NO! NO! NO!" Mom's latest boyfriend was on his feet, screaming at the flex screen. "YOU IDIOTS! YOU JUST HAD TO GRAB HIM! WHAT'S WRONG WITH YOU!"

Sitting next to her sister on the couch, Jessie was slowly munching her way through a bag of Tostitos and enjoying the show. William certainly wasn't the worst guy Mom had brought home, morbidly overweight, but that just made it more entertaining to watch him get this worked up. Besides, even if football wasn't her thing, and she didn't understand the rules, it was still kind of fun. There was that hint of that raw, competitive excitement she knew from playing softball. Something about getting invested in a game.

Sitting next to her on the couch though, Jackie was still fuming. *She'd* wanted to go hang at Ruth's earlier and, of course, Mom had told her she had to stay so they could watch the game *together*. That had been a huge screaming match that eventually devolved into a Cold War style nuclear standoff. Now Mom kept hovering over by the kitchen door with a sour face, while Jackie was camped out on the couch, radiating hostility.

That certainly put a damper on the evening.

Back on screen the blue guys kicked off and Jessie offered her sister the queso. "Want some?"

It was still the first quarter, so they had *a lot* of this left to endure. It'd be nice if Jackie could take a chill pill for the evening.

"I'm fine," she muttered darkly. Jackie glanced right back at her phone, doing her usual sulking where she refused to be happy, no matter what.

Suuuure. Jessie watched as the Bengals ran the ball back to the thirty-yard line, got tackled and then… it was first down? Right?

They played another couple of downs until…

"Interception by Marvin Watson! Back to the thirty, twenty–down at the twelve!"

"WHAT WERE YOU THINKING?" William was back on his feet. "COLLINS WAS WIDE OPEN! ALL YOU HAD TO DO WAS THROW IT!"

"Can you shut up!" Jackie abruptly snapped at him.

William wheeled on her, his mouth dropping open in exasperation. "Kid, do you understand what just happened?"

He called them both *kid*. Jessie suspected it was because he couldn't actually tell them apart. Which was dumb. He'd been around for nine months, and attitude wise, Jessie felt it was pretty obvious which one of them was which.

The name might have peeved her, but Jackie flat out *hated* it. Jessie cringed, she could almost see her sister's rage meter blast up to eleven, even as William kept on. "Not only did they just throw away their lead, but now they're about to–"

"NO ONE CARES!" Jackie screamed, "OKAY? DO YOU NOT GET THAT?"

"Jacqueline!" Mom's whipcord tight voice sliced like a razor from across the room. "Sit down and fix your attitude."

"Really?" she wheeled on Mom, venom in her voice. "Which one of us actually made me be here? Newsflash, it wasn't me."

"Just because you're sulking doesn't mean you have to ruin things for the rest of us," Mom spat back.

"Oh, sure I'm the one ruining things."

Jessie tried to hop in, keep things from blowing up again. "Jackie, maybe let's just–"

"Why? Why should–"

William interrupted, his boisterous voice booming over the announcer, as he waved for her to be quiet. "Kid, I'm trying to watch here."

"MY NAME IS *NOT* KID!" Jackie screamed so loud it hurt Jessie's ears. "And if you love the dumb game so much, why don't you go play it instead?" She sneered, "Or are you afraid you'd have a heart attack jogging down the field?"

Mom's furious voice interrupted, as she stalked over, grabbed Jackie's arm, and pulled her up to standing. "Jacqueline Isabell Fischer, you go to your room, *right now*."

Jessie slunk back a bit on the couch, knowing exactly how this would go. "Don't touch me." Jackie roughly jerked her arm free.

"Kid, listen to your mom," William snapped.

"SHUT UP!" Jackie screamed, then spun, taking three steps to the door outside. She wrenched it open, stalking into the night with a venomous, "SCREW YOU." Then the door slammed so hard the trailer shuddered.

In the aftermath, everything went dead still in the living room. Mom glared daggers at the door, until…

"What a brat," William muttered, then notched up the volume as a few orange guys piled on someone right in front of the goal line.

Jessie stared at the door a second, then noticed Jackie's coat still on its peg. In a flash she was up, snatching both their coats as she went.

"Jessie, wait," Mom called, "just…"

The trailer door closed behind Jessie, and she never heard the rest.

Outside the cold nipped at Jessie. Dusk had already faded to night, and a biting wind cut right through her sweater. Jessie slipped on her familiar purple overcoat, her eyes just catching Jackie as she disappeared into the gloom around the side of the mobile home. They had two flood-lights mounted to illuminate the gravel driveway in front of the trailer, but one had a blown bulb and the working one was pointed towards the car. It yielded enough light to get Jessie to the bottom of the porch steps, but there she paused, fumbling to flick on her phone flashlight.

Finally, it flooded out a splash of cold white light, and she hurried after her sister. Turning the corner, she caught sight of Jackie's own phone light bobbing off into the woods behind their house.

The field behind their house was grown up in a thicket of towering trees – pine, elm and oak – all clustered close together. A narrow deer path marked the main trail through the trees, and Jessie followed it back past where the path vanished, holding up one arm against the swishing branches.

Up ahead, Jackie's light flicked off.

Needle laden branches scraped her jacket as Jessie ducked beneath a particularly dense arch of pine limbs. Coming back up on the other side, she paused, brushing a few needles from her hair, then hesitated as she caught a low sobbing not far off. Her chest tightened as she continued the last little bit, to a spot where four giant pines had seemingly grown up together. Their trunks had widened out, merging until they formed almost a wooden wall at ground level. It was one of the few spots which screened them from the house that Mom didn't know about.

Jackie was there. The pale splash of light revealed her curled up with her back to the trees, sobbing.

"Hey," Jessie walked over, dropping down next to her sister and flicking off her phone light. That left only the pale moonbeams trickling through the canopy to see by. "I brought your jacket."

Next to her, Jackie sniffled, accepting the thick overcoat and slipping her arms into the puffy sleeves. Even in the dark, Jessie could glimpse the tears trickling down her cheeks. "I'm sorry," Jackie mumbled after a moment. "I didn't mean to…"

Jessie nodded. She knew, even without saying. Sometimes it felt like a miracle that they made it through the day at all when everything devolved into a fight.

For a moment the two sat there in silence, the icy breeze rustling the needles overhead, and Jessie tucked her already frigid hands into her jacket pockets.

It was odd, the things you could notice in the quiet. Sitting in the stark stillness of winter, she gradually became aware of her own breaths, long and even, while next to her Jackie's took up a sharper, strained tempo.

"Jess," Jackie's voice finally broke the stillness, "do you still want to leave?"

Jessie glanced over at her sister, her usually rosy cheeks dyed an icy blue in the moonlight. "Of course."

Jackie opened her mouth, then paused, before, "Like, do you *really* want to leave?"

There was something about Jackie's voice that gave Jessie a moment's pause. Like for once it wasn't just a daydream. Jessie hesitated. "You're talking about going to Nashville?"

Nashville was the one city they had an *actual* working plan to get to. It would cost a bit of money, but they'd scrounged up enough for a small emergency fund. They'd catch a Drive-Me to the Greyhound stop in town, buy two tickets to Nashville, then catch another Drive-Me to Grandma Luker's place. Technically, that was Mom's mom, but Mom had been feuding with her parents ever since high school, and they didn't go to see them much. Funny, how the proverbial apples hadn't fallen far from the tree, so to speak.

Honestly, if Mom hadn't been so stubborn, they would have moved in with Grandma and Grandpa last year. Mom had lost her job at the grocery store, and for a couple months, Jessie had been certain they'd lose the trailer. Not that it was much of a loss. The thing was falling apart, but still, that would have been game over. But in the final weeks, Mom had gotten a secretary job at the school district office. Then William had showed up, and here they were, almost a year later. Still stuck.

Jackie shook her head, her voice distant. "It's a lot further than Nashville, and we wouldn't get to see Mom again for a long time."

"How long?" Jessie frowned, suddenly a bit more on the fence. Nashville was close enough to escape, but Jessie had always implicitly expected Mom would cave and join them after a few weeks. Things would be like before, only somewhere else and… better… somehow.

"At least four years."

"Four…" Jessie's voice trailed off incredulous. "Jackie, we can't just… *leave* leave. What about Mom?"

"She'll be fine," Jackie said bitterly. "Probably better without us."

"Jackie," she scolded, "we can't. You know we–"

"Well, we have to do something," Jackie insisted, a spark of desperation in her voice. "What's the alternative, sit around waiting to get knocked-up like mom? End up just like her? Start the cycle all over again? Screw that." Jackie's tone bled cold despair. "Jess, I can't do two more years of this."

Jessie gulped. Jackie was scared, and for a moment she saw it too– both of them stuck here while life slipped on by. Jessie didn't want to leave Mom, but…

"Okay," she managed, a tentative nervousness building in her chest. "Where are we going?"

Back towards the house, she caught a shout on the wind. Mom. "Girls, come inside!" A pause then, "You're going to freeze out here!"

Jackie stared at the ground for a moment, like she wasn't quite ready to go back. The mention of the cold though, sent Jessie's thoughts straight to her legs, which were half numb beneath a single pair of jeans.

"Girls!"

She grabbed at her sister's arm, shivering, "Jackie, where are we going?"

"It won't be for a few weeks," Jackie said. She looked Jessie straight in the eye and added, "Jess, you have to *swear* not to tell anyone."

"Alright, I swear." Jessie's tone firmed up. Fine she was in, but, "Jackie, *where are we going?*"

Her sister gave a long sigh, then said about the craziest word Jessie could have imagined. "Mars."

Chapter 12
The Hunters and the Hunted

Sebastian's mouth fell open. "Mars? So your sister knew?"

"That can't be right," Cara insisted, shaking her head. "Maybe you're confusing being up here with–"

"That's just what I remember, okay?" Jessie shrugged, defensive. "I'm pretty sure she said Mars, because I remember thinking that it seemed completely crazy too."

Sebastian leaned forward onto the table. "Well, what else did she say?"

Jessie put up her palms with a blunt, "Nothing."

Cara frowned, "What do you mean *nothing*?"

"I mean it was *freezing* cold, and Mom kept shouting, so we went back inside," Jessie said pointedly. "Jackie gave her little, *I'm sorry, but not really* apology, then stomped off to our room. I wanted to help make things up to Mom, so I watched the rest of the game and ate too much queso. That's all I remember."

Cara watched as Sebastian's fingers rapped a little drumbeat on the tabletop, processing everything until, "But Jackie must have had a plan, right?"

"Yeah, probably," Jessie agreed, taking another bite of pizza.

"Well, did she tell you what it was? Because there aren't a lot of slots to Mars for adults, let alone people our age."

Jessie stared at him, then Cara, before throwing up her hands with an exasperated, "What part of *I Don't Remember* do you guys not get? Yeah, I'm sure she had a plan. She probably explained it later, and given that I'm up here, it probably made a lot of sense at the time."

Cara leaned in, "But does that like… trigger any other memories?"

Jessie gave her a blank, *seriously* stare, "No."

Sebastian opened his mouth to pry more, but Cara realized this was going too far and cut him off. "Why don't you eat, Jessie. Maybe that'll help you think of something else."

It probably wouldn't. But Jessie didn't need another reason to start back on her pizza, and it wasn't like their prying was improving things.

Meanwhile, Cara looked over at Sebastian, whose fingers were back to tapping his little symphony on the table. "Alright, having heard that, you still think this is military related?"

He considered the question a moment. "I don't know. But, be it the Space Force or CIA or… somebody had to put her in that pod. It wouldn't be the weirdest thing the military has done." He paused, adding an uncertain, "It almost sounds like Jackie got recruited for this, you know? Kind of like…"

He let the sentence hang, but Cara could fill in, kind of like a secret experiment. She wished he hadn't brought that up at all. Grabbing her fork, Cara busied herself cutting off the tip of her pizza slice with the long side before forking it into her mouth.

In the quiet though, Jessie chimed in, confused, "Kind of like… what?"

"It's nothing." Cara waved it off.

"Isn't it?" Jessie's gaze flashed from her to Sebastian, then back, suddenly even more on edge. "I've been honest with you guys, okay? What is it?"

Cara sighed, oh joy, here they went, right into the crazy side of the pool. Across the table Sebastian wet his lips. "Jessie, since you've come out of cryosleep, have you noticed anything… unusual?"

"You mean besides being stuck on a space station?" The girl cocked her head, skeptical. "I don't know, I guess I've been really hungry." She paused, her expression transforming in shocked understanding. "You think they did something to me?"

Cara jumped in, "Not necessarily, it's–"

Sebastian interrupted, "It's just a possibility."

A flash of worry creased at her face, but then faded to more of a stoic consideration. "You're thinking like… super powers?"

Put that way, it sounded extra stupid but… yeah, Cara mused, pretty much like super powers.

"Like I said, it's just a possibility," Sebastian added, his tone trying a little too hard to be reassuring.

For a moment, Jessie chewed on another bite, then abruptly pointed her fingers towards the parmesan cheese shaker at the end of the table. Her whole face tensed in concentration, both eyes pressed closed and her hand twitching like she was trying to telekinetically lift it from afar.

It didn't budge.

Jessie popped one eye open, then puffed up her cheeks again and let out a disappointed breath, "Dang it, that would have been really cool."

Cara rolled her eyes as she neatly trimmed off another bite with her fork. Amazing how those two thought in the same completely ridiculous, borderline magical terms. Might as well see if she had mind reading powers also.

Another employee picked that moment to pause at their table. "Hey, Sebastian, we could use a hand with orders. You can flirt with the customers later."

Instantly the boy's face turned beet red. Jessie looked away, blushing. Cara eyed him with a taunting grin, "Looks like work's calling, Pizza Boy."

Sebastian stood, his eyes narrowing on her. "We'll get back to this later."

"Sure thing. Until then we'll be at Kristina's place, working on the *less* supernatural options, maybe starting with Jessie's Codex." Cara's expression broke into a grin as she added a snarky, "Also, we could use some more breadsticks."

He scowled, and Cara added a mocking, "Pleeeeease, Pizza Boy."

Sebastian shook his head and hurried off, reappearing a moment later with another basket and a surprisingly not so acrid, "Enjoy, Klepto." Meanwhile, Cara focused back on her pizza, trimming off another bite. It actually was pretty good, and she hadn't eaten since dinner yesterday. It was only when she looked up that she noticed Jessie watching her, seeming very confused.

"What?"

Jessie's eyes drifted to Cara's fork, another bit of pizza impaled on the end. "What are you doing?

"Umm… eating my pizza?"

"With a fork?"

"Yeah," Cara glanced at her giant floppy slice. "It'd be really messy otherwise." She looked back at Jessie with a pointed, "Is there a problem?"

Jessie cocked her head. "I *guess* not. It's just… kind of weird."

Oh please, Cara thought. Besides, this was how Mom ate pizza too.

That said, her next bite, she couldn't help but be a little self-conscious. There was nothing wrong with using a fork. And she sure wouldn't swap it up now.

While Cara ate, Jessie at least seemed to have finally sated her hunger. Eventually, she settled down to nibbling on a warm breadstick, then anxiously fidgeting with her long blonde hair.

"Cara?" she asked, "what if they did do something to me? What if I'm dying or–"

"We don't know that, alright," Cara forcefully cut off the idea before it could get rooted. "We don't even know who put you in the cryopod, let alone why. If they did do something, Kristina will figure it out, and we'll handle it then. And worst case, if it really is the military behind all this, then we'll make a video and spam it out to the whole world that the Space Force is abducting teenagers. We'll work out something. But unless you can suddenly fly or punch a hole in the wall, worrying about it doesn't help."

Jessie nodded, although that didn't seem to stop her from worrying. They probably ought to get out of here, Cara mused.

Kristina had handed over the password for the fast WiFi in her office, which meant they could now check Jessie's Codex without the usual two-minute Medea Station lag just to load a page.

She was about to stand when Sebastian wandered back by. He reached over to grab the empty breadstick basket, talking fast. "We may have a problem, girls. Don't freak out, and try not to be obvious, but check out the line by the register."

Then, like he didn't want to draw any attention, he turned and headed back toward the kitchen.

Jessie instantly twisted in her seat in about the most obvious way possible, peering back towards the steadily growing lunch line. "What is it?"

Cara tried to be a bit more subtle. For a moment her eyes roved across the queue of people until…

A weight like a brick dropped into her stomach, and suddenly she was glad she hadn't eaten too much. "Jessie, just act normal," she hissed.

Jessie hesitated but finally turned back, leaning over the table with a whispered, "Who is it?"

Cara swallowed, her eyes flashing back to the man in a sharp Space Force uniform. "It's the Captain. The one from the shuttle bay who wanted to get your pod moved. He's ordering pizza."

Jessie's face paled.

Yeah… frick.

***

Jessie felt like her heart was about to hammer its way right out of her breast. "Do you think he followed us here?" She couldn't keep herself from glancing back towards the line.

"Jessie, stop," Cara snapped. "Just look at me. We're trying to be inconspicuous."

Jessie hesitated a moment, trying to memorize the different people, among them no less than three different men in uniform.

"Jessie!" Cara hissed.

Reluctantly Jessie forced her gaze back towards Cara, seriously wishing she'd taken the other side of the booth so she could see up front, "Which one is he?"

Cara relaxed back in her booth, doing an admirable job of seeming at ease. "Third guy back from the register. Black hair, captain's bars, poking at his phone.

Jessie nodded, her breaths coming short and anxious. "Do you think he followed us here? Should we run or–"

"I think he's probably just in the mood for pizza," Cara cut her off curtly. "Bad guys have to eat lunch too, you know."

That was a profoundly unsatisfying answer, especially when Jessie felt her entire body shivering in sudden anticipation. "What do we do then?"

Cara glanced around, "Nothing, the place is filled up. He can't sit anywhere near us. Let's just wait."

"And if he does head our way?"

"Worst case, he sees us," Cara said, taking the whole situation with an odd calm to her demeanor. "I'll stall him and you head for the kitchen. There's a door in the back. Leave and head right to get back to Kristina's."

Jessie chanced one last glance towards the front. The captain now had his phone put away and was standing at the register, gesturing toward something as he spoke. Cara was right though, the lunch rush had gradually swallowed up all the extra seats. Now every booth and table was filled, and up front they still had a line ten people deep. He couldn't sit here even if he wanted to.

"Jessie, stop staring," Cara snapped, angrily. "You'll give us away."

She sighed and tore her eyes away, fingering at her hair for a moment until Sebastian strolled back by.

"Sebastian," Cara gestured him over with an impatient scowl.

Jessie saw Sebastian roll his eyes, but he paused at their table. "You know, Cara, the way you've been acting, you'd better be leaving a *really* nice tip."

"Yeah, whatever," she mumbled dismissively. "Look, our officer friend over there, where's he supposed to eat? The whole place is full.

Sebastian shrugged like it was obvious. "He's probably getting it to go."

"I thought they didn't do disposable stuff up here?"

"They don't, we have little washable to-go tins. It's a couple dollars extra, but you get it off your order when you bring them back. No cardboard involved." He paused, "Do they not do that at the coffee shop?"

"Oh they do. Just with mugs. I should know."

Jessie hazarded another glance back to where the man had now ordered and was flicking on his phone while he waited. "So, he's leaving?" she asked, her mind flooding with a dozen questions.

"Yeah, probably," Sebastian nodded, then abruptly glanced back towards the kitchen with a curse. "I'll be back."

He darted off and Cara settled back in her seat. "We'll just wait a minute."

Jessie wasn't so sure, and not even being able to look at the man just made the buzz of questions worse. If the captain wasn't trailing her and Cara… where was he going? He must know that she'd escaped by now. Presumably the sergeant who'd tried to grab her up in the cargo bay guy would have told him. Right?

And what did he know about her and Jackie? The more she thought about it the more she wondered if waiting for the captain to walk off might be an enormous mistake.

"Alright, we're in the clear." Across the table, Cara breathed a sigh of relief. "He's headed out." She relaxed back in her booth, "Give it a minute, then let's get back to Kristina's."

And do what? Check out her Codex? Good luck with that. Her phone was a couple thousand miles away, and Jessie had *nooo* clue what her password was.

For an instant she straddled the fence. She'd be safe back at Kristina's, relatively, at least. But… Jessie looked back towards the front and caught a final glimpse of the man with all the answers as he hurried outside and vanished to the left.

Would they get another opportunity like this? For a moment Jessie felt the two fears balanced on a knife edge. What if he caught her, but then again, what if this was her chance?

What would Jackie do?

Even with her fragmented memories, Jessie could guess. Follow, make a mess, try to bluff her way out, possibly get them both thrown in cryosleep, the usual. Put that way, it was an easy choice, except… Jessie wet her lips, except somehow, by fair or foul, Jackie had actually gotten them halfway to Mars too. Maybe it was all just a question of perspective.

"Come on." Jessie stood.

"Huh?" Cara glanced up from scowling at her phone screen.

"We're following him."

Cara's mouth fell open, but before she could object, Jessie was already making for the promenade.

"Jessie," Cara's voice faded beneath the drone of a dozen others as Jessie wove through the packed tables. Turning sideways, she slipped past two men standing and talking near one booth, then shouldered her way through the ordering line that spilled out the front into the promenade. There at the entrance, she glimpsed their man from behind, a buzz cut of black stubble, in a speckled blue and black Space Force uniform. He was walking away from them with a a precise, intentional stride, like he had somewhere to be.

She took two steps after him, then a hand bit at her wrist, wrenching her to a stop.

"The frick are you doing?" Cara hissed. Jessie whirled to find Cara almost right in her face. She stood a forehead shorter, but her furious eyes more than made up for her lack of height.

"I… I'm going after him," Jessie said, forcing her voice to be firm. "He's getting away."

She tried to pull her wrist free, but Cara held on and instead pushed in uncomfortably close. Jessie caught a controlling sort of queen-bee gleam in her eyes that seemed dimly familiar from school.

"Jessie, stop it," she insisted. "This is stupid."

Yeah, it was, everything was stupid right now. She shouldn't even be up here… except she was. At least this way she might find out something useful. "Cara please, I need to do this," Jessie insisted. Usually she'd sit and talk and figure this out, but… she glanced back to see the captain had already disappeared in the milling crowd. There wasn't time.

"We're going back to Kristina's," Cara ordered, pulling her back towards Trio. "Then we can figure out–"

"NO!" Jessie's patience finally snapped with a volcano fury. She jerked her wrist free of Cara's grip and she found herself breathing hard in anger. "Look, Cara," she spat, "you're not the one with a giant enormous *blank* where your life is supposed to be. Okay? You're not sitting there trying to remember where you go to school, or if you have friends, or a dad. You're not wondering where your sister is, if she's alive, if you'll ever see her again." She pointed down the promenade. "You're not the one watching the only person on the entire damn space station who might know something just walk away."

Cara stared at her, lips drawn tight, her fingers clenching air in frustration and her voice slathered in sarcasm. "Do you not see how this is *exactly* like what happened earlier in the cargo bay?"

For once Jessie just snarked back, "Don't know, can't remember."

"Everything alright, girls?" Sebastian's upbeat voice butted in at precisely the wrong moment.

Cara whirled on him, hot with fury. "Don't you have a *job*?"

"Geez, Cara, did you wake up on the wrong side of the bed, or are you always this angry?"

Cara let out a low growl, but Sebastian stepped right past her and nodded to Jessie. He'd shed his pizza apron and was now just in a black shirt and jeans. "They won't miss me that much. I assume we're following that dude?"

"Yeah," Jessie said, smiling to have someone see things her way for a change.

"Awesome. That's him, right?" Sebastian pointed off to where the promenade began to bowl upwards like the sides of a giant valley. They could easily see over the heads of the bustling crowd nearby, and he'd picked out their man, Space Force fatigues and a dull chrome, pizza-shaped wedge in one hand.

"I believe so."

A few feet away, Jessie could see Cara, very stylish in her sunny yellow top, and just steaming. Amusingly enough,

Sebastian barely seemed to notice her simmering fury. He took two steps then glanced back at her. "You coming?"

"Idiots," Cara muttered.

"So, that's a yes?"

The act seemed to physically pain her, but Cara gritted her teeth and took a step after them, darkly muttering something about, "And *my* danger meter is the broken one?"

Chapter 13
Ariadne's Threads

Ten Minutes Later

"Who is that?" Jessie stared.

Cara might still think this was a terrible idea, but even so, she also found herself staring at the dark-haired woman who'd just come and sat down next to the captain.

Following the man had turned out to be extraordinarily easy, and *perhaps* less risky than Cara had assumed. Because of the way Medea bowled upwards in the distance, they'd been able to keep back a couple hundred feet. Usually that would have meant losing the captain in the dense crowds, but instead it had been like watching him climb a hill. Two hundred feet away, the station curved up, and they had a direct line of sight to track him.

For a while he'd kept walking, and Cara felt like they must have covered a quarter of the Medea Station ring. Somehow they'd gone even deeper into the endless barrage of colorful shops and restaurants. Some were even places Cara vaguely remembered passing Monday, before her ill-fated visit to Kristina's.

Eventually, the captain had stopped at an elaborate tiled fountain set right in the middle of the promenade and surrounded by benches and tables. In the center, a long sheet of water cascaded downwards from the ceiling thirty feet overhead. Around the edges, jets of water danced upwards in constantly morphing patterns that seemed timed to a musical score that Cara couldn't hear over so many voices. It vaguely reminded her of a miniature version of the Bellagio in Vegas. There the captain had stopped, finding a table near the fountain's base and eating his pizza.

They'd kept at a distance, expecting him to head on once he'd finished. But instead he'd waited around, thumbs furiously tapping at his phone with the concentrated focus of someone who took his job a bit too seriously. He seemed completely oblivious to the outside world. They probably could have strolled up behind him and he wouldn't have noticed.

That clearly wasn't the breakthrough Jessie had been hoping for. Cara had watched the girl's face slowly morph into a *disappointed, about to give up*, frown.

That was, until *she* showed up.

From two hundred feet back, it was difficult to make out much about the woman, but even from a distance, Cara could admire her power-suit style. She wore a black blazer layered over a black blouse and slacks, all matching the luxuriant, almost shiny black hair that hung down past her shoulders.

"Do you recognize her?" Sebastian asked.

Jessie hesitated, her forehead bunching up in concentration, "I... maybe? I'd have to get closer."

Of course she would. Cara watched the captain and power-suit lady talk a moment, the man throwing up his hands in agitation and power-suit flicking her hair in frustration. It wasn't a stretch to imagine that they were talking about Jessie, which might make this important enough to risk being found out. Her eyes fell on the continuously cascading waterfall and...

"Alright, come on," she gestured Jessie to follow before the girl ran off to do something crazy on her own. "Just try to walk so Sebastian and I are shielding you. I'll pretend like we're just talking and checking out the shops as we pass."

The waterfall poured down, perpendicular to the hallway, and as they came near, Cara tried to play the average teen, just gawking at the water-feature.

That turned out to be entirely too easy. As she got closer, she noticed the waterfall itself was acting *very* strangely. Instead of pouring straight down from the ceiling it… curved. You couldn't see it from head on, but from the side, the entire sheet gently slanted like the downward arc of a letter J and splashed into the pool below, off-center and at an angle. At first Cara assumed it must be some optical trick with a pane of invisible glass guiding the flow, but after staring a moment, she *definitely* didn't see any glass.

Thankfully, the captain and power-suit were still deep in conversation, as the three strolled by in a little knot. Even from across the promenade, Cara's heart pounded as she struggled not to stare. She tried to focus on keeping between Jessie and the two. As they walked by though, she did sneak a glimpse of the woman's face, rounded with a high-bridged nose and a stern complexion. Then they were past. A part of her screamed that they should run, but no one shouted and a quick glance back didn't reveal anyone following. Cara nodded them over to the back side of the water curtain, the three finding seats at the edge of the fountain.

"Did that help?" she asked Jessie, trusting to the constant crash of the falling water to hide their voices.

Jessie nodded, "Yeah, I'm certain I've seen her before. I just can't remember where."

Sebastian glanced back through the liquid veil toward the two hazy figures on the opposite side. "Nothing else came to mind when you saw her?"

"Not really, but I just got a glimpse." She paused, "It made me think of Jackie and I though, when we were both in those white clothes. I couldn't say why, but… I feel like the woman was there too."

Cara nodded, "So, good odds, she's probably involved. What if I walked by and grabbed a picture or–"

She glanced back through the water curtain and felt her chest constrict as the two figures stood and headed their way. "Frick…" she froze, then whispered, "everybody, look at my phone."

Jessie and Sebastian crowded around, all three staring down at Cara's lock-screen, an image of her and Maddie from last summer. She barely dared to breathe as she caught a glimpse of the captain and power-suit barely ten feet away. She heard the woman's severe voice, "...meet with her, then we'll deal with..."

Then they were past.

Cara looked up with a palpable relief as the two walked off. Next to her though, Sebastian was staring after them. "Did you hear them say something about a meeting?"

"Yeah," Cara nodded and didn't bother trying to argue. At this point, the curiosity cat had sunk it's claws deep into her also. Jessie was already standing to go, her eyes following the captain and power-suit.

Cara paused an instant, glancing back at the waterfall. From head on it was hard to notice anything wrong, but taking two steps off to the side she saw it again, the cascading sheet uniformly twisting like a stiff breeze pushing it to the side. If she'd had a pebble, she would have tossed it right on through the sparkling sheet, just to check if there was some invisible pane of glass causing it to curve. There had to be... right?

"It's the Coriolis Force," Sebastian commented.

"Huh?"

"The Coriolis Force. You know how when your shuttle got in, you walked down some stairs and felt like you wanted to throw up?"

How did he know... Cara glanced at him in surprise, "Yeah."

"That's the Coriolis Force. Same thing that makes us have Up and Down sides on the elevators. When you drop something in spin gravity it curves to the side, because... complicated space magic reasons..."

Sebastian ran out of words there for a second, before finally continuing, "Anyway, this place is called the Coriolis Fountain. If you hang around, you'll notice the water jets all twist when they shoot up. It's worth a watch sometime."

Jessie opened her mouth and for a moment nothing came out until, "So... the water always curves like that?"

"On the station, yeah. It'll always curve anti-spinward."

Her face lit up, "That's so cool."

Cara agreed and made a mental note to figure out what *space magic* and *anti-spinward* meant. Preferably sometime that didn't involve admitting how clueless she was to Sebastian. Meanwhile, the captain and power-suit had vanished into the crowd, but as she watched, Cara saw them slowly pop up a couple hundred feet ahead, visible as they walked up the sloping side of the station. "They're up there," she pointed.

Sebastian talked as they followed. "There's actually a lot of cool stuff up here that most people don't realize."

"Like what?" Jessie asked, seemingly more upbeat now that they were making some tangible progress.

Sebastian glanced around then pointed to a pastry shop up ahead. "Does that place look familiar at all?"

As they passed by, Jessie shook her head, but Cara spared a glance, her gaze lingering on a miniature ferris wheel out front that spun with brownies, macaroons, and chocolate cake…

It did seem weirdly familiar. The restaurant itself was mainly just a long bar with some seats, showing off cupcakes, donuts… general kryptonite for anyone with a sweet tooth. It sprawled out longways along the promenade instead of running all the way to the back, a telltale sign the Space Force was using real estate behind the wall. Meanwhile, a smattering of half occupied tables spilled out into the wide promenade, completing the straight-out-of-Paris feel.

At one end of the counter, a holo-sign showed a cupcake pierced by an arrow and…

"Oh my gosh!" Cara's mouth fell open. "It's Cosmic Confections, from *A Stellar Christmas*." She glanced at Sebastian, shocked he even knew about the movie to reference it. "They actually filmed that up here?"

"Parts of it."

Jessie blinked, "Hold on… you're talking about a movie?"

"Yeah," Cara nodded, casting a final glance at the shop and making a note to take Maddie there sometime. "It's about what you'd expect from the title. A down-on-her-luck, fervently anti-war reporter gets assigned to do a Christmas piece on her pastry loving, space bound sister. There she meets a sweet Space Force hunk and discovers that, through the magic combination of cupcakes, chocolate, and big strong arms, your principles *don't* have to matter."

Cara noticed Jessie cock her head in bewilderment and added, "Mom made me watch it. She's a major, and she just ate it up."

She noticed Sebastian shaking his head. Hey, wasn't her fault Mom was a sucker for military romance.

Up ahead, the man and woman were still just walking and Jessie asked excitedly, "Did they film anything else up here?"

"Parts of *007 - Starsight*," he said. "But mostly that was in the CIC and shuttle bay. I believe they did some of the zero G stunts on the Saratoga."

"Huh," Cara mused. Calvin, her painfully recent *not*-boyfriend, had drug her along to see Starsight. She hadn't paid much attention, but… "They didn't film that motorcycle scene up here, did they?"

"Oh heck no," Sebastian shook his head, chuckling. "The military would have popped off a few missiles if they'd tried."

He glanced ahead and abruptly picked up the pace. "Actually, speaking of interesting places," he pointed into the distance, "looks like our friends just picked the most interesting of all."

Cara saw right as the duo vanished into a side hall a couple hundred feet ahead.

"Come on," Sebastian broke into a jog. "We'll lose them in there if we don't hurry."

"In where?" Jessie asked, hurrying to keep up.

"You'll see."

Chapter 14
Higher Than the Clouds

"Whoa," Cara paused at the giant, floating hologram of Earth in the middle of the dimmed room. Displayed in vibrant color, the holo-sphere towered at least fifteen feet high, making an imposing centerpiece. Smaller floating tags marked out prominent landmarks, and circling above, a stylized Space Force emblem trailed a distinctive silver arc. That could only be Medea Station moving in its endless orbit. The base of the large globe was ringed with six smaller holo-projectors, all but one taken by people in civilian clothes, busy zooming in on particular spots.

Meanwhile, on the far wall, a twenty-foot flex screen displayed a massive panorama of Earth, almost imperceptibly drifting by a thousand miles below. It took a half second for her to recognize the geography since *west* was currently oriented as *up*, but finally it clicked. They were floating right over Greece, a paint-brushed swath of forest green speckled with clouds and nestled amid the Mediterranean's deep cerulean blue. Dozens of smaller islands dotted the expanse, while on the far left, the golden infinity of the Sahara gradually crept into view.

Two steps ahead, Jessie had also ground to a stunned halt at the sight. "Wow!"

"Yeah," Cara murmured, finally tearing her eyes away from the display and casting them after Sebastian. He was… gone?

Cara didn't see the boy anywhere. Where had he gotten off to?

What about… her eyes roved the room for a second. It was crowded with about ten other people, while a hallway led off to the left. None of them were the man and woman from earlier though, and Cara swore beneath her breath as she realized they'd lost them.

Hurrying over to the hallway, she found something reminiscent of a movie theater. A corridor with muted lighting and a patterned carpet stretched off for the next hundred feet, far enough for the curvature of the station to become noticeable. Along the right side, she could see several side doors branching off, with large lettered *Reservation Only* signs plastered on the front. Meanwhile, down at the end, a pair of theater style double doors with a giant *Theater 1* stenciled above the mantle were just swinging closed.

Still no Sebastian.

Presumably the doors at the end were the actual Earth Viewing Theater that Medea was known for. It wasn't too hard to guess that would also be where they'd find Sebastian, along with the captain and power-suit.

Turning back she found Jessie staring wide-eyed. "This place is amazing," the blonde enthusiastically declared. She walked up to the hologram and waved her hand through part of Antarctica with an eight-year-old grin. "Up close, everything is just so… big."

"Yeah," Cara nodded, grabbing her arm, "Come on, I think everybody else is already in the actual theater."

Jessie cast one last glance at the massive holo-sphere but reluctantly followed when Cara tugged. The two made it down to the end of the carpeted hall, past the *Reservation Only* doors and a dimly lit service entrance tucked away in back. Pushing through the double doors, Cara found herself confronted with a flight of steps upward. Oh great, she gulped, not stairs again. The one flight she'd stumbled down from the shuttle bay when they'd landed had honestly been more than enough to last her for a lifetime.

Jessie cheerfully brushed past, took two steps up and froze, looking back at Cara in alarm, her hands poised like she might fall. "Did– did the station just shake?"

Cara shook her head and slowly started up the stairs, feeling the phantom shove on her entire figure at each step, "It's that stupid Coriolis Force that Sebastian talked about," she said. "It gets you when you go up stairs. It's not as bad as up in the shuttle bay, but you might want to use the rail."

Jessie nodded and seemed to take that advice to heart, clinging to the handrail like a life raft until they were both at the top. The girls emerged into the bottom tier of… well, it was basically an old fashioned movie theater. A dimly lit room with steep, stadium seating rose up towards the back, and on the wall where the screen should be…

"Frick." Cara blinked, feeling almost dizzy and more than a little terrified as she stared through a thick movie screen sized pane of glass and out into… space.

At least it wasn't just emptiness. There might be a vacuum outside, but far below, the vastness of Earth consumed the entire view. The same greens, blues and golds from the entry room radiated from the planet below, but somehow deeper, more vibrant, more real.

It was beautiful, but as Cara watched, she had to clutch the rail again to keep from stumbling backwards, because the entire planet was spinning. And not the normal, once every twenty-four-hours sort of spinning, more like, every thirty seconds the view of Earth flipped upside down, then thirty seconds later it flipped back right-side up.

Next to her she heard Jessie's awed, "Wow!"

If her own mind hadn't twisted into a yarn ball just from trying to watch, she might have shared the sentiment. Earth wasn't exactly whirling below, but her eyes still struggled to keep up with the gently panning views of sunny Greece and the Mediterranean Sea below.

Completely overwhelmed and feeling like she was about to fall over, Cara finally looked away. She sucked in a deep breath and massaged her forehead. Okay, she just needed a second.

Letting her eyes trace back across the ranks of raised seats, she caught Sebastian hurrying his way back down to them. Otherwise, the room wasn't terribly crowded. About a dozen other people were scattered throughout, watching. She'd heard a lot of cool stuff about this place, but now that she actually saw it, Cara didn't know how they weren't all sick from visual overload.

One alarm did dimly register though– the captain and power-suit woman were nowhere to be seen. With the light pouring in from Earth, she could easily distinguish the faces, and she saw no one even close.

The moment Sebastian reached them, she caught the concern on his face too. "We have a problem."

"Two problems, actually." Cara said, and added a queasy, "Why is the Earth spinning?"

"I think it always does that, Cara," he chuckled at her sour expression, stepping past her over to Jessie. "Pretty cool, isn't it?"

"It's beautiful," Jessie whispered, her gaze transfixed by the vast spectacle below. "I've seen a few pictures, but it's not the same at all."

"Yeah," he agreed, "it always seems a lot bigger in person."

"Seriously though," Cara asked, "what is going on out there? She looked back towards the two, trying but mostly failing *not* to notice the giant twirling planet in the background.

"It's not the planet spinning," Sebastian said after a moment's serene quiet, "we are. The station spins to create artificial gravity. From up here, it gives the illusion that it's Earth flipping around. The big screen in the other room corrects for the spin and broadcasts a stable image."

"Oh," Cara swallowed back a churn in her stomach like she was about to be sick, "great." Maybe she needed to go back to the other room then.

She looked away in a hurry and Sebastian seemed to notice. "You okay, Cara?"

"Not really," she gulped back the taste of bile.

Earlier she might have bristled at him touching her, but now Cara didn't mind at all. Sebastian took her by the arm and guided her down a few steps, the pulsing Coriolis Force from the stairs not helping either.

"Here, sit down for a second." Sebastian helped her down to a seat on the bottom step. "Motion sickness?"

"Sure, we'll call it that." Cara leaned forward, her head between her knees as she sucked down a few deep breaths to calm her twisting stomach.

"Some people have a hard time getting used to all the spinning when they first arrive," Sebastian said. "They say most folks acclimate after a few weeks, but I suppose it's not exactly fun in the meantime."

"Yeah," Cara felt the worst of the nausea passing although she still made sure to take extra deep breaths. "I assume we lost our two friends?"

"Not exactly," Sebastian said. "I'm certain I saw them go down this hall. I'm pretty sure they didn't come all this way just to slip out the back door. So if they're not in here, that means they're in one of the reserved theaters."

"What, so they can puke in private?"

He chuckled but shook his head, no. "That lady said something about a meeting, right? Well, if she wanted to have it in private, the reserved theaters are about the best spot on the station, assuming you can get a slot in the schedule. Problem is, we can't follow them. From what Dad said, when they first opened the theaters, they had a plague of people just wandering in, so now they're locked." He held up the back of his wrist where the subdermal implant would be. "Unless of course you have the right passcode."

Cara nodded, understanding, "Well, frick."

Up at the top of the stairs, Jessie finally tore her eyes away from the grand scene, her face almost glowing in the gentle blue-green light. "This place is incredible." She frowned, apparently noticing Cara. "Are you alright?"

"Yeah," Cara stood, only a little wobbly now. "Just… maybe next time you two can come back on your own. I'll stay outside."

She caught a blush on Jessie's face and added, "It seems mystery woman gave us the slip. Sebastian says she's in one of the private rooms, except we won't be able to get in."

Jessie nodded, disappointed, but with an expression as though she'd half expected something like that. "So there's nothing else we can do?"

"I mean, we could wait at the front until they come out," Sebastian suggested. "But that could take quite a while."

That was hardly a satisfying answer and after a moment he added, "Let's get back to the entrance and figure things out from there."

Cara couldn't agree more. Any plan that got her out of the nausea room sounded fantastic. Holding the rail that led down the steps, she reached for the door at the end but hesitated. Her eyes peered through the slit window and out into the hallway where a young woman was strolling right towards them...

She knew that girl. From Kristina's dress store. The register girl, Josephine. The face was burned into her mind from the humiliating debacle on Monday. For a second, Cara bit her lip at the embarrassing prospect of having to pass the woman as she came in.

Except Josephine abruptly turned at the last side door. She didn't swipe her wrist though. Instead, Cara's jaw dropped as the door swung inward and the captain they'd been following stepped out into the hallway.

Hoooooly Frick.

The two exchanged a few words that she couldn't hear, then the captain gestured Josephine inside. And they were gone, leaving the door to gently glide closed from within.

Cara didn't really think. She bodily jerked open the theater door and sprinted. It wasn't more than twenty feet to the reserved room, five steps, with the access door drifting shut from within almost in slow motion.

Closing, closing, closing–

Her hand caught the handle. The door was so far closed she was sure it must have been too late. But then she gave it a tentative push... and the door inched inwards. Not much, but enough to tell her it hadn't latched.

Yes.

She didn't say it aloud, but her heart did a victorious somersault. Back at the main theater, Sebastian and Jessie stepped out. Putting a finger to her lips for them to *shush*, she nodded towards the door.

"There're in here," she mouthed, peering through the glass to check that the coast was clear.

"You're sure?" Sebastian whispered, crowding in behind her.

"Yeah," Cara nodded, breathless, "I just saw one of Kristina's people go in."

It wasn't until Cara said it that a more troubling thought popped to mind. What the frick was one of Kristina's girls doing meeting with these two? Had Kristina sent her or…?

It seemed borderline impossible that Josephine could randomly be friends with the people who'd frozen Jessie. So was Kristina selling them out?

Suddenly Cara *had* to know what was going on inside. "Quiet," she warned.

Then, pushing open the door, she slid inside with Sebastian and Jessie right behind.

Chapter 15
Davani

The three teens found themselves crowded at the base of another dimly lit stairway with glowing LED strips marking the steps. Barely daring to breathe, Cara crept towards the top, her shoes quiet as mice on the thin carpet. This stairway extended up higher than the one in the big theater. Reaching the top, she found herself at the back, gazing down over a much smaller viewing room.

The design was the similar to the other theater. Two tiers of plush lounge seats were laid out with an aisle running down along the left wall. Directly ahead, a massive window gave an up-close and gut-twistingly personal perspective on the slowly turning planet below. But instead of being giant and theater sized, this room reminded her of the time Dad's friend had gotten them box seats to a Rams game. Both rows were only six seats long, and Cara caught her breath as she spied three figures seated in the front and backlit by the soft glow of planet Earth.

Cara had only heard Josephine speak once or twice back at Kristina's, but she could still easily pick out the woman's perky soprano voice below with just a hint of nervousness tucked in as well. "So, are you enjoying the view?" Josephine was asking. "Earth from this height is an uncommon sight to see in person."

"It a tad nauseating, actually," the other woman answered, her voice a lower alto, with a severe, almost haughty inflection. "But I suppose that's not why we're here, is it."

"Of course." Josephine sounded taken aback, like she wasn't sure what to make of the frigid woman. She continued with a more upbeat, "I apologize, but you were a little vague as to what exactly you were looking for."

"I prefer not to discuss it over text," the woman said cryptically. "I'm sure you understand. That said, I'll be needing quite a lot. At minimum, I'll need twelve tops in US size 4, and I'll take up to twenty if you have them. I'll need at least ten pairs of leggings, all mediums. I'd prefer black or grey, but I'll consider any alternatives. A dozen pairs of size 6 jeans. And of course, I'll require the undergarments to go with all that, at least a half-dozen bras, plus socks, four pairs of size seven flats and–"

"Whoa, hold on," Josephine held up her hands, stunned. "That… that's a lot of tops and leggings. And," her voice turned almost apologetic, like she hated being the one to break the news, "no offense Ms Davani, but I don't think you're a size 4."

"Obviously." The woman's deadpan tone chilled significantly as she added, "If I was, I wouldn't be meeting here with you, I'd just go to the store." She let that hang a half second before adding, "I was under the impression that, along with clothing, you also supply a certain amount of discretion. Is that still correct?"

"Well, of course," Josephine stammered, "I'm just–"

"Good," Ms Davani snapped, as though that settled the matter. "There'll be no more questions then. Now, I don't particularly care about the style for any of this. Obviously I'd prefer anything matching, but I'll take what you have." There came a crinkle of… was that paper? Who still used paper?

"I have a complete list here along with a few other items as well," Ms Davani continued. "This has the minimum of what I need, as well as what else I'd be willing to accept beyond that. Obviously, since the Persephone is leaving for Mars next week, I'm on a very tight schedule. So I need to know now if you can acquire what I'm looking for before then."

"I…" Josephine hesitated, and Cara didn't have to guess what was running through the sales girl's head. What in the heck did this Davani lady need with a dozen wrong sized shirts? And not even in a particular style, just… whatever? That was beyond stupid, especially up here where everything cost a minimum of three times the usual price. Cara had only browsed Kristina's store briefly, but she'd seen enough of the prices to know Ms Davani was about a drop a fortune on a bunch of useless–

Cara's entire train of thought crashed to a halt as the pieces all clicked into place. She glanced back at Jessie, who was crouching down next to her, eyes wide. Frick, the clothes were for her… weren't they? Those were the sizes Cara had picked out for Jessie just a few hours ago. That also explained all this secrecy. Having Ms Davani walk into Kristina's store and buy out everything in a bunch of sizes that obviously didn't fit her would raise some glaring questions, wouldn't it?

But why? Why would she be in the market for a bunch of clothes for Jessie and presumably Jackie as well? Cara bit her lip. This lady wasn't secretly Jessie's mom, was she? The thought briefly bounced through her head, before being discarded. No, it couldn't be, wrong last name. Maybe a rich, eccentric aunt? With military connections? And who was able to get them to Mars…?

Cara shook her head. No, that didn't make any sense either. There were just too many puzzle pieces that wouldn't fit. Davani didn't seem friendly at all, but she sure was going to a lot of trouble for Jessie.

Josephine had gone silent, but now she spoke up. "You understand, this is going to be a big stretch to get by the end of this week. I mean, this may raise some questions if it all just vanishes at once. It's going to be difficult."

"I presumed that was what I'm paying for," Ms Davani said. Down below, Cara saw the silhouetted woman casually checking her nails. Apparently the thousands of dollars she was about to throw down barely qualified as a distraction. "Now the real question is, can you provide what I need *in full* or not? If not, that's fine, I'll take what you have. But I need to know *now,* not on Saturday when I'm out of time."

"I'd have to check, but…" The paper crinkled as Josephine scanned it over.

Cara leaned back to think on all this. She glanced at Sebastian, only to see his mouth hanging open too. Well, at least he wasn't the only confused one here. So if she had this correct, Josephine was robbing Kristina to sell clothes to power-suit woman on the side because she'd… forgotten to pack any for Jessie?

No, she realized. Ms Davani hadn't forgotten, she hadn't had time

The realization dawned on Cara like a crisp spring morning. Jessie had seen the Super Bowl, right? So give Jackie a week or two afterwards to make the arrangements. Cara swallowed, in that case they might have been cryo-frozen as late as last week.

But even if the pods were classified, Cara doubted their clothes were, and she hadn't seen anything to wear in Jessie's pod. So, assuming all eight crates had contained pods with people in them, what about the other six pods besides her and Jackie? Their clothes were probably sitting in a crate somewhere up in the cargo bay. They'd probably been shipped off weeks ago. That as all fine, except that Jessie and Jackie were last minute arrivals. Ms Davani would have only had so much weight she could pack for herself, so now she was scrambling to find them something to wear on Mars.

Down below, Josephine had a dozen questions as she delved into particulars. Looking over though, Cara saw Jessie's face had gone almost kleenex white. "Hey," she mouthed with a breathless whisper, "you okay?"

Jessie weakly shook her head, no.

Cara caught Sebastian's attention and pointed back down the stairs. In a moment all three of them had retreated to the small landing by the door, and the voices from the room had dissolved into indistinct mumbles. It was as far as they could go without locking themselves out, and the three crouched down almost elbow to elbow in the tight space.

"I do remember her," Jessie whispered, her arms pulled tight, almost shaking. "From when Jackie and I were in white. We were in a room and Ms Davani was there too."

"Do you remember why you were there?" Sebastian asked.

"A little," Jessie murmured. "We did some sort of weird physical exam, and we were waiting for the results. I was nervous because Jackie had lied about our ages and I felt awful about leaving Mom, but Jackie really wanted to go, so..." Jessie swallowed, "I think she told us we'd be working some sort of job on Mars but..."

Cara could fill in the rest of what Jessie must be thinking, *but... obviously not.* Seriously, what sort of boss iced their employees to smuggle them off world? She'd heard Maddie's dad complained about some awful superiors in the past, but this was a whole new level of negligence...? Malfeasance?

Whatever.

Even by military standards, this was royally screwed up.

As much as it pained Cara to admit, "I think it's time to call Kristina," she said. Then she hesitated as a second idea hit her. "Sebastian, you didn't happen to record any of that? Did you?"

The boy shook his head, no, and Cara mouthed a curse. That would have been a genius idea all of ten minutes ago. Then they could have walked away with some actual evidence. Still, this was way out of their league.

Jessie's faint whisper intruded, "Guys, do you hear that?"

"One second." Cara held up a finger for quiet. Should they run back upstairs and try to record a bit more or...

"Guys," Jessie hissed urgently, "I think we should–"

"Who are you–" the captain's sharp voice demanded from close by. All three teens spun, horrified, to see the captain standing at the top of the stairs, with Josephine a step behind.

For the briefest instant, the captain seemed baffled at finding them there. But then he saw their faces. Even through the gloom, Cara saw the switch of understanding flick on and, before she could react, the man had rushed halfway down the stairs.

"FRICK!" Cara lurched towards the door, pushing Jessie in front of her and reaching for the handle. It dimly registered that the door swung inwards, and crowded onto the landing as they were, there was no room for it to move. Even so, her fingers desperately grabbed at the cold metal handle, right as the juggernaut of a man hit them like a tsunami.

The momentum alone sent her and Jessie tumbling backward. Jessie smacked the wall with a sickening *thunk* and Cara crashed hard, her hand ripped from the door handle and the back of her head stinging from the impact.

Sebastian's furious voice tore the air. "What's your deal!"

Cara dimly saw him grappling with the captain, a wild fist connecting with his chest. Fighting through the pain and shock, a vengeful Cara threw herself at the man too. She'd never been in a real fight before, but crashing at the captain from the side, she wrapped herself onto his right arm. The captain was built like an ox though, and Cara could feel his corded muscles surging against her entire body weight even as his voice boomed, "Reyna, get down here!"

With her one free hand, Cara pounded as hard as she could. At least one desperate blow connected with his face, and her fist came away stinging like she'd just punched his teeth in. The captain grunted in pain but then crushed forward in the tight space, body slamming Sebastian against one wall. The boy gasped and his grip slipped. Cara suddenly understood what a bull rider must feel like as the captain bucked beneath her, surging around and fairly hurling her against the stairs.

Cara crashed hard on the steps, liquid fire lanced through her shoulder and a scream ripping from her throat. With a strength born of raw panic, she tried to stand, but her whole body hurt and…

She couldn't move her arm.

Horror coiled around her chest. Her shoulder hung terrifyingly limp, and the joint blazed with an agony like she'd showered in lava.

Cara dimly saw Sebastian still frantically fighting. Then the captain slammed him against the wall a second time. Sebastian wavered, dazed, and the captain coldly planted an elbow right in his gut.

Sebastian crumpled.

Through the haze of pain, Cara half crawled towards the door with her good arm. If she could just get outside, she could scream for help and…

Something grabbed her hair. Cara shrieked as her head was wrenched around, and she found herself face to face with Ms Davani's icy expression.

"Well, well, who do we have here?" Ms Davani murmured, pulling Cara's hair until her head was wrenched all the way back and Cara could barely move without her scalp flaring in agony. For an instant, Davani's disdainful eyes hovered bare inches from Cara's face. She gave Cara an appraising once over with a frigid, almost mercenary, dispassion. For an awful instant, Cara felt like a slice of meat being examined at the supermarket.

Apparently Cara didn't make the cut. The woman snorted in disdain, her grip loosening, and Cara slumped down. She gasped for breath as the torture in her shoulder blazed like an inferno.

"I think you dislocated her arm, Damien," Ms Davani remarked.

The captain snorted, "Better than the little brat deserves."

Ms Davani let out an annoyed sigh, then knelt down, one hand grabbing Cara's arm. Her shoulder screamed, but Cara couldn't have fought the woman if she'd tried. "Now stay quiet," Ms Davani said with a perfunctory sort of friendliness, "this'll only take–"

Cara's arm popped and her whole world swam. For an instant, Cara could hardly breathe, her shoulder blazing with a hellish pain. But then the tide of torment went out, leaving her huddled on the stairs, almost scared to move for fear she'd hurt her arm again.

Down at the base of the stairs, Jessie clutched her arm where she'd crashed against the wall, her face streaked with panicked tears as Ms Davani advanced on her. "And look who it is?" Davani sneered. "Our little run-away."

Jessie tried to scramble away, her back bumping against the wall. The door to the outside sat barely four feet away but hopelessly out of reach.

Jessie glanced at the floor, but Ms Davani leaned down, snatching Jessie's golden locks and yanking them so the whimpering girl had to face her. "What are you doing here, Jessica?" Ms Davani asked with a terrifying sweetness to her voice.

"Please," Jessie's voice choked with tears, "I just want to go home."

"And leave your sister all alone?" the woman *tsked*. "Jacqueline would be so disappointed."

"Please, I don't want to–"

Ms Davani shook her head, "A bit late for that."

Reaching into her pocket, the woman pulled out a little bottle that looked for all the world like nasal spray, adding an amused, "I was wondering when I'd have to use this."

Jessie tried to push it away, but Davani used her knee to pin the girl's one good arm then jerked hard on Jessie's hair. The struggling girl's head was forced back as Davani wedged the tip up one nostril and gave it several quick pumps.

A part of Cara's brain screamed that she was killing Jessie. "No!"

She made a stumbling lunge at Ms Davani, got one step and dimly saw the captain's hand come up. Her whole world went sideways and next thing Cara knew she was curled on the floor, tears in her eyes and her face lit up with a white-hot fire where she'd been struck.

"Ahh, now that felt satisfying," the captain chuckled.

Ms Davani rose from Jessie a moment later, leaving the girl with a faraway, drugged-out haze in her eyes. She strode straight over to Cara, kneeling in front of her with a frosty glare. "So, you're the girl who stole poor Jessica from me. I don't suppose you have a name?"

"Screw off, bitch," Cara spat, throwing every ounce of hatred she could muster into the words.

"Ahh, a brave one then." Davani grinned, wetting her lips like she enjoyed the challenge. Cara tried to swallow back the terror bubbling in her throat.

Davani held up the nasal spray, with a mocking, "Tell me, darling, have you ever tried Serenity?"

The drug?

Cara shook her head a terrified no, her eyes shying away from the woman's vicious grin. Her gaze danced up to the top of the stairs, where Josephine was watching, her mouth hung open in shock. From her expression, she might as well have just discovered that her new business partners were closet Nazi psychos.

Davani reached for her hair and Cara's head was rudely wrenched back, the desperate plea slipping out, "Please, no."

"Now, now, I thought you were going to be brave?" Davani's grip tightened on Cara's hair. "Besides, I think you'll like it," the woman added with a sneer. "They say it hits incredibly fast."

Davani glanced past Cara to Josephine up at the top, seeming to register the hesitance on her face. "We're not going to have a problem, are we?"

For a second Cara had the wild hope Josephine might do something, until, "No," the woman said flatly. "But you should know, that girl is the one who got caught shoplifting yesterday. She's been working it off at the same place as me. Her name's Cara, I'm not sure about the boy."

Helpless tears stung at Cara's eyes. Sure, just sell her down the whole fricking river, thanks a lot.

"Hmmm," Davani nodded thoughtfully, "in that case, I'll make sure she gets some extra special treatment. No need to worry."

Before Cara could dwell on what horrible fate that entailed, Davani pushed the spray bottle towards her. "No… NO!" Cara screamed, squirming and clawing it away.

"Damien, hold her," Davani snapped.

The captain took two steps over and his fists closed like chains around Cara's wrists.

"NO!" She tried to lash out with her feet, but faltered as Davani jerked her hair back, and her scalp lit up in a searing inferno. Cara pressed her eyes shut as the woman jammed the nozzle up her nose. A sharp mist burned her nostril, one… two… three times. Then the pain dimmed, the bottle vanished, and Ms Davani released her hair.

Cara slumped to the floor, sobbing. No, no, no. She desperately tried to fight the drug, willing herself to be alright. She had to… she had to…

The thought turned slippery. She had to…

Cara's vision defocused as the most wondrous calm lapped at her like the tide rolling in. The feeling strengthened, washing over her and sucking her down into the bliss. Suddenly she was lying on a cloud. Her muscles didn't hurt, her arm didn't hurt, nothing hurt. Far away, her mind dimly protested that something was wrong… but this was beautiful. What could be wrong? Everything was perfect, and as Cara watched, the world around her slowly dissolved into the most incredible display… of purple.

Chapter 16
Person of Interest

Out on the main Medea Station ring, Kristina leaned back in her chair at Skytide Cafe. She flicked at her tablet, pretending to read a book while *very* slowly sipping her way through a small mug of coffee. Mostly though, she kept a razor eye peeled for one Sergeant Carrington. It was a slight gamble, but she felt confident he'd come by here... eventually.

Medea Station lived and breathed on what was termed the *Panama Schedule*– basically a continuously rotating mess of twelve-hour shifts that, through some arcane witchcraft, kept everyone at under fifty hours a week. For the military, that was a big deal.

And since Perry was, generally speaking, a benevolent military dictator, everyone normally got lunch breaks. Being unofficial and all, lunch on Medea usually started sometime after eleven and ran until about two, with servicemen rotating off their duty stations to ensure there was always someone watching all the screens. She'd picked Skytide since it was on the quickest route from the service elevator over to the majority of the commercial side of the station.

That said, Kristina had been here since twelve. Obviously, reshuffling all those frozen crates up top would take a while. But, given that it was nearly three, she was starting to wonder if Carrington had skipped lunch entirely.

That would be a shame, she mused dryly. Then she'd have to scheme up some new way to get kicked off Medea. She shook her head with a grim humor and continued to nurse at her dwindling cup. Josh here always brewed the coffee stronger than she preferred, but the military folks seemed to love it. Incidentally, that was why the black coffee at her own shop also tasted like trash. Market research.

Service here sucked though. Josh was perennially understaffed, which was one mistake she'd been trying to avoid. Next Exodus Week she'd follow Miranda's lead and just schedule extra people for the entire month. Assuming, of course, that she was still even working on Medea by then. With the current Jessie situation, that was looking more and more like an open question.

Sitting there, struggling to occupy herself and hoping that no one noticed that she'd foregone her own coffee in favor of her main competitor, Kristina was about to throw in the towel and try something else. Then her eyes caught a heavily muscled man in Space Force fatigues traipsing down the promenade with… was that a black eye? Kristina suppressed a chuckle and glanced back at her screen. Jessie sure had done a number on him.

She'd already paid an hour ago, and clicking off her tablet, Kristina slipped it into her purse and promptly followed right after Milo Carrington.

Based on her own data analysis, Kristina had guessed Carrington really only had three serious possibilities for lunch. It would either be a protein shake at Shake-em-Up, Mexican at Las Estrellas, or American at Game Time Bar and Grill.

Those guesses were based off skimming through his Codex check-ins. But they also lined up nicely with her own, longer term surveillance program of daily walks around the promenade. The station was only about a mile around, and quick enough to walk a circuit on slow days. She'd taken to recording walks, scraping the station directory for pictures, then running the footage through facial recognition to build a daily travel map for… pretty much everybody at this point. She'd never really expected to use it, but it was a little scary how much she could pull up on random people.

Anyway, Carrington was apparently in the mood for some comfort food. He headed straight to Game Time and Kristina waited two minutes on a bench outside, answering a few frantic questions from Melody before following him in.

She found the bar mostly empty and Milo sitting near the center, sipping something dark and fizzy. Confidently strolling over, Kristina grabbed the seat next to him and called to the bartender, "Zed, vodka martini, shaken, not stirred."

The bartender gave an exaggerated sigh and went to work with a little shake of his head. Ordering the *James Bond Special* was one of her favorite icebreakers when she needed to strike up a conversation. Zed always disapproved, apparently he thought it was a stupid drink, but she was used to his scowls by now.

As expected, she glanced over to see Carrington eyeing her in surprise. She met his eyes with a playful grin. "You ever tried one?"

"Can't say that I have."

"Would you like to?" she offered innocently. "My treat."

He gave a reluctant sigh, raising his own fizzy glass. "Wish I could, Miss, but I'm on duty."

"That's a shame. You don't know what you're missing." She shook her head, then offered a hand. "Kristina Andrews, by the way. I'm the coffee shop lady."

"Milo Carrington." He regarded her a moment, warming significantly as he realized who she was. "I thought you looked familiar. Turns out you're the most important woman on the station."

Kristina let out a girlish giggle, "I'm glad someone thinks so."

He nodded at her drink. "A bit early in the day, isn't it?"

"Depends on how your day is going."

He shook his head with a dour chuckle, "I hear you there."

"You having a rough one too?"

Milo's hand edged toward his black eye, "You *would not* believe."

Zed strolled over, setting the signature martini glass in front of her, with a sarcastic, "Enjoy, Kristina."

"Thank you, Zed," she taunted back with a prim smile.

Carrington chuckled, massaging his forehead. "So tell me, what's with you and your James Bond drink?"

"Well, at first I just wanted to try it. Then Zed gave me so much grief about how martinis ought to be stirred that I just had to keep on ordering them."

This time Carrington burst into a full-throated laugh. "I suppose I've heard worse reasons."

"Exactly," Kristina took a sip. "And I do like vodka. If I'm going to be drunk, at least it gets me there quickly. Helps me forget I'm up here."

He cocked his head in surprise. "You don't like it on Medea?"

"It has its moments. But mostly it's like living in an alpine fortress. Looks beautiful on the flight in, then you realize you're stuck there, you can't really go skiing, and it's a nightmare getting anything delivered. As someone trying to run a store, it feels like every day is a battle."

"Really?"

Kristina shook her head with a dismal expression, "I don't even want to talk about the fights I have trying to get the right things shipped up here. I'd give an arm and a leg for a reliable supply chain. It wears you out after a while."

"Hmm," Carrington mused, nodding to himself.

Kristina mentally crossed her fingers. Take the bait, take the bait, take the bait…

"You know, I might know some people who could help."

Kristina tilted her head, folded her arms and made sure to add a skeptical challenge to her voice, "Really?"

"Oh, yeah," Carrington assured her, taking a long draught from his glass. "There's an art to getting things shipped up to Medea that most people just don't realize." He gestured to her, "You're fairly new up here, aren't you?"

"A few months," Kristina agreed.

"Yeah, you just haven't had time to learn all the ins and outs of the station. There are *hard* ways to do things and *easy* ways. I'm personally an *easy way* sort of person."

Kristina raised her drink, "Cheers to that."

Zed picked that moment to stroll by and deposit a hamburger and fries in front of Carrington.

For a while they talked on and off as he ate. Kristina giggled at his jokes as she polished off her martini, then switching to apple cider. She actually did love vodka, but she also legitimately needed to be sober for this… mostly sober. She slowly teased out a bit more about the *arrangement* he'd been hinting at.

The technical term was somewhere between *smuggling* and straight up *theft*. It mostly seemed to involve *borrowing* other peoples', and sometimes even the Space Force's, cargo allocations. Those were essentially expensive credits the Space Force auctioned to determine what *stuff* actually got sent up to Medea.

He talked like it was fairly common, which might explain some of her own, very legitimate, frustrations about getting supplies delivered in a timely manner. Ever since she'd arrived, it had bothered her how the Space Force seemed to get so many routine orders completely wrong. She'd written it off as general incompetence, but now she wasn't so sure.

It took a while, but as Carrington finished up with his food, Kristina grinned drunkenly. "You know, I think this day is turning around already."

"Same here," he toasted with his freshly refilled Dr Pepper.

"I know you've got to get back to defending the station and all, but…" Kristina gave a sarcastic snort, and the two burst into laughter.

When she got herself under control she added, "Do you think you could come by my shop right now, just for… ten minutes? I could show you a bit of what I need."

He glanced at the time on his phone, then shrugged, "Sure, why not? That's part of the fun of being a Non-Com, you disappear for half an hour and no one asks questions."

"Wonderful," Kristina declared in an airy voice. She stood with a wobbly, "Ohhhh," and felt his arm steady her.

"You okay, Kristina?"

"I'm good," she insisted, waving him off. "Like I said, there's a reason I like vodka, but I'll be fine." She took a tentative step, making it seem like something of an effort and added, "Let's go out the back." She gave a conspiratorial whisper. "I've got a reputation with my people as a severe, sober sort of person up here. I'd hate to ruin that all at once."

He laughed, but nodded, and leaning just a bit on his arm, Kristina made for the service hallway in the back.

In between Zed's bar and her coffee shop was a decent sized maintenance closet. The door code for which was, incidentally, the same as the passenger elevator code… and pretty much every other low security door on the entire station, 3687 or ENTR. No cameras either.

As they passed, she pretended to be confused, stopped at the closet, and punched in the code, "It's just right through here."

She pulled open the door and led him inside, flicking on the lights to illuminate his confused face. One hand slipped into her purse, touching the soft grip of the uncovered taser and snaking her fingers through the wrist strap loop. She turned back, pulling the door shut behind her and…

"Kristina, are you sure this is– OWWW!"

She spun and kneed him right between the legs. The man curled forwards with a sharp breath, his eyes nearly bulging out of his head. Kristina jabbed with her taser and caught Carrington square in the shoulder with a hundred thousand volts. He staggered two wild steps forward, and Kristina didn't really think, so much as move with muscle memory. She planted one foot dead in his path, and with a hand wrapped behind his neck, she body slammed the behemoth of a man face first into the floor.

In a flash she had a knee jammed into his back, using her weight and the sheer surprise of it all to pin him down. Earlier she'd pre-connected three extra-heavy zip ties into a large triangle. Whipping it out, Kristina dropped her purse and used both hands to deftly slide the ties around his left wrist.

Carrington recovered enough to struggle. But sitting on his back, she already had the leverage advantage, and she wasn't drowning in pain either.

She snatched his other wrist and grunted, wrenching it back and forcing his hand into the zip-tie triangle.

Zzzzzp, zzzzzp, zzzzzp.

Three sharp tugs cinched the ties tight before Carrington could truly recover to fight back. Reaching into her purse, she quickly added a second zip-tie around his wrists, just to be safe. After that it was the work of only a few seconds to stitch two more together and sit on his legs to stop him kicking as she snagged them around his ankles.

Zzzzzp… and done. The whole struggle lasted about twenty seconds and when it was over, Carrington was moaning obscenities on the floor… but doing little else.

She bodily rolled the bound man over so he was face up, then cheerfully straddled across his lower abdomen. He furiously tried to twist her off, and Kristina's expression split in a leopard smirk. "Opps, I guess this isn't my office after all."

There was pure hatred in the man's eyes, even with his face still screwed up in agony. "Who are you, bitch?"

"Now now," she *tsked,* staring down at him with a smile, "no need for all that foul language. I am a lady after all. And I believe *I'm* the one asking the questions right now."

"Screw you."

In response she jabbed the uncovered taser electrodes right in his gut. Carrington emitted an agonized grunt, clenching his teeth as she felt his whole body go rigid.

One… two…

Kristina let off and the sharp electric clicking faded. "Alright," she grinned, "got that out of your system?"

He swore and spat at her… which was all the more pathetic since the spittle didn't even make it to her face. Kristina shrugged, "Guess not." Then blasted him again for another two seconds, letting the snapping electric discharge do her talking for her.

When it was over Carrington was gasping for breath, until he finally managed a weak, "What is this?"

"Well, if you'd stop being so unpleasant, I'd tell you. I just need some information. Nothing complicated."

For a second he looked like he might cuss her out again, but she wiggled the taser temptingly and Carrington seemed to reconsider. His breaths came sharp and furious, but he finally managed, "What about?"

"The girl."

His body tensed. "What girl?"

Kristina rolled her eyes. Seriously? She was sitting on top of him. He might as well have been hooked up to a lie detector. "The one from the frozen section that got unboxed earlier today? Gave you that shiner? Ring any bells?"

He stubbornly didn't answer. Kristina let out an aggravated sigh, lowered the taser and…

"Wait! Yes, okay," he sputtered at the last minute. "I might have bumped into her. The one in white."

"Indeed," Kristina inquisitively leaned forward onto his chest, watching him wince as she casually planted both elbows in his gut, "I'd like to know a bit more about her."

"She's classified."

"Okaaaaay," Kristina leaned down further, watching him squirm as her elbows dug deeper… deeper… "Anything else?"

"AHHHHH– Alright! Alright!"

She let up enough for most of the pain to vanish.

"I don't know much."

"Let's keep it basic then." Kristina crossed her arms and sat back. "What interest does the Space Force have in a teenage girl?"

"I don't know."

Kristina grinned, "Wrong answer."

"No I… AGHHH."

She jabbed the taser into his stomach, the electrodes punching right though his Space Force uniform and turning him rigid as a tree trunk for another two seconds.

When it was over she pulled it back and gently blew across the top like a smoking gun.

"Want to try again?"

"I'm not *need to know*, okay," Carrington insisted frantically. "Don't you understand how the military works? They don't tell me."

Kristina ignored him. "You know, I don't usually get to experiment with this baby." She held up her taser enthusiastically. "It's hard to find volunteers. But now that we're here, I think this experience can be… enlightening. And the thing is," she leaned over, again planting her elbows deep in his gut as she whispered in his ear, "I know you have some theories."

She sat back upright, leaving him gasping. "So, let's try this again. In your *professional* opinion, why is the Space Force stuffing young girls in refrigerators and shipping them to Mars?"

Carrington let out a long sigh, then a reluctant, "They're not."

Hmmm…

"Explain."

"Look, classified cargo still gets labels, alright. If you're shipping super-secret bombs, the truck still gets labeled as carrying explosives so you know what you're dealing with. You're just not supposed to look inside." Carrington paused for breath. "The classified crates have e-tags with basic information. The ones with the cryopods…" his voice trailed off a second, "they were listed as Radar Subsystems with a note to avoid magnets."

Kristina's mouth dropped open an inch. "All of them?"

"Well, four of the eight. The rest were other parts of the array. But you get the idea."

"So then, who swapped the radar array out for Ice Princess?"

He gritted his teeth, clearly not wanting to say, but his eyes fixed on the taser as it danced another six inches lower… "Probably Captain Tallier."

"I'm not familiar with the name."

"He's a passenger for Mars. I think he's Corps of Engineers. He and this woman, I don't know her name, but they…"

His voice trailed off, hesitant, and Kristina could guess what was coming next. "It's alright," she nodded, "I won't tattle."

He growled like he didn't believe her at all, but admitted, "They dropped a *significant* sum to make sure those crates get… let's call it special love and care."

"And what does that actually mean?"

"The usual. Expedited off Medea, no questions asked. Express service out to the Persephone and they magically vanish until Mars."

"And you arrange that?"

"Let's just say I know some people."

Kristina nodded, biting at her lip and regarding her taser for a moment, as she let that sink in. Finally, she took a deep breath and asked the *big* question. "Alright, so what's in the other seven crates?"

Carrington didn't meet her eyes. "I didn't check."

"BS," Kristina snapped, leaning in so her face was barely a foot from his. "You checked enough to know exactly who Jessie was when she showed up. At least enough to try and put her back in the box." She caught a flash of shock on his face at her knowledge and sparked the taser electrodes like an electric whip-crack. "Let's try again," she said grimly. "What's in the other crates?"

Carrington swallowed, "A bunch of women. One in each pod," he declared quietly

Kristina drew in a sharp breath, and in a flash all the pieces dropped right into place. "*Dermo.*"

Her eyes focused on Carrington like lasers and her tone turned acrid. "Let me guess, all of them were… young?"

"Early twenties… probably." Carrington wouldn't meet her gaze.

"And did Captain Tallier happen to drop *why* exactly they were trafficking a bunch of young girls to Mars?"

"Kristina, come on, you know I don't ask those questions. It's how I'm still in business."

"But I'm sure you have a theory?" She cracked the taser electrodes again for emphasis, and forced an icy smile. "I'd like to hear that."

Carrington rolled his eyes, "Look, it's just business on my end, okay. Boxes passing through."

"Not what I asked." She dropped the taser to his midriff.

"Fine, okay." Carrington frantically tried to squirm away from the weapon. "If I was *hypothetically* guessing, which technically I am, there's only one reason to be secretly sending a bunch of young women to Mars." For an instant he did meet her gaze, and Kristina could read the truth in his eyes. "It's exactly what you think it is."

Kristina sat back a moment, one hand massaging her forehead. Oh, just perfect, so she'd stumbled onto a human trafficking ring. Well, this was about to blow up like a tactical nuke.

Sitting beneath her the sergeant jostled. "You got your answers. Let me go?"

Kristina nearly laughed, amazed that he expected her to just let him walk out after admitting something like that. "Where did you move the boxes?"

When he didn't answer, her calm slipped. "Look, I already have Jessie. I know you were moving them." Her tone turned dangerous, "So where?"

"A side room. Somewhere curious people won't stumble over them. It's by TT 60-175-0."

Kristina had been around Medea long enough to know that was the fancy polar coordinate way of saying up in the cargo bay, about thirty degrees around from the passenger elevator.

"A heavy lift shuttle is scheduled to dock sometime late tonight," Carrington added, "then they're off to the Persephone. Satisfied?"

"Not really," Kristina said coldly. "But I'll pretend like I am."

Standing and stepping away from the man, she grabbed her purse and idly rummaged inside.

"Hey," Carrington swallowed, suddenly anxious as he rolled so his eyes could follow her. "You can't just leave me here. I told you what you wanted."

"Yeah, yeah, I know," Kristina said distractedly. She dug around until she found a smooth plastic case. Popping it open, her fingers touched on a feathered dart with a needle tip and a syringe body filled with a clear liquid like water.

Before Carrington could make more of a fuss, she turned and calmly plunged the needle dart into his thigh.

"WHAT THE–"

Kristina watched the pressurized liquid drain out, while Carrington tried to struggle away and lit off in a hurricane of obscenities. Impressive really, particularly with his booming voice. She should have recorded it, might have earned him a job as a drill instructor. He was definitely about to need a fallback career.

The last of the liquid drained out and Kristina coolly tugged loose the dart, tossing it back in her purse. "Will you shut up, Carrington."

"You psychotic–"

"It's not going to kill you," Kristina snapped.

"Of course you'd say that, you lying piece of–"

"You should consider this a favor," Kristina primly cut him off. "You get to go to sleep, wake up, and forget all about this little indignity. Sound good? I'll even cut you loose once you're out."

The answer was another rude expletive.

"Or not." Kristina shrugged. "I guess I could just leave you here."

She puffed out a long breath. It'd take a few minutes for the tranquilizer to kick in. Had she forgotten anything or… oh yeah.

"Last question," Kristina said, "And if you're honest, I give you my word I'll cut you loose. The girl, Jessie, how in the world did she beat you in a fight?"

Carrington sneered, "She didn't win. She cheated, same way you did– cheap shot to the groin."

Ahhh, that made a lot more sense. Kristina nodded, a part of her quite pleased that Carrington had taken two hits right there in the same day. It must have been exquisitely painful. "Alright then, fair enough." She pulled a pair of scissors out of her purse and held them where he could see, waiting as the drug gradually took effect.

Well, if nothing else, this settled what to do next. She needed to get Jessie to Colonel Perry and let him root out this mess.

As Carrington's eyes glazed over, Kristina spent a moment checking her phone. She'd stuck it on silent for this bit of subterfuge and now she shot Cara a quick *everything alright* text.

One minute… still no response, which… of course not. Kristina almost wasn't surprised. The girl had one job, *one* job, and she couldn't even…

Her phone emitted an alert, three ascending chimes, *Dong-Ding-ding.*

That noise specifically marked the alarm she'd set on the dress store stock room. Given the theft issues she'd been having, she'd splurged for an IR laser wall that triggered every time someone went in or out. It had already paid off for catching Cara earlier.

She flipped to the camera feed. Maybe that explained Cara ignoring her. If the girls wanted to play dress up for an hour that wasn't the worst…

Those possibilities vented straight to vacuum when she saw Josephine rummaging around in her stockroom, hastily piling tops across one arm.

Kristina's face turned dark. Josephine had specifically requested off today and she had gone to a lot of effort trying to staff around her absence. So what exactly was she doing rummaging through the closet?

At her feet Carrington was blissfully asleep. Kristina clipped loose the zip ties, stuffing them in her purse so as not to leave a trace. The drug would ensure he didn't recall any of this, which incidentally meant that Carrington was going to be *really* confused when he woke up. Then she stood and strode out the door.

Josephine had some explaining to do.

And where on this madcap carnival ride of a station was Cara?

Chapter 17
Starlight

Cara felt like death. She awoke to a sharp throbbing in the front of her head. The her mind swam in a dreamy haze where she couldn't think straight, and through the knifing pain, she heard voices.

"Catherine, stop making this hard," a man said. "Just throw her back into cryo. We'll overdose the other two and be done with it."

"You're missing the point, Damien," a woman's voice insisted. Ms Davani, the thought dimly pricked at Cara's mind. "You can't just hop people in and out of cryosleep. The body isn't meant to take that kind of shock. Definitely not twice in the same day."

"So what, she's a teenager. She'll get over it."

"She'll be *dead*," Davani snapped hotly.

"We don't know that for sure."

"Because no one's been stupid enough to try it."

Cara's eyes crept open to find the room glaring back. She was laying on her side, one cheek cold and numb from being smushed against the floor. All around, more of the beige-white cargo crates were piled up like so many of the twins' building blocks. She tried to move, but her shoulders ached, and her hands wouldn't budge. A jolt of panic stabbed past the pulsing in her head. Her wrists were tied.

Across the room, Davani and the captain bickered. "That pod was an *investment*," Davani spat. "I paid for eight spots, not seven. That's all money straight down the drain if we put Jessica back in there."

"Catherine, I'm not stupid. I'm just saying it doesn't matter. They ship to the Persephone tonight. There's no time." The captain paced. "I agree it's a loss. It's unfortunate, but there's nothing we can do."

Davani hesitated an instant then tilted her head towards Cara. "Let's take the other girl then."

A long pause, "The brunette?"

"At least she'll survive the trip." Davani glanced over and Cara pressed her eyes shut.

The voices came nearer. "Are you out of your mind?" the captain snapped. "What about her parents? You don't think they'll notice she's missing?"

A foot nudged at Cara's chest like Davani was trying to rouse her, and she lay perfectly still, barely daring to breathe. "Kids go missing, it happens," Davani dismissed.

"Not on a space station it doesn't."

The foot bumped at Cara again, followed by a pause, then, "Oh, stop playing, I know you're awake."

Someone kicked at her chest, and Cara's eyes flashed open. She gasped in pain and curled into as much of a ball as she could with her wrists tied behind her. Laying on her side, she looked up to see a smug Davani staring down. The woman knelt with a smile that chilled Cara's blood. "What do you think darling, you want to go to Mars?"

Hell, no. Not unless Davani fricking assaulting her was supposed to make them best friends. Cara met Davani's glare, letting all her furious loathing spill out in two venomous words, "Screw off."

Davani's eyes narrowed but she held her smile. "You sure, darling? It's the only way you walk out of here alive. If you beg, I might consider it."

Oh right, survive to go live in whatever nightmare Davani had dreamed up on Mars? Cara swallowed back her fear, leaving just a lot of serious rage issues. "Try to," she hissed, "and my dad will end you." She glared at the captain, "*You* in particular."

"Right," the man scoffed.

"The name Rosenfeld ring any bells?" She caught the hesitation on his face at the name. Oh, it sure did, didn't it. The Space Force was a pretty small world after all. Wasn't that the ultimate fricking irony, she was about to be murdered by someone who'd probably worked with her parents. She wanted to scream, except it wouldn't do much good, and she didn't want to give Davani the satisfaction.

Davani sneered and aimed one more kick at Cara, the blow glancing off her knee and leaving it stinging. "Damien, let's take smart-mouth here." She added an ominous, "I think I'd enjoy having her around."

"Catherine, you're not…" the captain's voice trailed off. He glanced at Cara then gave a sharp sigh and nodded towards the exit. "Let's talk."

The two vanished outside, the door thudding behind them. Cara finally remembered to breathe, and as the anger dimmed, the desperate fear rushed back. Davani was going to kill them. Actually kill them. She gave her wrists a desperate flex only to find them tied just as tight as a moment before. Frick.

From where she was lying on the floor, she could see there wasn't another way out either. The room didn't have much in the way of decor. Several stacks of smaller crates were scattered about and a pile of cardboard boxes had been haphazardly set near the front door. In her peripheral vision, Cara glimpsed two battered desks pushed up against the wall and stacked high with the general office detritus of the station – old flex screens, tablets, a minifridge – that sort of stuff. None of it looked like it would help her survive though. Mostly it just marked out a room that no one seemed to care about, and which would probably be dead last to get checked. A horrible hopelessness settled on her like a shroud. What was she supposed to do?

"You know that was really dumb, Cara," Sebastian's voice startled her from behind. Twisting, she rolled over and found herself almost face to face with the boy. He was also bound and lying on his side, but had a grating positivity in his voice. "I'm pretty sure kidnapping 101 is *don't* antagonize the kidnappers."

Cara let out a growling sigh and looked… anywhere that wasn't his stupid face. He sounded like Maddie when she was trying extra hard to cheer everyone up. "What does it matter if Davani hates me?" Cara muttered. "They're going to kill us anyway."

"Not if we get out of here first."

Cara's eyes jumped back to Sebastian, studying the boy, not certain if he was being serious or just putting on a brave face and whistling past the graveyard. Behind the forced half smile, she could see the tightness in his expression. He was scared, but she also caught a glint of genuine optimism there too, and it was enough to spark an ember of hope in her breast. "You have a plan?"

"Let's just say I've been staring at your backside long enough to get some inspiration."

Cara wrinkled her nose, "Really, are you ever *not* a child?"

"Just get up." Sebastian twisted to push himself upright. "You awake, Jessie?"

"Yeah," The girl's voice came back, shaky.

Bunching up her legs Cara rolled up onto both knees, a fact made easier by the strangely weak gravity. Combined with the containers taking up a quarter of the room Cara could guess they were in the cargo bay. In a moment she met Sebastian on her feet while Jessie scrambled upright five steps away. "So what is this plan of yours, Sebastian?" she asked quietly.

Instead of answering like a *normal* person Sebastian dropped down on one knee, right fricking in front of her and Cara's chest abruptly coiled tight, "Ummm, what are you…"

"Turn around," he nodded toward her.

She cocked an eyebrow with a skeptical, "Why?"

His expression tightened. "Cara, can you just trust me for once? Turn around and get down on both knees, try to pull your palms apart and press your elbows tight."

She didn't see how this would help, but they were about to die anyway, so… she lowered herself down, feeling her wrists bump against his knee.

"Perfect," Sebastian said. "Now, I want you to raise your wrists, then smash them down as hard as you can across my knee."

Cara craned her neck around as far as she could to stare at him. That mostly sounded like a good way to dislocate her arm again. "You want me to *what*?"

"Look," Sebastian's expression twisted like he *really* wanted to strangle her, "they zip tied your hands together. And not even with the heavy-duty sort. If you apply enough force, they'll break, but…" he gritted his teeth and let out a hiss, "Cara, can you *please* just trust me?"

Ohhhhh, *right*, easy for him to say. He wasn't the one about to pop his shoulder out of its socket. Just the memory of that pain sent a chill like liquid ice running down her spine. She understood the stark reality, if they stayed here they were dead, but… Cara willed her arms to push down, once, twice.

They didn't budge, not with the agony from before seared into her mind.

"Cara, come on. We're running out of time."

She preemptively gritted her teeth, the anger and frustration gripping at her, "Sebastian, if you're screwing with me I'll… I'll…

Cara jammed her wrists down and… *pop*.

Her hands were free.

The force bounced her a little in the weak gravity. Balancing on unsteady knees, she stared at her wrists in open-mouthed astonishment. Finally she glanced back to see his smug grin, "Told you."

Cara swallowed, still in shock, even as Sebastian nodded for her to move behind him, "Get mine."

Five feet away, Jessie was staring, "How did…"

"It's the angle," Sebastian explained. He got down on both knees as Cara maneuvered herself so one leg was positioned a couple inches beneath his wrists. "The zip-ties aren't really that strong, but your arms don't have the leverage they need to snap them. Your knee forces your wrists apart though and…"

Cara interrupted with a breathless, "You're good to go."

Sebastian basically sat down really fast and… *pop*.

Jessie was next and as her wrists snapped free, Cara could hear Davani and the captain still arguing outside, nearly shouting. From the sound of it, the captain had talked Davani out of taking her along, but now the woman wanted to hold off throwing Jessie back in the pod for another twenty-four hours.

Cara swallowed and looked at Sebastian. "So what? Do we try to fight them?"

Sebastian gave her a *what are you smoking* sort of look. "Not unless Jessie really *is* a super soldier, which umm…"

They both glanced at the blonde girl who gave a bemused shrug. "Let's assume no."

Sebastian nodded, "Fair enough. In that case," he turned and pointed at a ventilation grate set high up on the wall near the ceiling, "that's our way out."

He jogged over, and Cara followed, staring at the metal vent covering fastened to the wall eight feet up. Yeah, *grate* plan, she nearly laughed at her own pun, except for the cold irony that smothered her ember of hope. The vent might be large enough to squeeze through, but that ignored the bigger problem of how they could get it open. The thing was screwed into the wall, and just because she could jump five feet in the low gravity didn't suddenly make her Supergirl.

"Sebastian," she sighed, "how are we–"

He wasn't listening. Instead his eyes lingered on the grate a few seconds before he spun away, mumbling. "Alright, we need a uhhh…" He beeline over to the desks piled up with junk in the corner, and grabbed a battered Keurig coffee machine that looked like it had survived at least five years past its retirement date.

"Jessie, hold this." He shoved the bulky machine into her arms then turned back towards the grate with a frenetic, "Cara, you'll have to stand on my shoulders."

Cara rolled her eyes. She hated feeling like a killjoy. "Sebastian, I can't just pull off the grate with my bare hands."

"Yeah," he knelt down beneath the grate and gestured her onto his shoulders, "That's what the coffee machine is for."

Did he even hear himself right now? Was she supposed to smash her way through?

"*Get on,*" he insisted with an urgent hiss.

"Sebastian, are you sure you can pick me up–"

"Cara, you weigh like forty pounds up here. I'll manage." He looked her right in the eye adding those two really scary words from before. "Trust me."

Cara hesitated, not sure that she did. But she could still feel the traces of pain from where her wrists had been cinched together. He'd figured that out, so maybe…

"Alright," she whispered, situating herself so that she was sitting on his shoulders. His hands locked around her thighs, and Cara took a deep breath, "Okay," she nodded.

Her heart gave a flutter as the boy effortlessly rose, gravity almost vanishing for a second. She leaned down, her arms gripping him as the spin gravity momentarily left her feeling like they were about to tip sideways. But then it was over.

Letting up her death grip, Cara found herself perched on Sebastian's shoulders, face to face with the vent grate. Thin slanted strips of metal gushed out a chilly breeze while four little screws in the corners stared back at her.

"How am I supposed to–"

"Use the coffee machine," Sebastian explained. "The power plug prongs on the end should slot right in."

Jessie handed it up. Grabbing the wall plug, a skeptical Cara pressed one prong into the screw to find he was right, the prong fit right into the groove. She gave it a tentative twist and…

No way… the screw actually turned.

Cara nearly forgot to breathe as the little ember of hope in her chest burst into a bonfire. They could do this. They could actually do this.

Tuning out everything else, Cara's whole world focused down to the four vent grate screws. Alright, here went nothing.

Chapter 18
Dark Times

Cara twisted the wall plug like her life depended on it… which it did. Already she'd pulled two screws out, letting them slow motion tumble to the floor with satisfying *dings*. Beneath her Sebastian shifted. "How's it going?"

"Almooooost…"

She gave another twist with the power prong, then jiggled the screw, finding it two-thirds of the way out but still tightly stuck in its socket. "Frick."

"Push on the grate," Sebastian suggested beneath her.

Cara didn't see how that was supposed to help, but she tried it anyway. To her surprise, the screw instantly came loose. Two seconds later, her shaking fingers had twisted it right out. She was about to start on the last screw when she took her hand off the grate and the thing hinged down, sliding completely out of the way and dangling from the one remaining screw. Well, that worked too.

She heard Sebastian mumble a quiet *yes* under his breath, then shifted to move her close. "Can you make it in?"

"Yeah," Cara grabbed onto the edge of the duct, feeling an unexpected grittiness beneath her fingers. Pulling back one hand, she cringed at seeing her palm coated in a thick black layer of grime. Oh well.

With Sebastian to give her a boost in the weak gravity, she easily hoisted herself high enough up to peer inside. Cara found herself facing a gloomy, three-foot-long shaft that abruptly terminated with a thick steel gray plate blocking the way.

"What the?" Cara blinked. That didn't make any sense. She frowned and pulled her head back out. She could actually see the square outline of the air shaft along the back wall. A long rectangle wedged in where the wall met the ceiling, plated with the same ubiquitous dark plastic they used everywhere up here. She could even feel the air breezing past her face. So how was it blocked?

"Sebastian, why is there a plate here?" she gulped.

"Huh… uhh, hold on," he said.

Back on earth, Cara probably couldn't have managed a pull up if her life depended on it. Here though her fingers easily gripped the duct, holding up her much slimmed weight as the hands supporting her vanished. A second later, Sebastian hopped up to peer inside, drifting next to her for an eerily long second before, "Oh, I think it's to hold back-pressure on the room."

He floated back down to the floor below.

Uhhh… what? Cara felt like an idiot asking but, "Which means…?"

"Just pull it up and it should open. These rooms are designed to be temporary lifeboats if the cargo bay depressurizes. The shuttle bay has some too." His hands returned, pushing her up as he explained. "The plate clamps shut if there's a pressure drop. It keeps the air sealed in here. It's a safety thing."

Greaaaat. Sticking her head into the claustrophobic space, Cara tried to ignore the thick layer of grime smearing the front of her shirt as she squirmed close enough to grab the plate. She found it hanging, barely open, with a rubbery seal on the reverse side. Pulling it towards her, the plate swung up and a blast of cold air washed over her. She blinked, staring into the pitch blackness behind.

"Okay, push me up." She shivered but crawled an arm's length in, trying to pull up her legs, which were still hanging

out, while also holding the plate open. "I think we're good to–
"

"WHAT THE– GET THEM!" Davani's shouts sliced through the room like a knife.

Cara's heart almost stopped in her chest. The world behind her exploded in screams and curses, punctuated by Sebastian's panicked, "CARA GO! GET HELP!"

Frick. She wiggled further in, only to have the plate fall back down wedging right in the small of her back. She pushed her whole body upwards knocking it back up, then shoved her way forward, right as a hand bit at her ankle.

Captain Damien's furious shout echoed in the tunnel around her. "Get back here, you brat!"

Cara kicked, lashing out with a desperate strength and felt her heel connect with something hard.

"AHHH– BITCH!"

The hand on her foot vanished, and knocking the plate back up, she heaved herself forward. Her torso slid into the narrow air vent as she wiggled into the space. Her head bumped the far wall in the gloom, and she tucked her legs in to pull herself through into the cramped main vent. The last traces of light vanished as the plate dropped back down, plunging her into a chilly darkness.

Behind her, Cara could hear her friends' muffled shouts past the blowing air. Sebastian's "NO! DON'T TOUCH HER– AWWW!" His voice collapsed into pained moans, while Jessie shrieked, "No, don't! Please– OWWW!"

"SHUT UP!" Davani roared. "Damien, get the other one back! NOW! YOU, it's back into cryo."

"NO!" Jessie screamed, tears in her voice. "You can't! Please! We're not even–"

Davani snapped, "Damien, hold her!"

No, Cara blinked, tears coursing down her face. She tried to rub them away, but instead just left a streak of grime and dirt on her face. She was shaking so hard she didn't even know what to do... she... she... Sebastian's words drummed in her head – GET HELP.

Right. Help.

Staring into the inky blackness, Cara had no clue which way to go. Maybe it didn't matter. The whole station was a circle anyway. Surely both ways had to go somewhere, and anywhere was better than here. The vent was so cramped she could only really inch forward on her elbows, sliding one forward, then the other, but that was still progress. Feeling her way ahead in the pitch blackness, Cara tried to ignore the awful sense that the walls were closing in and began crawling… somewhere.

The vent stretched on forever. A stiff breeze nipped her cheeks, and Cara could feel her elbows thick with grime. She could barely even move her hands enough to wipe them on her filthy clothes, and the vent floor beneath felt like an ice block on her fingers. The only sounds were the gentle whispers of the air duct – a faint whistle as the air squeezed around her, and the faraway hum of a fan.

She didn't know how far to go. Obviously, Damien would immediately check the next room over, but would he know which way she'd gone? Maybe? Assume yes.

How far had she gone then?

Not sure, Cara began a slow count at each shuffle, "One… two… three…"

Numbly counting, she soon got to a hundred. But each shuffle couldn't be more than four inches so what… thirty-three feet? She bit at her lip, trying to fight back the despair as the numbers came up woefully tiny. How far around even was the station here?

Suddenly she wished she'd paid better attention in math. Medea was a circle which was pi times the diameter but… the diameter in the shuttle bay was… frick if she knew. Best guess, three, four hundred feet maybe? And pi was like… three, so nine hundred feet around? Maybe twelve hundred?

Frick. That couldn't be right, could it? Cara's heart sank even as she counted past one hundred and fifty. That meant she needed to go like… a thousand shuffles just to get decently far away?

She tried the division over and over in her head. But each time, four hundred multiplied by three came up exactly the same, twelve hundred feet. The miserable reality sank in. There was no way. Already she was breathing hard, trying to keep going with a mumbled, "One-sixty-three, one-sixty-four…"

She reached two hundred and slumped down a moment, her elbows aching. A part of her wanted to scream at the infuriating hopelessness as her cheek rested against the miserably cold duct and she felt the grit staining her hair.

"Keep going," she mumbled to herself. "Just keep going."

Ignoring the pain in her elbows, Cara blindly forced herself on with only the steady rhythm of counting to keep her sane amid the cold darkness. At this point, she didn't even know if she'd passed another exit. She must have, right? She'd been crawling like this for ages. She checked the count in her head, two hundred and twenty-seven. Maybe seventy feet.

Yeah she'd probably passed an exit. But then, where was the next one? Was there even another one? At some point the vent had to loop back to atmospheric recycling? She could be stuck up here until she froze and died and…

NO! The stern thought hammered in her head, smashing aside everything else. Cara shoved back the swirl of macabre images and held the nipping panic at bay. No, there *was* another exit, she clung to the thought. There were plenty of rooms, so logically, there had to be an exit into one of those. Forcing herself ahead through the inky night, Cara kept counting. Silently praying for a way out… anything to escape this nightmare.

"Three hundred and seventy… seventy-one… seventy-two…"

Catching a slight change in the venting breeze Cara froze… was that…

She reached over, barely daring to hope, and her numb fingers bumped against something that moved. A rush of relief swept her like a tsunami, and squirming forward she pushed up the seal plate with her head. It moved and she caught a welcome splash of light spilling through from the other side.

She wriggled a step forward… then froze in panic.

No, no, NO!

This vent still had the grate on it, she realized, icy dread sloshing in her stomach. Even if she'd had a real screwdriver, she couldn't open it from the inside. Her breath drew sharp until she was nearly hyperventilating… she was trapped.

Pulling back into the dark passage, Cara felt a nausea like she would puke. The breeze chilled her skin and she lay there, the terrible reality sinking in. She couldn't get out. She was going to die in here. No one would ever find her, and they'd kill Jessie and Sebastian and…

For a moment the sheer horror clawed at her, trying to drag her down. But no… she couldn't, a part of her determinedly fought back. She was going to make it. She was *going* to make it. She *had* to make it.

But how?

Cara momentarily shoved away her looming panic and paused, trying to think the situation through. Okay, *rationally*, in the worst case, she could go back. It would suck, but she could count back three hundred and seventy-two crawls and know she was close. She doubted Davani would have bothered to put the grate back up, so she could at least escape the vent system. Besides, even if Davani had blocked her in, the vent hadn't been attached that firmly the first time anyway. She could probably kick it out from the inside or…

Or… the possibility flicked on like a light bulb. Kick it out… she could kick it out.

Shuffling another ten counts forward, Cara felt with one foot until she found the hole. She slowly squirmed her way backwards, which probably made more sense than going in headfirst and tumbling out into the room anyway. In a moment she was wedged halfway into the side vent, her heel against the metal grate.

Taking a deep breath, Cara desperately prayed that this worked, then slammed her heel against it. It made a horrible boom, but at this point, she just wanted out. She smashed it again, putting everything she had against the grate.

And again.

She felt the grate budge.

It was the flicker of hope she needed and Cara unleashed two more ferocious strikes, wedging the vent loose, then a third to finish it off. Behind her light poured in. Worming backwards, she squeezed out of the vent, gently dropping to the floor with relieved tears in her eyes.

It was only then that she thought to look around. Her heart nearly jumped into her throat as she realized Damien could have been waiting for her… except he wasn't. Pausing to catch her breath, Cara finally looked at herself. Her hands were coated with a nasty shade of black, and her jeans were stained even worse. She'd nearly worn holes in her shirt at the elbows, and the yellow fabric was smudged beyond recognition with a nasty coat of vent soot. She looked worse than the twins after a finger painting session. But she was alive.

And – she forced herself to stand – she had to save her friends.

Three more breaths to calm herself, then Cara jogged for the door outside. There had to be someone out in the cargo bay, right?

Peeking out, Cara found herself staring across the familiar scene of the cargo bay, crammed to the brim with crates and rising upwards around her like a sports stadium. She didn't see Captain Damien, although that didn't mean much. He was probably rapid-fire checking every room he could. Regardless, she needed to find the elevator. Hopefully Victor was still on sentry duty.

She didn't know which way to go, but the place was a circle anyway. Blindly guessing, Cara went right, breaking into a full-on bounding sprint in the weak gravity. She whizzed past another door in the string of side rooms just as it opened. Glancing back she nearly tripped when she saw Captain Damien barrel out into the hallway.

Frick.

He moved like he was heading back the direction she'd come from, then did a double take as he realized it was her. Cara looked back ahead, and her heart hammered as she put on a terrified burst of speed, running with long looping strides to give herself a lead. She didn't have to glance back to guess that he was coming after her. No point being quiet either.

"HELP!" she screamed, her voice echoing in the cavernous chamber. "SOMEONE HELP!"

She ran.

She moved faster than she'd ever run, calling on a desperate strength she hadn't known was there. "HELP!"

Up along the curving valley of the station floor, she glimpsed the elevator. Victor stood there, visible amid a break in the fields of crates. His eyes traced towards her voice. "HELP! PLEASE!"

For a second his mouth dropped open in shock, then Victor broke into a run towards her, stumbling to a stop in the weak gravity, as Cara fairly barreled into him. "Help," she panted.

The man's eyes went wide, probably at seeing what a mess she was. "Cara, what are you doing up–"

"He's trying to kill us."

"He… who? Cara, everyone else left half an hour ago. What are you…"

Victor's voice trailed off as he caught Damien charging down the arc of the station, shouting, "Don't let her get away!"

Cara froze, fighting panicked tears. "Please, you have to stop him. He's trying to kill us."

"It's alright." Victor gave her a reassuring nod, one hand straying to the pistol at his side, as he turned toward the rapidly approaching captain. "Hold it right there, sir." Victor raised a palm and Damien stumbled to a stop about ten paces away. Victor's tone was sharp. "Who are you?"

"He's a kidnapping, murdering–"

"Cara." Victor silenced her with a glower.

"Captain Damien Tallier," the captain introduced himself between deep breaths, all the nastiness from before abruptly vanishing. He pulled out a wallet and flipped it open to reveal his military ID, then nodded at Cara. "Thanks for stopping her, private. I think she's having hallucinations. You need to call a doctor right away."

Cara blinked. Wait… what?

"Her friend's in trouble too." Damien thumbed back the direction he'd come, somehow managing to sound genuinely concerned. "He's passed out… I think they were doing drugs. She ran when I tried to stop her."

Victor's gaze flicked to Cara, and she felt a sudden unease at the indecision in his gaze.

"Victor, you have to believe me, he's–" Cara took a step back and the soldier grabbed her wrist.

"Hold it right there," Victor said, "neither of you are going–"

"NO!" Cara panicked, realizing exactly what was happening, and hysterically trying to worm her wrist free. "He's playing you! Don't you see?"

Victor's grip just clamped down tighter. He turned to Damien, "Sir, what are you doing up here? The next shipment isn't until eleven."

"I was just inspecting some of the gear for Mars," Damien explained strolling closer, now five steps away... four... three...

"Must have lost track of time. Then I found the girl and her friend. I tried to help, but she panicked and–"

Damien swung, his fist stabbing Victor's jaw with a sickening crack. "NO!" Cara screamed.

Victor's grip on her wrist slipped and she bolted.

Behind her she heard the shouts of a fight, a grunt of pain. No whip-crack discharge of Victor's gun though. Skidding to a halt at the elevator, she smashed the call button a half dozen times, desperately hoping for the door to glide open.

It didn't.

She glanced back to see Victor slumping to the ground, and Damien three dozen paces away, glaring at her with murder in his eyes. He didn't try to grab Victor's pistol, they both knew it would be palm print locked. But if everyone had already left, then she didn't have anyone else to help and...

Damien catapulted himself towards her, and Cara ran.

She didn't know where.

She just ran, her breath ragged as she pressed her body to the razor edge. Behind her she could hear Captain Damien's feet pounding the floor, so close that she was terrified to look back. Her legs were ready to give out and she didn't know where to go when...

"What's going–"

A dark-haired woman appeared out of the crates, stepping right into Cara's path barely four feet ahead. Cara had only an instant to react and crashed straight into the lady.

In the weak gravity Cara went slow motion tumbling, landing in a tangle of limbs on top of…

Her eyes went wide as she saw who the woman was.

Kristina?

Chapter 19
Better Angels

"Owww, what are you–" Cara saw Kristina's eyes go wide in shock. "Cara?"

"Help," Cara pleaded, her chest heaving.

Behind them Captain Damien's voice boomed, "Stop that girl! Space Force business!"

Cara glanced back to see the captain barreling up barely ten feet away, and she knew it was over. She tried to summon up the strength to keep going, but found she didn't have it. She could barely catch her breath.

Then, to her absolute amazement, Kristina smoothly rolled to her feet and, without an ounce of hesitation, bounded straight at the man.

It was like something out of a dream. Kristina hurled herself at the stunned captain, sweeping beneath a snappy punch and smoothly planting an elbow in his stomach. In the weak gravity, the man literally lifted off the floor and flew back a foot, flailing even as Kristina kept her forward momentum and clawed onto him like an angry lynx.

He fell in slow motion, the two struggling on the way down. He landed one punch straight in her side but Kristina barely seemed to notice. They crashed to the floor with Kristina on top, hammering him repeatedly with one elbow.

The captain snarled in pain, but got his arms up to shield his head like a boxer. Snatching at her hands, the two frantically grappled. Then Damien abruptly shoved, and Cara's brain skipped a cycle in utter disbelief as he hurled Kristina off with a roar. In the weak gravity he might as well have been Superman. Kristina went flying a foot up into the air, scrambling in shock, and the captain's leg lashed out, stabbing her right in the chest.

The force of the kick booted Kristina ten feet back, and she crashed to the floor with a gasp. Cara stared, rooted in shock and certain her boss must have broken a rib. The captain unsteadily pushed himself up, standing with a furious growl. Blood oozed from his nose and two scarlet nail marks traced his cheek. "You two are dead," he hissed. "You hear me?"

Kristina must have, because she winced, rolled onto her side with a pained inhalation, then shoved herself upright. She staggered, even in the weak gravity, and grabbed her chest. "We'll see," she gasped coldly. Then she rushed at Damien.

Cara had finally regained her breath enough to sit up, and she watched in stunned awe as Kristina hammered at the larger man. He took a haymaker swing at her, which she blocked with one arm, then rushed close and threw an elbow that grazed his cheek. Her knee came up, aiming for his groin but instead connecting with his thigh, and Kristina latched onto the man. She held him close, trying to drag him to the ground while landing another sharp blow to his head.

But Cara could see it wasn't going well either. Clearly, neither one was exactly sure how to fight in the low gravity. Finally, the howling captain bear-hugged Kristina, pinning her arms against his chest. He easily lifted her and bodily slammed her against the nearest crate.

Kristina shrieked in pain even as she furiously clawed his chest. Her legs frantically vined around his, her whole figure struggling to bring him down. "CARA!" she shouted, through panting breaths, "my purse… please."

Her purse had flown several feet away in the crash and scrambling over, Cara grabbed it. Darting close, she kicked at Captain Damien. "Let her go!"

Cara caught him right above the knee. Something gave a horrible pop, and the captain screamed, one hand instinctively dropping towards his knee. Kristina's hand slid free, snaked into the purse and re-emerged with… a translucent plastic gun?

Cara watched in awe as Kristina smashed him on the head with the weapon. Something in the gun gave a sharp, synthetic snap, but that was enough. Captain Damien's eyes rolled up in his head, going an eerie white, and the man collapsed on the floor, even as Kristina slumped down with a moan, "Owwww."

Cara gawked, frozen in place and open-mouthed. What the frick?

Down on the floor Kristina groaned and sat up, one hand gripping her chest as she gasped for breath. "Cara… where have you been?"

"Me?" Cara blinked, "What about…" the words piled up in her throat before coming out in a rush, "Why do you have a gun?"

Kristina briefly regarded the weapon. It was assembled from a cloudy, semi-transparent plastic, and her striking Damien on the head had left a long crack running right up the hilt, splitting off a piece along the back of the barrel. "Well, I don't anymore," she snapped, adding a darkly muttered, "*Dermo.*"

"Kristina, what's going on?" Cara demanded, confused… and scared… and *way* too hyped up on adrenaline. She wasn't sure what to think.

Kristina rose to a wobbly sort of standing and grimaced. "It's complicated." Moving with less than her usual precision, Kristina took her purse from Cara and dropped her shattered weapon back inside.

"Complicated how? You have a pistol."

"Dart gun, technically," Kristina clarified, as though that somehow made it better.

"Same difference," Cara snapped.

Kristina's breaths were coming more evenly now and despite her obvious pain, she knelt down next to the captain, her hands quickly searching though his pockets and coming away with a phone and a wallet for her troubles. "Let's just say I haven't always been in retail." Kristina thumbed through the wallet a moment, before apparently deciding there was nothing there and tossing it onto his chest. "I might also work for a uhhh… let's call it a three letter agency. Hence the light weaponry."

Cara stared and suddenly everything made perfect sense. Her head might have exploded at the obviousness of it all. She put a palm to her forehead. "Oh my gosh, you're with the CIA."

"Something like that," Kristina agreed.

Cara unconsciously ran a hand through her hair, pacing, "*Hoooooly shit*, that makes so much more sense."

All the pieces clicked into place. The kung-fu-whatever stuff Kristina had used on her. The fact that Kristina had caught her stealing at all. Kristina mysteriously knowing all the station elevator codes. Her cavalierly going off to interrogate Sergeant Carrington. Her pistol. Kristina was a spy… well, a friendly spy but…

"What are you even doing here?"

"I was trying to catch a thief." Kristina gave a few tries at unlocking the phone before apparently giving up and discarding it on the captain's chest as well. The man hadn't stirred and only the steady rise and fall of his lungs marked that he was still alive.

Kristina managed to stand, and leaned up against the nearest crate. "I discovered Josephine casually looting my storeroom earlier. It took a bit of prodding, but eventually she broke down and confessed everything. Claimed she was supposed to meet a man and a woman up here who wanted to buy a *very* large cartload of clothes."

"Yeah," Cara nodded, "that would be Ms Davani and," she nodded to the unconscious captain, "that guy."

"Hmm," Kristina nodded, unfazed. "And you happen to know this because…?"

Cara blinked. "Josephine didn't tell you?"

"Tell me what?"

Cara felt a stab of fury. That icy-hearted witch.

"Ms Davani," Cara explained, "she's the woman who put Jessie and her sister in cryo sleep to take them to Mars. We followed her down to the observatory, and Josephine was there too. She was talking with Davani about all the clothes she was trying to buy.”

“Davani and the captain, they…” her voice faltered at the awful memory, “they drugged us – Sebastian, Jessie and I – and brought us up here. They had us locked in a room back that way,” she pointed. “They were planning to kill me and Sebastian, and Davani’s going to put Jessie back into cryosleep, which is probably going to kill her too.”

The urgency from before flooded back as Cara continued. “We tried to get away but they found us and I had to crawl through the vents.” Cara gestured at her shirt, the front of which had transformed from a flowery yellow to soot black at this point. “But we have to go. We need to get the Space Force to stop Davani before she puts Jessie back in cryo. The captain just took out Victor, we have to call for help and…”

Kristina puffed out a breath, “Right, okay,” she mumbled, taking a few steps then sucking in a sharp gasp and pressing a hand to her chest. “You said Victor was…?”

“He’s back there.” She pointed toward the elevator. “He looked like he was out. The captain caught him by surprise.”

Cara hadn’t run that far around the ring that was the cargo bay, and Kristina’s expression darkened as her eyes followed the curve of the deck to see Victor sprawled on the floor near the elevator. In a moment the two were crowding around the limp figure with a battered jaw. Kristina knelt, resting a finger on his neck, then sighing, “Well, he’s alive. But he’s in a bad way.”

The woman muttered a curse, then grabbed for his pistol, which was still clipped in the holster at his side.

“That won’t work,” Cara warned, “it’s–”

“Hand print locked.” Kristina swore again, glancing over the standard issue Sig Sauer before tossing the weapon away. “I was hoping it was one of the normal issue ones.”

Most military guns weren’t palm print locked, specifically so that anyone could pick them up and use them in combat. According to Mom, the Army had experimented with coding everything to specific soldiers back in the last war and it had flown about as well as an unpowered helicopter. Noncombatant sentry's guns *were* ID locked though. There'd been a big deal where someone had snapped, stolen one off a sentry and used it to shoot up a dining hall back when she'd been a little kid.

Kristina eyed Victor with a frown, and Cara could almost see the gears clicking in her head. Finally her eyes snapped towards Cara, "Does this lady have a gun?"

"Huh?"

"Davani, did she have a gun or weapon? Anything?"

"Uhhh…. I didn't see her with one."

"Alright then." Kristina nodded, took a deep breath and stood. "Let's go."

"What?"

"You wanted help," Kristina said bluntly. "Well, here I am."

"But… shouldn't we call the Space Force or–"

"Yeah, if you think we have a half hour for them to kit out reinforcements and get up here," Kristina remarked, calmly walking back the direction Cara had just come from. "But I don't think there's anyone else up here, and I'm assuming we don't have that long."

Cara watched her a moment, mouth agape, before realizing, "Wait… I don't even know where Davani is keeping the pods."

"I do," Kristina called back cryptically. "Hurry up, Cara."

"Wha… you do?"

"Carrington might have let it drop." She looked back and shot Cara a wry grin. "Told you I could handle him. Just took a little feminine persuasion for him to spill everything. I was going to let Colonel Perry know, but I wanted to find you and Jessie first. Plus the Josephine thing came up and… well, yeah. Come on."

More than a little amazed, but not sure where else she was supposed to go, Cara jogged to catch up.

Kristina moved at a quick, but obviously painful pace, her breaths short and shallow and one hand pressed to her chest like she was trying to hold it in place. "Kristina, are you sure you're okay?"

Kristina took another short breath, her tone strained. "Would you believe me if I said yes?"

Cara just eyed the woman, skeptical.

"Nothing's broken, if that's what you're worried about," Kristina added.

"A doctor tell you that?"

"It'd hurt more if it was broken. Probably just bruised. I'll be fine. The low gravity made it look worse than it was."

Cara cocked an eye. "You sure you don't want help?"

She thought to herself, *or maybe a doctor*?

Kristina fixed her with a glare, "Do we have a choice?"

Cara swallowed and didn't answer. Fair point.

"Speaking of backup though…" Kristina pulled out her phone as she walked and dialed someone, pausing a moment before, "Perry, it's Kristina…" a pause, "Yeah, the problem Kristina… Why does it matter how I got this…. Fine, okay, I bummed your number off someone. That's not the point." Her expression wrinkled in frustration. "Look, I need you to send a squad up to the cargo bay. It's somewhere near TT 60-175-0. I'm not sure beyond that, but just follow the shouting and you should find me."

She paused a moment, listening, "No, I really don't have the time to explain, but someone's about to get murdered– also your son's up here. I think he's locked in a room somewhere. Just send people with guns. You'll need to arrest a woman called Davani and there's a captain laid out not far from the service elevator. I'll explain when you get here. And send a medic, would you?"

Cara could still hear Perry's voice faintly shouting from the other end as Kristina calmly hung up on him. "Alright," she chuckled, then winced at the effort, "that should get some help headed our direction in a hurry. Come on, Cara. Let's go find this Davani woman and defrost Ice Princess."

Chapter 20
Ice Princess

Kristina laid out her plan as they headed back in the direction of the door where Cara had emerged from the air vent. "They should be in one of these side rooms, and we should have the element of surprise. So we charge in, and you let me deal with Davani. You grab Jessie, and if Davani isn't down you run, understand? You don't look back, you just run and find the help that Perry is sending.

Worst case scenario, if you can't find anyone up here, Jessie's implant should still be coded for the passenger elevator. You can take that down to the promenade and get help there. Either way, you'll need as much of a head start as you can get. So run and don't stop until you find help."

"But… what about you?"

Kristina didn't answer for a moment. "I'll take care of myself," she said grimly. "Main thing is making sure you and Jessie don't end up dead."

"But…" Cara bit her lip at that part. Yesterday she would have told Kristina to have fun and *possibly* try not to die. But Kristina had just saved her life, and she was very obviously hurt. What would happen if she had to fight Davani alone? Cara swallowed. What would have happened if she'd run off during Kristina's fight with the captain? Her boss was clearly good in a tight spot, but…

"Kristina, what if you need help with Davani or–"

Kristina rubbed her forehead. "Cara, you know you are just about the *worst* employee I've ever had."

"I'm just trying to help," Cara snapped, indignant. "Is that such a crime to–

"Then do your job." Kristina fixed her with a serious glare. "You have *one* job, okay? Look after Jessie. Not look after me, not go sightseeing, not piddle around. *Look after Jessie*. That means you need to get that girl out of this mess, as quick as you can. Understand?"

"But…"

"Cara, right now Davani and Captain Smash-Face back there are about to go to jail *forever* for human trafficking. But that means you or Jessie have to be alive to testify and put them in jail. Got it? You get the chance, and the fight doesn't go well, you run. This is bigger than you or me."

Kristina paused, turning to lay a hand on Cara's shoulder, her voice softening. "I need you to tell me you understand that."

Cara hesitated, torn, until finally, "I understand."

"Good." Kristina turned and kept walking.

Yeah, she understood, didn't mean she cared, but… whatever.

Kristina took a few more shallow breaths before adding, "I'd also appreciate it if you could keep this whole CIA thing quiet."

Cara glanced at Kristina. She might have phrased it as a suggestion; however, it was pretty obvious the CIA woman was telling, not asking.

"Yeah," Cara nodded, hesitantly. "Umm… who else knows, just Colonel Perry?"

Kristina didn't answer, just kept walking and Cara shot her a wary look, reading between the lines, "Wait, Perry *doesn't* know?"

"No," Kristina's voice turned chilly, "and I'd prefer to keep it that way."

"But you have a gun. Isn't that the sort of…"

Cara's voice died in her throat as Kristina's eyes honed on her with an arctic glare. "No, it isn't his business. Do we have a problem, Cara?"

Yeah, they kind of did, because if Kristina was rolling around with an actual weapon and keeping even the station commander in the dark, then what the heck was she up to? Catching the dangerous glint in her eyes though, Cara was smart enough not to push. At least not until they'd found Jessie. "No… ma'am." She swallowed hard and forced the words out.

Kristina shot her an unconvinced glower, but finally nodded, with a curt, "Good."

For a moment Cara didn't dare ask another question, but soon Kristina's frostiness seemed to thaw and a more pressing concern bubbled up in her throat. "Are you sure you'll be able to take Davani?"

"Most likely." In answer Kristina's hand slid into her purse and pulled out…

"What the frick?" Cara stared, not sure if she should be surprised or flat out worried. "You have a taser too?"

"Stun gun, technically. Tasers are usually the ones with range." Kristina held up the palm-sized brick with uncovered electrodes, and pressed the trigger to give an experimental lightning snap. "You should get one, very handy and dirt cheap. Plus, no one questions it if you're a girl."

Kristina paused, glancing at a set of guide numbers on the wall, before, "Ice Princess should be right down there."

She pointed two doors down, and Cara gulped. Okay, this was it.

"I'll go first." Kristina had at least stopped massaging her chest as they got to the door, although her breaths still sounded sharp and pained. Her voice lowered to a hushed whisper, "I want you to follow. Run in, grab Jessie and go."

Kristina pointed Cara to stand a few feet away as she gently tested the door handle, slow motion pushing it halfway down to ensure it was unlocked. She hesitated a second, motionless, then hissed, "Any reason why Jessie is being so quiet?"

Cara whispered, "Davani probably drugged her."

Kristina nodded, and tensed, "In that case, assuming she can still move, it's doubly important that you two get a head start."

Cara nodded, fighting back a sensation like a flock of sparrows dive bombing in her stomach.

"On three," Kristina said with an almost surreal composure. "One, two, three…"

Kristina smoothly forced the door open, stormed inside, and everything immediately went wrong.

Inside, the bright LED lights shone down on a row of frost flecked cryopod crates with their lids popped off. A wave of chilly air poured out of the room, pricking at Cara's arms like an arctic breeze. She saw Davani standing at the pod control panel… and Jessie was gone.

The raven-haired woman spun at the squeak of the door and in a flash seemed to size up Kristina. "You're too late." Her eyes danced to Cara with a venomous bite. "And to think I was worried I'd have to track you down. Change your mind about Mars, darling?"

Kristina raised her stun gun, somehow hiding all the pain Cara had seen just a moment before as she strode closer. "Give it up, Davani. Perry is already on the way."

Davani sneered, "Thanks for the notice." She deftly reached back to tap something on the cryopod control panel and the machine took up a low hum. Kristina moved to attack, and faster than Cara could follow, Davani plunged one hand into her purse. It emerged clutching a collapsible police baton which she snapped out to its full two-foot length with a loud *crack*.

Cara swallowed as she saw Kristina hesitate, and Davani's venomous grin drew wide. "In that case, I'd better make sure all they find are bodies up here."

Davani lunged, swiping with her baton, and Kristina danced backwards almost floating in the low gravity.

Cara bolted for the pod.

As the two women dueled, Cara skidded to a halt at the pod. She had to swallow back a shriek when she saw everything she'd feared, Jessie, lying prone in the pod with an expression of utter calm. It was a look that Cara now bitterly recognized as being drugged out of her mind on Serenity.

Her eyes flashed across the adjacent rows of pods and the awfulness of what Davani was doing sunk in. The tops of all the boxes had been pulled off, probably to make sure the rest of the girls were still there. Right next to Jessie's pod lay a frozen pale girl who might have been Jessie's clone, except with shorter hair. The next down was a young girl with jet black locks, then more that she couldn't see. All clothed in white and encased in a thin layer of frost with that sickening Serenity smile. Davani's personal kidnapping collection.

Cara's eyes darted back to Jessie's pod, and something else registered. Jessie might be locked inside, but she hadn't been frozen… yet. Her cheeks still shone with a vivid rosy-peach, not the frosty pale of her sister the next pod over.

In desperation Cara hammered a fist on the red emergency thaw button. Except this time, the coffin emitted a harsh *beep beep* of protest and nothing happened.

No.

Cara pounded it again… and again… *beep beep… beep beep.*

No, no, no… "Frick!"

She punched it so hard her hand hurt. The control screen remained stubbornly unchanged and a mockingly helpful computer voice chimed, *"Due to safety concerns, emergency override is unavailable during deep-freeze initiation. For pod shutdown protocols, please access the control panel and follow the instructions in your Cryo-tech user manual."*

The frick? Cara swallowed a lump in her throat, panicking and nearly in tears. What sort of genius had designed this garbage?

Panicking, she poked at the control panel, but nothing worked.

Behind her, Kristina shrieked in pain.

Cara glanced back to see her boss battling Davani…

And losing.

Kristina already had a ribbon of red sliced across one cheek. She charge close even as Davani slashed the baton across her chest. Kristina jabbed with her stun gun and the room crackled with the sharp snap of electric discharge.

Davani shrieked, but before Kristina could finish the fight, Davani staggered out of reach, wildly lashing with her baton. She landed a horrible sounding crack on Kristina's shoulder and Kristina dropped the stun gun with a gasp.

Before she could recover, Davani had closed on her, raining down brutal blows. Cara froze.

She knew what she was supposed to do. Run. Honestly, now that she was here, all her bold, hero talk from outside felt like so much hot air. It was easy to talk about danger, but now that Davani was right there, cold and vicious, and ready to spin and start flaying her with the baton, it felt so much harder to do… anything. She could almost feel the agony even now, Davani beating her to within an inch of her life… maybe further, and not even blinking an eye.

But running… that also meant Davani won. It meant leaving Jessie to… die. It meant leaving Kristina, who'd just saved her life. It meant running out of the room and knowing she was signing both their death warrants as she did.

Twenty feet away Kristina was backed against the wall, her forearm streaked scarlet from Davani's strikes. Suddenly she lunged forwards, grappling with the woman and landing an elbow right across her face. Davani stumbled back a step and went down, while Kristina's shout echoed in the tight room. "CARA RUN!"

Cara swallowed a horrified lump in her throat as the two crashed in a heap, Davani on top. She stepped towards the door and…

Davani taunted, "That's right, darling… better run."

Cara froze.

Run.

That felt like all she'd done since she'd gotten to Medea. Run from Kristina, run from station security, run from Captain Damien, run from Davani… run. She hated it. Every time she ran, it seemed like things got worse. The memories flashed through her head. Kristina pinning her to a wall… because she'd tried to run. Finding Jessie… and running. Sebastian shoving her into a freezing air vent… to run from Captain Damien. And now Kristina and Jessie were about to die… and she was going to run.

For an instant Cara felt a ferocious stab of anger at the vile woman. She saw Jessie in the pod, drugged so she couldn't fight even as Davani murdered her. She heard Sebastian shouting in pain as he tried to cover her escape through the vents and paid the price for fighting back. She sat with Jessie, trying to comfort a terrified girl who'd lost her memories and didn't even know why. She saw all of Davani's kidnapped prizes in pods behind her, each trapped in their own little icy hell. She was back at the observatory, struggling for her life as Davani forced a dose of Serenity up her nose. She felt Davani casually jerk her hair until her scalp screamed, heard Davani joke about kidnapping her too… and for a single instant Cara was a thousand times more furious than she was afraid.

Then she saw the stun gun.

The weapon lay forgotten on the floor, and Cara lunged, scooping up the stunner. Davani was still grappling with Kristina on the ground, both women desperately struggling over the baton. Charging Davani, Cara glowed with a matchless satisfaction as she jammed the stunner electrodes into Davani's lower back and death-gripped down the trigger.

The stunner crackled with power, and Davani shrieked.

The woman writhed like she'd been stabbed, her head snapping up to clock Cara right on the jaw. Cara's eyes defocused, and she stumbled back, dazed and tasting blood.

Cara's gaze re-focused to see a shocked Davani spin on her with death in her eyes. Except Davani had forgotten one thing.

Her baton.

She'd let go of it.

Crack.

Davani tumbled off as Kristina, now clutching the business end of the weapon, lashed her across the chin with the handle.

Davani gasped, a streak of fresh blood across her face. Cara dived at the struggling woman and planted the stunner right in her chest without an ounce of sympathy. Davani let out a banshee wail, desperately kicking Cara off in the low gravity.

Before Davani could recover though, Kristina was up, twirling the baton like an expert.

Crack.

As Davani struggled to stand, Kristina caught her across the face so hard Cara winced. Once… again… again…

Moving almost slow motion in the weak gravity, Davani crumpled to the floor, out cold.

Next to her Kristina dropped to the floor panting as she mumbled, "And stay down… bitch."

Chapter 21
Keeper of Secrets

For a second Cara stared at Davani, half expecting the awful woman to try and get back up. But she didn't.

As her breaths slowed, Cara finally let the stun gun slip from her fingers and wiped her stinging lip. The back of her hand came away slick with blood.

A few feet away, a battered Kristina massaged her arm, while a smear of blood on one cheek lent her a slightly more deranged than usual look. Kristina hissed in pain and swore, before glancing at Cara. "Let's *not* do that again."

"Sounds good," Cara gasped. She made clean her blood stained fingers on her blouse, before remembering it was still filthy from her crawl through the vents. After a flash of indecision she settled for wiping off the sticky redness on one of the rare, unmarked patches on her leggings.

Catching her breath, and shivering against the frigid chill that drenched the room, she nodded Kristina towards the humming cryopod with a single urgent word, "Jessie."

Kristina nodded. Stumbling to her feet, she hurried over with Cara a half step behind, offering a frantic explanation, "It won't let me shut anything down. I tried but…"

They paused, Kristina fingers dancing across the screen while Cara touched the smooth glass canopy where a white watery mist had flooded the interior, hiding Jessie inside. The canopy was cold beneath her fingers, too cold.

Beep Beep.

Kristina swore.

"I think Davani may have locked the controls or–"

"No, it's just complicated... maybe..." Kristina stared blankly at the control screen. Watching over Kristina's shoulder, Cara understood what the CIA woman meant. The entire screen was awash with a verbose word soup that hurt her brain to even look at.

Menus, drop-downs, and icons were stacked on top of each other, and when Kristina keyed in *Help* there were so many opaquely titled sub-results that Cara couldn't even guess what they were looking for.

Help - Cryo-Preservation
Help - Deep-Freeze
Help - General Maintenance
Help - Preparation.
Help - Storage

Cara's eyes glazed over just reading down the endless list, and her mind struggled to summon any ideas of what to do next. In desperation she slid alongside the canopy, her fingers trying to find a grip on the chilly glass and pull it open.

She finally found a tiny bit of purchase and pulled until her fingers slipped, leaving the tips raw and smarting.

The canopy didn't budge.

Kristina was still staring at the screen, but with an utterly lost expression that Cara remembered from the first time Mr Defrieze had told them to open Photoshop in school.

Her chest burned in panic. What were they supposed to do? Sure they could probably figure it out with a few hours to delve through the complexity. But they didn't have hours. Touching the ever more frigid glass, Cara guessed they were down to minutes... at most.

She needed... Cara glanced back at the control panel, where Kristina was futilely fighting her way past a parade of angry beeps. That tablet controlled the whole system, right… so what if…?

Her eyes danced back across the room to where she'd left Kristina's stunner on the floor, an absolutely insane idea brewing in her head. It was the sort of thing she normally would have dismissed out of hand, except Jessie was dying in there… and it wasn't like they had a better plan.

Bolting across the room, Cara grabbed the stunner, shouldering her way in beside Kristina.

"Cara what are…STOP!"

Cara jammed the stunner into the tablet right next to the power button. The metal electrodes bit at the composite touchscreen and she squeezed the trigger. About a bajillion volts, amps… whatever the frick… pulsed straight into the tablet electronics.

The tablet flickered, then went black. And down below, the whirring compressor fan died like an exhausted AC unit.

For an instant, Kristina stared in horror, until she seemed to notice that the cryopod had died as well. Cara caught a glimmer of relief, quickly replaced by a scowl. "Give me that." Kristina snatched away the stun gun with a huff.

Above the broken tablet, a single red led strobed a sharp alert. Pressing the big, red emergency stop button, Cara couldn't believe it when the glass canopy popped open with a hiss and a puff of icy air. Apparently they'd shorted out whatever software overrides were keeping it closed, and as the white vapor cascaded out like a misty waterfall, Cara saw her friend laying inside. Jessie's face was a rosy, just-in-from-the-cold shade of red, and reaching in Cara found her friend's fingers as cold as popsicles.

She might have hesitated, except for the urgency in Kristina's voice. "Cara, grab her legs, let's get her outside where it's warm."

Normally that would have been a struggle, but in the weak cargo bay gravity, Cara found Jessie almost scarily light. Her friends limp figure would have made it struggled to lift Jessie all by herself, but with Kristina's help, the two had the blonde girl outside in a flash.

Kristina vanished to collect her purse from inside, while Cara busied herself propping Jessie against the wall. She tried not to panic as she frantically squeezed some warmth back into the girl's icy fingers, "Come on Jessie… wake up… please."

Kristina reappeared a moment later. "If she's been drugged, you won't wake her up."

Cara shot the woman a glare, but Kristina shrugged it off and sank down beside her with an exhausted sigh. "Perry will be here soon. Let the doctors handle it, Cara."

Cara was loathe to do that, but as her driving panic slowly dimmed, she felt the fatigue of the last hour persistently washing over her like waves on the shore. She knew she had to do something, but she wasn't sure what and…

Cara finally slumped down between Jessie and Kristina, all the strength suddenly going out of her arms and a note of despair in her voice. "We still have to find Sebastian. Davani might have killed him or–"

"Doubtful" Kristina said, "she seemed pretty focused on Jessie. I imagine she was saving you two for afterwards. Either way, Perry will have the actual manpower to search the bay. He'll find him." She hesitated before adding, "You did well, Cara."

The words felt strange coming from Kristina. Surprising maybe, and also uncharacteristically sincere. Cara managed a nodded, "Thanks," followed by a tentative, "I don't suppose this means I'm off dish duty for the rest of the week?"

"I don't know about that. I still need the help."

"Oh, come on," she let out a disappointed sigh and folded her arms. "You're with the CIA, what does it matter? The whole place is just a front anyway."

Kristina rolled her eyes. "I assure you my accounting books say otherwise." She turned towards her purse, and busied herself digging around for something. "Speaking of which, don't take this personally but…"

Almost faster than Cara could blink, Kristina whipped out a syringe-tipped dart and plunged it right into Cara's thigh.

For an instant Cara gawked in open-mouthed disbelief. When she recovered enough to lean forward and grabbed for the dart, it was already too late. Kristina caught her from behind, one arm pinning Cara's elbows to her chest, while the other hand clamped down over her mouth.

Kicking frantically, Cara tried to worm free, but Kristina's arms cinched her in place with an impossible strength. She tried to dislodge the syringe, but found herself powerless as the drug rapidly drained into her veins. Cara screamed, but all she could force out was a muffled, "MMMHHHMMM!"

"Now, Cara," Kristina's almost motherly tone belied her crushing grip. "I told you *not* to take this the wrong way."

Kristina had just drugged her. How the frick was she supposed to take it? Throwing all her strength into a desperate squirm, Cara tried to break free. She shoved hard with her elbows and managed to slip one hand loose. Then Kristina's grip tightened until it felt like she was fighting against steel bars. Cara could barely move.

Cara furiously clawed behind her with her free hand. Kristina wasn't going to get away with…

Kristina's fingers pinched Cara's nose. With her mouth still covered, her lungs strained to pull in air, and a spike of panic pulsed down her spine… she couldn't breathe.

"Cara, stop," Kristina hissed in one ear. "Now!"

Cara desperately grabbed for Kristina's hand, her lungs frantically sucking a trickle of air past the woman's palm. But not enough.

She kicked hard, but Kristina barely seemed to notice and she could only manage a terrified squeak of protest.

Then Kristina's fingers slipped from her nose, and Cara finally drew in a wonderful breath of fresh air. For a moment she almost couldn't suck in the air fast enough, and in her ear Kristina mumbled, "Now, you think you can behave and *not* shout?"

Cara had no intention of doing a single fricking thing Kristina said *ever* again. But her brain was screaming for air, so she frantically nodded. Kristina's hand fell away and for a moment she gulped down air. Even as a slow sort of exhaustion nipped at the back of her mind.

"The frick did you do to me?" she gasped, still reeling at Kristina's sudden change of heart.

"It's just a tranquilizer. You'll go to sleep and when you wake up, you won't remember any of this. It's nothing awful."

It took a moment for that to sink in, and when it did there was really only one question "But… why?"

Kristina sounded almost surprised she even had to ask. "Cara, I have an extremely delicate dance going on up here with this whole intelligence officer deal. And we're both quite aware that you're going to blab everything you know the first chance you get."

"Well, now I sure will, you psychotic… mmmmhhh!"

Kristina's hand clamped back over Cara's mouth and the woman let out an exasperated sigh. "See, that's what I'm talking about," the CIA woman said with perhaps a hint of remorse. "Like I said, it's nothing personal. You just know too much."

Even after everything they'd been through during the last twelve hours, Cara had the sudden burning urge to punch Kristina right in the face. But pinned there, barely able to speak, she didn't see how. Instead she felt a cloud drifting over her mind. It was like… like being really tired, that sort of exhaustion where she couldn't hold onto thoughts. She was drifting, and as she did, Kristina's voice softened.

"Trust me, it may not seem like it, but you don't want memories like these anyway. They'll just make life difficult."

If it was such a great deal, then why hadn't Kristina asked first, Cara thought sullenly.

"This is a lot easier," Kristina said. "And don't worry, I'm not going to try and steal your glory. You did really well today, hun. I'll make sure everyone knows it. And uhhh… I'll see what I can do about your job."

Cara felt like she had a snarky comeback sitting around somewhere, but her brain seemed to have lost it. Instead, a hazy veil fell across her senses. Whatever Kristina had dosed her with wasn't like the Serenity. There was no wondrous euphoria followed by a blissful haze… she was just really tired and couldn't seem to keep her eyes open.

"It's going to be fine," Kristina whispered, her hand finally lowering from Cara's mouth. Cara felt herself slipping away, no matter how she tried to hold on.

"You're a real bitch," Cara mumbled past the exhaustion.

Kristina chuckled, "Likewise, hun, likewise."

Cara drifted off as the tranquilizer finally sucked her under. The last thing she felt was Kristina's hand gently stroking her hair. "You did well, Cara. *Spakoni nochi, milaya.*"

Chapter 22
Messy Days

Cara awoke to find that everything ached. Her head pounded like she'd had *way* too much to drink, and something soft kept irritatingly poking at her thigh. She dimly heard a familiar boy's voice cheerfully humming a tune. "Wake–up–sissty."

"Eli, stop pestering her."

Given the circumstances, Cara's first word was a mumbled, "Huh?"

The poking abruptly vanished, replaced by an earsplitting, "MOM, DAD, SHE'S UP!"

Given the throbbing in her skull, Cara really would have preferred not to be. Soon though familiar voices clustered near, and she inched her eyes open against the glaring light to see, "Mom… Dad…?"

"Cara." Her dad leaned over her, momentarily blocking out the light. "How are you feeling?"

Cara blinked, adjusting her eyes, and taking in the room. She was in a bed in… what looked like a hospital? Well, at least judging from the muted colors, and the weird railing down at the base of her bed. Her eyes fell on the snowy white shirt she was somehow wearing and… OH FRICK…

She bolted upright, remembering– "Jessie, is she…" Cara caught herself mid-sentence, panicked eyes tracing her parents' expression. They weren't supposed to know about…

"It's alright, Cara," Mom said, surprisingly *not* upset with her for a change. "Jessie and Sebastian are both fine."

Wait, whaaaaaat?

Mom added, "Kristina told us all about what happened."

Oh frick… she had?

"And your father and I are both very proud of you."

Cara blinked in surprise, the words not computing.

"You are?"

Mom's expression softened with a *very* uncharacteristic smile. "Of course, Cara. Kristina told us all about what you did. It was very brave of you, saving all those girls. Kristina even said you saved her life too."

The twins crowded in also, just tall enough to peer over the edge of the bed, their hair the usual pair of uncombed bird's nests and both their eyes shining with an eager gleam that would have terrified Cara if she'd been babysitting. "Did you really beat up a bunch of people?" Eli demanded.

"And blow up a cryopod?" Leo added.

"You two, stop annoying your sister." Mom turned her icy glare on the pair of five-year-old terrors. "Go play with your tablets." She vanished a moment as she shooed them outside.

Dad's gaze followed the commotion before turning back to her. "You'll be happy to know that Perry's people picked up that Davani woman and Captain Tallier in the cargo bay. They also tracked down Sergeant Carrington about half an hour ago."

The mention of Davani and the captain brought back a flurry of memories. She remembered her, Jessie and Sebastian spying on the two and… they'd been found out… and she'd been drugged and…

And then she didn't remember anything at all. Cara tried to force the memories back to mind. Something must have happened, but… after Davani drugging her, she had no clue what.

She could remember a little though. "So, the captain," she asked, "was he with your command?"

"Damien Tallier?" Dad's face creased in a dark frown. Captain was several steps below colonel, so she doubted Dad had known him that well, but even so he nodded. "He was.

202

Always seemed like a bit of an odd one, but I don't think anyone ever suspected what he was really doing. Don't worry though," Dad added, more encouraging. "I don't think he or Davani will be bothering anyone for a *very* long time."

Mom reappeared over the bed, her expression only a *little* strained. As she did, Cara glanced down at her pristine white outfit and a second, slightly more awkward, question popped to mind. "Ummm, where are my clothes?"

Mom sighed, "Cara those clothes were filthy. They were covered in dirt and there was blood on your leggings... I just threw them away."

"Wait... my yellow top? I liked that top."

"Well, Kristina promised you could come by and she'd get you a new one for free. Honestly, after being drug through the air ducts, you couldn't really tell what color it was anyway."

Cara blinked in confusion. "Air ducts. What are you talking about?"

Mom hesitated, "Well, Kristina and Sebastian both said you crawled through the air vents to escape that awful Davani woman."

"Uhhh.... okay."

Mom must have read her bewilderment, because she pointed. "The dirt's still in your hair. Once you're feeling up to it, you need to take a shower."

Cara felt at her head and... was shocked when her palm came away lathered in a sickening looking grime. The frick had she done?

Meanwhile Mom and Dad both eyed her with concern. "Are you feeling okay, Cara?" Mom asked. "You were out for almost three hours. Kristina said Davani gave you a nasty knock to the head, but the doctor was getting worried."

"I..." Cara wasn't sure what had happened. Davani punching her would sure explain the aching that lanced down her left jaw and radiated across her entire face when she spoke. "I guess. I don't really remember."

Dad frowned, "You don't remember at all?"

"Well," Cara concentrated a second before coming up frustratingly blank, "I remember we, uhh... Jessie, Sebastian and I, followed the captain and Davani to the observation bay. We got inside and they were meeting with one of Kristina's shop girls. I think she was robbing Kristina. Then they found us and we tried to run but they…" Cara hesitated a moment, shuddering at the horrible memory. "They drugged us and that's all I remember."

Mom's expression turned extra dark. "That vile…" she spun without completing the sentence and vanished into the hallway. She reappeared an instant later accompanied by a man in blue medical scrubs, "…that she can't remember anything after being drugged."

"Well, ma'am," the nurse explained, "I'm sorry to say that's not unusual. Especially when she's had a concussion."

Mom didn't like that answer. For about a minute, she lapsed into drill sergeant mode and let the man have a piece of her mind about quality medical care and attentive doctors. By the time she was done, even Cara felt like Mom had overdone it. Cara could guess that she'd spent the last few hours working herself up about the situation and now the unfortunate nurse was receiving an extra dose of overcompensation in parenting. Surprisingly though, the man didn't get defensive. He just nodded along, made a few notes on his tablet and promised to let the doctor know, reassuring Mom that they'd probably send her for an MRI.

Woohoo, Cara thought sarcastically, more tests to tell her she still couldn't remember.

Just what she wanted.

After Mom's tirade had subsided and following a few more questions, Cara finally managed to slide one in herself. "So… you said Jessie and Sebastian are alright?"

Her parents traded knowing looks and Mom finally said, "They're outside." She nodded towards the door. "We were all worried when you didn't wake up for so long. You must have gotten hit pretty hard."

"I guess so," Cara agreed, massaging her still throbbing head. Stupid Davani.

Dad nodded, "Do you think you're up to seeing them?"

As opposed to what? Sitting here being awkwardly grilled by her parents for the next hour? "Yeah, of course."

Mom hesitated, "You're sure? If you start feeling bad just let us know, alright? You've been through a lot and–

"Mom, I'm fine."

That wasn't strictly true. Honestly, she felt horrible, but… she got the feeling even Sebastian would be better than Mom and Dad at taking her mind off things.

Mom nodded, almost teary eyed, then grabbed her in a crushing hug. "I love you, Cara."

"Yeah…" Cara winced, struggling to breathe, "I love you too, Mom."

From the fuss Mom made, Cara would have thought they were saying goodbye forever, but finally she got her parents out of the room and in walked…

"Maddie?"

"OhmygoshCara," her best friend burst in. "Why didn't you tell me?"

"Huh?"

"About Jessie and Sebastian and the cryopods and the kidnappings." Maddie gestured like she was trying to keep in her bubbling excitement. "I can't believe I missed everything."

"I wouldn't quite say you were missing out," Sebastian commented wryly as he and Jessie wandered in behind Maddie. Cara's gaze instantly jumped past the several purpling bruises on the boy's face and straight to his arm, which hung across his chest in a sling.

"Sebastian…" her eyes widened and Cara sat all the way up in bed, "are you okay?"

"Oh this," he casually nudged his injured arm like it was no big deal… except he must have moved something wrong. Instantly his eyes went wide and he sucked in a sharp breath, his expression screwing up in agony. "It's– nothing."

Maddie rolled her eyes with an exasperated huff. "He's been trying to show off ever since they bandaged him up."

Cara bit at her lip, from the bruises on his face he looked like he'd taken an awful beating. "What happened?"

"Well," the pain on Sebastian's face seemed to be gradually dimming as he said, "turns out, you *can* break an arm if someone kicks it hard enough. I guess Davani wasn't very happy after you escaped into the vents and she was looking for someone to take it out on." He managed a wry grin. "It happens. How were the vents anyway? I heard you were a mess when they found you."

"I... don't actually remember," Cara said. One hand unconsciously brushed at her hair and her fingers came away smudged with more rough grit that she wiped on the side of her bed.

She didn't think it was *that* bad, but from the looks she got, she might as well have said she'd been teleported to Jupiter or something. Maddie cocked her head in skeptical surprise, Jessie's mouth dropped open an inch and Sebastian shot her a confused look. "Like, you just don't remember the vents or–"

Cara shook her head. "Basically everything after the observation deck. They were saying I had a concussion and... well..."

Sebastian stared, as though he wasn't sure what to make of that. Finally Maddie piped up, "*Oh–my–gosh.* Cara, you're like... a hero, and you don't even remember?"

Okay, whatever had happened, that was probably taking it a little far.

"Well, what happened to you guys?"

Sebastian shrugged with his one good arm. "I was stuck laying on the floor with a broken arm for half an hour," Sebastian said with a vanishing attempt at humor. "So... not fantastic. They drugged Jessie and tried to throw her back into cryo, so she only woke up about an hour ago when the serenity wore off."

Jessie spoke up. "I don't remember much of anything after you got into the vents," she explained. "They told me you and Kristina saved my life though, so... thank you." She paused, then quickly added a more enthusiastic, "Oh, and they found my Mom."

"They did?"

Jessie nodded excitedly. "I just talked with her. Apparently I'm from Cookeville, Tennessee. I guess Jackie and I have been missing for the last week. It sounds like the police just kept telling her that we'd run away. She sounded really happy to hear from me. I guess the Space Force showed up at our house too."

"For real?"

Jessie nodded and Maddie picked that moment to jump in with an eager, "And you know the best part about all this, Cara?"

"Uhhh…" maybe the fact that they were all alive and only had one broken arm between them? Or that Davani was in jail? For some reason she doubted that was what Maddie was aiming at though.

Fortunately, Maddie couldn't hold it back for too long. "I haven't posted *anything*, because I wanted you to be the one to break the news." She solemnly crossed her heart. "But Calvin and Amy are going to absolutely *die* when they hear about all this."

Jessie frowned, "Who?"

Before Cara could say it honestly didn't feel that important, Maddie had already launched into her rapid-fire explanation. "Well, we used to think Amy was our friend before the whole Mars thing. But it turns out she's secretly a backstabbing witch. *Literally*, the day we left, she hooked up with Calvin, Cara's *ex-*boyfriend, which means Calvin was probably cheating way before that. But *now*, with Cara being a hero and all, we'll get to show everyone that they're just a pair of lying, cheating… cheaters…" Maddie's words finally outran the rest of her thoughts and she trailed off with a noncommittal, "… so, yeah."

Cara sighed, she'd actually forgotten all about that mess. But, admittedly, it would be nice to stick it to Amy for a change. Speaking of which, it was probably what… mid-afternoon back home? Enough time for the daily rumor mill to have spun up again. Wouldn't that be fun? She could see how many other people had already broken their Codex streaks with her. "How's that all going anyway?"

Just the look on Maddie's face kind of said it all. That bad then? Well, Cara mused, on the plus side, at least she hadn't planned on going back to Earth anytime soon.

Behind Maddie the door outside squeaked open, distracting Cara's gaze as a familiar looking man walked in.

"Uhhh…" Maddie said, hesitantly, "let's just say it'll be a lot better when you tell everyone what happened and how you–"

"That's something we need to discuss," the man's voice interrupted from the back of the room.

Everyone except Sebastian spun as none other than Colonel Perry strode into the room. Apparently Maddie and Jessie had both been introduced, because Jessie nervously fidgeted with a strand of hair and Maddie offered a polite, "Hello, sir."

Perry's eyes focused on Cara, "Hello, Cara. I understand you can't remember much, but otherwise you're feeling better?"

Cara nodded, "Yes, sir."

"Good." Perry glanced around the four. "I'm sure you all are very excited about today's events. However, I'm going to have to request that you refrain from discussing this with anyone else." His eyes honed on Maddie, "*Particularly* on Codex."

It took Cara a moment to register what Perry was saying and when it did, a spike of indignation stabbed at her. Sebastian beat her to voicing her frustration, "Wait, the Space Force is just going to bury this? Dad, you can't let them pretend like–"

"*This mess*," Perry interrupted him very pointedly, "is not going anywhere. I can assure you of that. I just got off an *extremely* unpleasant call with General Galvan and two members of the House Armed Services Orbital Defense Subcommittee. To put it lightly, they were all extraordinarily curious as to how a captain had managed to successfully replace more than a half dozen crates of classified equipment with smuggled girls. There were also a number of questions raised about how they had gotten them all the way up to Medea. I assume that over the next few days a whole bunch of heads are going to start rolling back at Shepherd and Vandenburg when they sort out who precisely is responsible."

Perry paused a moment, adding, "You *are not* to repeat this, but I'm also going to be starting my own investigation up here on Medea to root out everyone else responsible. That process is going to be long and complicated and an accompanying media circus will not help at all. It might even tip off anyone who actually was involved." He eyed the four of them, adding, "There's also a *very* important ODI review coming up in May."

Oh… Cara was starting to grasp what was going on. ODI was the Orbital Defense Initiative, which was basically like… the masterplan for the entire US Space Force – budget allocations, mission objectives… all that stuff. In that light, this *was* kind of a bad time for a salacious media scandal… like, a *reaaaaally* bad time.

Perry continued with a stern, "I've been informed that, if there is no appreciable progress made by the time that review begins, then Congress will consider that to reflect very poorly on the Space Force." He paused, arms crossed before adding, "Obviously, that would be a bad thing."

Yeah… obviously, Cara mused.

Given that Jessie was probably the only one of the four who didn't instantly know what the ODI was, Cara wasn't surprised that she was the first to speak up. "So… what's going to happen then?"

Perry demeanor softened. "Well, Miss Fischer, we're still in the process of assembling evidence. To begin with, we'll be taking statements regarding today's events. The doctors are telling me that your memories should start returning over the next few days, so if you don't object, we'd like to keep you here overnight and debrief you tomorrow. After which, you and my son will both be catching a shuttle back to Earth. I've already made assignments for your necessary security detail, so you can be sure that you'll be perfectly safe during the rest of your stay on Medea. If you'd like we can arrange for a tour of the station as well."

Cara saw Jessie pause a moment at that news, like she wasn't quite sure what to make of hearing that she was leaving. Finally though, the girl nodded and asked, "What about my sister?"

"We don't have the facilities here to properly wake people from cryosleep, so we'll be sending all the pods back to a specialist facility on Earth. We'll want you to be there when your sister wakes up to help smooth her transition. The Space Force will ensure you both get the best care available."

"There's also the issue of…" Perry seemed to consider his words a moment, "let's call it the media. Obviously we've already contacted your mother and we're actively tracking down the parents of the other girls." He fixed Jessie with a serious look. "When you get back home, it's critical that what happened today *not* become widely publicized. At least for the next couple of months. As part of that, the Space Force has already spoken with your mother and arranged for a victim compensation settlement for both you and your sister, provided you don't publicly discuss any of this. It should be plenty to get you both through college, at which point the remainder is yours. Consider it a token of how apologetic we are about everything that's happened to you."

Whoa, what? From the bed Cara couldn't see Jessie's face, but for an instant, the blonde girl froze like a statue, one hand covering her mouth. When she finally spoke, her voice came out shaky, breathless, "You… did?"

"Yes," Perry said with a nod. "All we ask is your discretion while we investigate. You can rest assured that Davani and Captain Tallier will both be stewing in jail until we finish with our inquiry. At which point you, my son, and Cara here will probably all be called as witnesses for their trial. Given that one of you is scheduled to be on Mars," he nodded to Cara, "That's going to be very– *interesting,* logistically speaking."

Perry paused with a sigh and glanced around the group of teenagers. "Now, with that said, can I trust the four of you *not* to speak of this? That means no posting on Codex and no slyly mentioning it to other friends who might post it on Codex. If people ask what happened, you deflect the question or refuse to answer. If reporters come by, you simply say that you have no comment. You don't discuss it at restaurants, or the store, out walking, or anywhere where someone might overhear you.

Basically, treat everything that happened today like it is classified until you're informed otherwise. Is that understood?"

From Perry's tone, he clearly expected an answer. Starting at one end of the group, his iron eyes focused on Cara, who nodded with a, "Yes, sir."

His gaze moved to Sebastian, "Yeah, Dad."

Then Maddie and her pouty, "Fiiiiine."

Apparently that wasn't good enough because Perry's eyes narrowed until Maddie puffed out an exasperated huff. "Yes, *okay,*" she fumed. "I won't tell anyone about all this awesomeness or post about it online. Happy?"

It seemed he was, because Perry's gaze continued on to Jessie, who'd turned away still somewhat in shock from the news and was rubbing at a sudden dampness in her eyes. She looked back and gave a nod. "I understand..." she sniffled. "thank you."

"Of course," Perry said sympathetically. "And I want you to know that I'm truly sorry about all this. I'll be working very hard to ensure that everything is set right."

He waited a second, as though expecting more questions, but when none came, Perry nodded. "I'll leave you all be then. Let me know if you need anything, and we'll get it arranged."

The teens nodded, a moment later the door bumped shut and Perry was gone.

For a moment no one spoke until, "Wow, he's kind of serious," Maddie broke the quiet.

"Tell me about it," Sebastian agreed, then added, "Hey, anybody up for Asian food? They've got a pretty good Japanese place and it sounds like Dad just said we can order in whatever we want."

That sounded amazing actually, Cara thought. It was nearly past dinner time, and by this point she felt like she'd been beat up enough to deserve at least one tasty meal.

"Ohhh," Jessie agreed, "and can we get ice-cream too?"

"Don't see why not," Sebastian said. "They've got a Handels up here."

Cara added in, "And something from Cosmic Confections."

At the very minimum, she wasn't going to leave this stupid station without grabbing a snack from the one sort of… not really… touristy place. At least she could say she'd eaten somewhere she'd seen in a movie. Even if it was a sappy romance movie.

Actually, speaking of movies, Cara reached for the remote and clicked on the flex screen situated across from her bed.

"I don't suppose anyone would object if I bought a movie to watch while we're here?"

Sebastian glanced up, excited. "That'd be great. We could watch *007 Starsight,* that's Medea Station themed."

"Yeaaaaah," Cara mused, "or we could watch… something else."

Cara settled back in her bed clicking through movie options as Sebastian started working out orders and everyone else grabbed a spot to sit. She couldn't help but grin a little – ice cream and cookies. Mom definitely wouldn't have approved, too much sugar.

But whatever, she doubted anybody would mind, not today. They'd earned at least one night off. They could figure out everything else in the morning.

Chapter 23
Kristina

Kristina hated being stuck in the infirmary, even if she *did* have a bruised sternum… and a bruised face… and a bruised arm. So what? It wasn't like she had broken something. Didn't mean the doctors could keep her trapped here forever. Besides, she had two stores, a dozen employees, and several thousand customers who needed her *right now*.

A pair of overzealous nurses had caught her earlier when she'd tried to walk out, but that just meant she'd picked the wrong time of day. It was currently a little after nine, and if she waited until everyone on night shift started getting tired in a couple of hours, she might just be able to sneak away and…

The door to her room creaked open, and turning her head, Kristina wasn't terribly surprised when she saw who it was. "Perry, back again already?"

They'd spoken earlier, but only discussed the basics of what happened – where were all the bodies, who was Jessie – those sorts of things.

She'd hidden her shattered gun and the darts after Cara passed out, just in case someone went rummaging through her purse. But that didn't mean there weren't a host of other lurking land mines from today to tread around.

As much as she usually enjoyed playing verbal games, it still hurt to talk, so Kristina didn't bother beating around the bush. "What can I do for you?"

"I'm not sure just yet," the man remarked, strolling over to her bed with critical eyes. "I suppose I ought to thank you for saving my son's life," he said pacing at the foot of the bed. "But then I find myself wondering why you didn't just report the girl in the first place and save everyone a lot of trouble?"

Ahhh, there it was, Kristina mused. She'd expected something along those lines. Why hadn't she just turned Jessie in to the Space Force? Yes, it might not have seemed like the right decision at the time, but reporting her was still what you were supposed to do. Cara and Sebastian could get away with it, because they were, well... teenagers. No one expected them to make intelligent choices. Sadly though, she was an adult, which meant she was accountable to a slightly stricter set of rules.

That said, she'd also had several hours to consider precisely this conversation. "You should know that I strongly considered it," Kristina said, leaning back on her pillow and working to keep her voice level. "But I was concerned for the girl's safety."

Perry put both hands on the bed frame and leaned in with eyes like razors and a skeptical voice. "Her safety?"

"Well, don't take this the wrong way, but with two of your own currently behind bars, was I entirely wrong?"

"So instead you tried to hide her?"

Kristina glanced at the ceiling a moment in exasperation. "I *tried* to keep her in my office for two hours until I could work out which way the winds were gusting. Perhaps you forgot, but she *was* in a box marked classified. Surely you can understand my confusion. Besides, I'd hardly call that *hiding* her."

Kristina hesitated a second, reading Perry's unconvinced glower, and added. "And yes, clearly it didn't work out quite as I intended, and you have my sincere apologies." Kristina met his gaze with an unwavering look of her own. "But I wasn't trying to *hide* her... you know that."

Honestly, she doubted if anything she said mattered at this point. Policy was probably to kick her off the station for a security breach, regardless of the *why*. The irony was that, yesterday, she likely would have celebrated and sent Perry a thank you gift basket. Being up here was basically a punishment anyway. The last couple months she felt like she'd been getting nowhere, and if she'd gotten run off… oh well, what a shame.

But suddenly, after a single frenetic afternoon, she almost didn't want to go. It had actually been kind of fun. Not the whole *almost dying* thing, of course, that always sucked. But fighting Davani was hardly the first time she'd walked close to that edge, and Kristina doubted it would be the last. And investigating, helping the girls, feeling like she was doing something positive with her life for a few hours… that was a nice change of pace. She might almost hang around if she thought she could do a little more of that. That, and after leaving her stores on autopilot for the afternoon, she very acutely felt the siren call of her miniature business empire. It might sound stupid, but the dress store *needed* her. It'd be a shame to lose it, especially after all the work she'd put in.

If she was about to get run off Medea though, Kristina didn't see the point in piddling around. She shook her head. "Just tell me what the damage is. Am I being kicked off the station?"

Perry didn't immediately answer, which perhaps was an answer in and of itself. Kristina cocked her head. Ohhh… what was this?

She levered herself up on her elbows, ignoring the needle pain in her sternum as she watched the Colonel rap his fingers on the railing at the foot of her bed. Finally Perry sighed, "That would imply that something had happened."

Kristina's eyes went wide as she grasped his meaning, and she started laughing. It hurt like being jabbed with a steak knife, but she couldn't help herself. She could read between the lines. This was all very embarrassing for the Space Force, wasn't it? Which, incidentally, meant that if she wanted to keep her job, then…

Kristina winced, forcing back her amused chuckles long enough to ask the one important question. "Davani and her crew are all still going to jail?" Kristina probed. "Right?"

"You have my word," Perry nodded. "This will come out eventually but… not now. That's from up top."

"And here I thought you were the top?" Kristina chuckled, ignoring the pain. She could read the irritation on Perry's face, which made her laugh even more. This was beautiful.

"Everything alright?" the Colonel asked, clearly *not* sharing her amusement.

"It's fine…" Kristina clutched at her chest, settling down to a broad smile and taking a few deep breaths until the pain diminished. "I'm fine," she nodded. "Just uhhh…" she gestured to her chest, "ran into a door and banged myself up. Painful things, those doors."

She met his eyes and Perry got the message. "Good," he nodded. "You'll be debriefed later, and there'll be a few forms to sign."

"There always are." Kristina settled back on her bed, still grinning.

"And *don't* do it again."

"Of course not," she said sweetly.

Kristina assumed that would be everything. Pinkie promise not to cause any more problems and everyone moves on with their lives. However, for a moment Perry lingered, regarding her with a calculating glare.

Kristina blithely brushed it off. "Was there something else the matter, Perry?" she asked, a peppy cheerfulness weaving into her voice now that she was in the clear.

Perry rapped his fingers on the bed frame a moment before, "How?"

"You mean how do we make so much coffee?" Kristina grinned. "We have these big machines that–"

"How did you take down Captain Tallier?" Perry snapped, serious. "The man has fifty pounds of muscle on you, not to mention combat training."

"Oh, that," Kristina shrugged, and let out a long puff. "I suppose I almost didn't. As you said, he has fifty pounds of muscle on me, not a fun fight. I think Cara blowing out his knee helped though.

Perry pursed his lips a moment, and Kristina saw the skepticism written across his face. She had the sense that deep down, he suspected that was a lie. He had a look in his eyes like he knew her story was an iceberg with a tiny tip visible above the waves and a whole world beneath the water that he couldn't see. But then again, there was no one to contradict her, now was there? Tough luck.

Finally, the Colonel nodded, satisfied, at least for now. "You rest up, Kristina."

He headed for the door and she called, "Will do… sir."

She caught him stiffen slightly and fought back another chuckle. There it was again. She didn't really understand why it bothered him. Shouldn't have. But it did.

Maybe he just didn't like her?

That was probably fair. She had caused more than her share of problems today.

Oh well, Kristina settled back onto her pillow. She ought to get some sleep, at least for a few hours. She could sneak out of here later tonight. There was still an awful lot to do for the next few days. And when she got around to penning it, this was all going to make for one *very* fascinating report.

TO BE CONTINUED

Afterword

Thank you for reading *Medea*. If you're excited to continue this adventure and learn more about Kristina there's a sequel book in this series called *Starbound* that continues her story.

If you enjoyed the book and want to help others discover it, I'd also encourage you to leave a review. Those reviews are very important to the continuing success of the book. For those reading on online that can be as easy as flipping to the end and offering a rating.

If you're interested in my other works, I've also penned several Biblical historical fiction novels. I'd encourage you to start with *The Days of Elijah*. You can learn more about me as an author at *www.jnoblewrites.com* as well as reach out to me at *Johntheauthor1@gmail.com*.

With that out of the way, I won't say a whole lot more except that Medea was a fun little book that I very much enjoyed writing. Hopefully you enjoyed it also, and if so… well, I'll see you in the next book.

UNTIL NEXT TIME